Evie sat up and bumped her head on the drawer

"Police officer," the mean-sounding man said. "Come out of there."

Police officer? Evie curled her fingertips around the top of the desk and said, "Okay, I'm coming out." She sounded like the lone holdout in a hostage crisis. Slowly rising to her knees, she stopped when her nose was level with the desk blotter, and stared across the top.

The gruff voice belonged to a tall, formidably built man whose face was set in a scowl. He was definitely a cop—blue uniform, lots of stuff attached to the belt, the whole package. And he didn't look happy. Clearly he wasn't welcoming her to town with a big ole Heron Point grin.

She spoke into the middle of the lap drawer. "You don't have your gun drawn, do you?"

Dear Reader,

An Unlikely Family is the third and last book in my Heron Point, Florida, series, and that means it's time for me to say goodbye to Claire and Jack, Helen and Ethan, and now Billy and Evie. This story about the hapless island cop who searched for years but couldn't find the right woman seems an appropriate way to end the series. After all, the Heron Point books are about finding love in the strangest place with the person you'd least suspect. No one would ever have thought that bad boy Billy would follow his heart to the new elementary school principal.

But this book, more than the others, is about how the most unlikely folks come together and, through struggle and perseverance, form a true family, complete with all the caring and love that defines such a special bond. And it's about one unique little girl who needs everyone in her thrown-together family, and on her quirky island, to support and cherish her.

I hope you enjoy Billy and Evie's journey and get the chance to visit again with the characters from the first two books, *An Unlikely Match* and *An Unlikely Father.* And if you want to see Heron Point for yourself, just follow Florida's Route 19 and take 24, a narrow two-lane road, west to where the cedar trees blend with the Gulf.

I love to hear from readers. Please visit my Web site, www.cynthiathomason.com, e-mail me at cynthoma@aol.com or write a letter to P.O. Box 550068, Fort Lauderdale, FL 33355.

Wishing you the warmth of the Heron Point sun,

Cynthia Thomason

AN UNLIKELY FAMILY
Cynthia Thomason

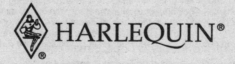

HARLEQUIN®

TORONTO • NEW YORK • LONDON
AMSTERDAM • PARIS • SYDNEY • HAMBURG
STOCKHOLM • ATHENS • TOKYO • MILAN • MADRID
PRAGUE • WARSAW • BUDAPEST • AUCKLAND

ISBN-13: 978-0-373-71393-6
ISBN-10: 0-373-71393-2

AN UNLIKELY FAMILY

Copyright © 2007 by Cynthia Thomason.

This edition published by arrangement with Harlequin Books S.A.

® and TM are trademarks of the publisher. Trademarks indicated with
® are registered in the United States Patent and Trademark Office, the
Canadian Trade Marks Office and in other countries.

www.eHarlequin.com

Printed in U.S.A.

ABOUT THE AUTHOR

Cynthia Thomason writes contemporary and historical romances as well as a historical mystery series. She has received the National Readers' Choice Award, nominations for *Romantic Times BOOKreviews* Reviewers Choice Award and the Golden Quill Award. She and her husband own an auction company in Davie, Florida, where she is a licensed auctioneer. They have one son, an entertainment reporter, and a very lovable Jack Russell terrier. Learn more about Cynthia at www.cynthiathomason.com.

Books by Cynthia Thomason

Don't miss any of our special offers. Write to us at the following address for information on our newest releases.

Harlequin Reader Service
U.S.: 3010 Walden Ave., P.O. Box 1325, Buffalo, NY 14269
Canadian: P.O. Box 609, Fort Erie, Ont. L2A 5X3

This book is dedicated to those hardworking faculty members who educate our children. Having been a teacher, I know it takes much more than a textbook to do the job right.

CHAPTER ONE

THE PAVEMENT ahead of Evie Gaynor's Chevy Malibu shimmered hot in the sultry Florida sun. Two days after leaving Detroit, she'd clocked thirteen hundred miles and experienced a twenty-degree spike in the temperature. Since entering the state, she'd gone from her air-conditioned automobile to a chilled fast-food restaurant and a convenience store to pay for gasoline. And with each stop, she'd removed another article of clothing until now she wore only a camisole, capris and sandals.

The road she was driving was nearly deserted, but Evie had expected that. Claire Hogan, the town mayor, had told her Heron Point was a weekend tourist destination. On Friday afternoons the population swelled with Gulfside visitors who came to sample the fine food and browse the upscale gift shops. Since this was only Thursday, the influx had yet to begin.

Once she'd turned off the main highway onto the thirty-mile stretch to Heron Point, Evie had enjoyed a lush, green landscape. Taking advantage of the quiet drive, she picked up her cell phone and punched in the number from her notebook, propped open beside her. A woman answered on the first ring. "The Pink Ladies Cottages," she practically chirped.

Evie introduced herself as the new principal of the elementary school and confirmed her reservation for one of the cottages which she assumed would most probably be pink.

"Oh, yes, dear, we're expecting you." The woman gave directions and verified Evie's assumption by adding, "You can't miss us. Our buildings are true baby-girl pink, just like our delightful beds of impatiens."

Evie disconnected and rolled down her window, fully expecting another blast of steaming air to hit her face. Instead, an undercurrent of cooler, salty freshness promised a respite from the stifling heat. She ran her fingers through her hair and enjoyed the feel of it whipping against her cheeks.

After a few miles, the panorama changed. Dense hummocks of cedar trees dotted the horizon and the ground rolled with gentle hills identified as Indian Burial Grounds. She crossed a narrow bridge spanning a wide inlet. At the end a placard announced her arrival in Heron Point, population just over two thousand.

She passed a marina, a tavern and a small grocery before turning onto Gulfview Road. She had every intention of driving straight to her pink-painted destination. But when she saw a sign pointing down a road that read Heron Point Elementary School, she simply couldn't resist. She drove by the entrance of the clean, freshly painted parsonage-turned-schoolhouse. The dazzling white exterior had just enough sage-green Victorian trim to give the building an air of whimsy. And Evie fell in love with it.

She pulled around to the parking lot in back and got out of the car. She didn't have a key, but she walked up to the rear entrance and gave the knob a firm twist. The door opened with a subtle creak. Stunned, since no one seemed to be on the property, Evie looked around, waited a few seconds and then stepped over the threshold.

The back foyer smelled of old books, cleanser and something unmistakable to buildings where children gathered. Evie called it the smell of learning, and it varied according to the age of the student body. In this school, it was a pleasant mixture of crayon and pencil shavings.

She walked down the central hallway and looked into rooms identified with numbers on the doors. Desks were scattered haphazardly, waiting for a maintenance crew to finish the summer spruce-up and set them back in rows. The last door before the front entrance made her feel at home. The sign on the panel read Principal. There was no name under the title, but she anticipated seeing her own in a few days.

She entered her office much as a new student might enter his classroom for the first time, with an exhilarating rush of uncertainty. Reaching up to her ear, she twisted the diamond stud earring in her left lobe, a habit she'd developed over the years whenever she felt apprehensive. The smooth metallic finish of 14-carat gold and the slightly rough edges of the rose-cut stone were familiar, and she relaxed. She took a deep breath, comforted by the realization that she belonged right here in this eclectic hodge-podge of bookshelves, supply cabinets and wooden chairs.

The principal's position she'd seen advertised a few months ago in an educational journal had been her wake-up call, her chance to stop spinning her wheels as an assistant administrator working for an impassive school board. Here, in tiny Heron Point, she could truly have a positive impact on America's next generation. And maybe make a difference in her own stagnant life, as well.

Careful not to disturb anything, she progressed to the inner office—hers. It was smaller than the reception area and well-organized, with a desk in the center, a credenza behind and file cabinets along one wall. She walked behind the desk to a corner window that afforded a view of flowering shrubs and towering pines. It was paradise, a sunny, inspiring space that caused Evie's eyes to well with tears.

And then she heard a gentle ping, much like a tiny pebble ricocheting off a smooth surface. "What was that?" she asked the otherwise still air. She spun around, expecting to see that someone or some *thing* had disturbed her solitude. But she was quite alone in the stuffy office. A trickle of perspiration ran between her breasts. She again felt for her earring and discovered it was missing. Ah. The ping. She dropped to her knees and began searching frantically.

She scraped her fingers over the rubber mat under the chair and mumbled threats to the earring. She never heard anyone enter the room until a deep voice commanded, "Come out from under that desk right now. And don't try anything funny."

Evie gulped back a gasp, sat up and bumped her head on the desk drawer.

"Police officer," the mean-sounding man said. "Come out of there."

Police officer? Well, that was good, wasn't it? Evie curled her fingertips around the top of the desk and said, "Okay, I'm coming out." She almost laughed. She sounded like the lone hold-out in a hostage crisis. Slowly rising to her knees, she stopped when her nose was level with the desk blotter and stared across the top.

The gruff voice belonged to a tall, formidably built man whose face was set in a scowl. He was definitely a cop—blue uniform, lots of stuff attached to the belt, the whole package. And he didn't look happy. Clearly he wasn't welcoming her to town with a big ol' Heron Point grin.

She spoke into the middle of the lap drawer. "You don't have your gun drawn, do you?"

"No, but hear this sound?" She flinched at a muffled pop. "That's me unsnapping the holster just in case."

She stood and held her hands high enough so he could see them, figuring submissive and obedient was her wisest course of action. "I don't have a weapon," she said, "so, if you don't mind, I'd prefer it if you'd snap up again."

He did. "What are you doing in here?"

She felt the back of her head where a small bump had formed. "I lost my earring," she said. "It was a gift from my father, and I would be heartbroken to lose it. It rolled…" She stopped when she realized that was probably the least significant part of the story to this man in blue.

He frowned, obviously lacking any sympathy for her. "Looks like a case of breaking and entering to me."

She checked her fingertips. No blood from a head injury, thank goodness. Just a dull pain behind her eyes. "You're wrong. I did enter, but I didn't have to break anything to do it. The back door was unlocked."

"I don't buy that," he said. "This building is a school. It's closed for the summer and is locked every night."

Okay, forget submissive. No one had ever called Evie a liar to her face, and she was running out of patience with this guy, cop or not. "I'm well aware this is a school, and I'm telling you I opened the back door and walked in."

"You shouldn't have," he said. "It's nearly dark. No one has any business being in this building this time of night. You're violating public property even if you didn't pick the lock."

She released a frustrated breath. "Oh, for heaven's sake. I'm not violating anything. Besides being part of that public you're sworn to protect, I'm the new principal of Heron Point Elementary. And this is my office, or soon will be."

He cocked his head to the side and studied her. His frown deepened. Was he drawing a conclusion based solely on appearance? Did he find her lacking in stature at five feet four inches? She followed his gaze downward and sighed. A jersey-knit camisole was definitely inappropriate for the head of a school. She tugged its thin strap back up to her shoulder. Give me a break, she thought. I've been driving all day. She was glad he couldn't see her feet. One flat, flowered sandal had slipped off somewhere under the desk.

A corner of his mouth twitched. He rubbed his jaw and continued staring. "You're the new principal?"

She squared her shoulders. "I am. And you'll pardon me for saying so, but with your attitude, I'd guess you've spent more time in a principal's office than I have."

He folded his arms over his chest and grinned. She detected a dusting of fine dark hair on his left forearm, broken by a patch of white where his wide leather watch strap began. His ball cap covered most of what appeared to be thick black hair.

"That's a pretty good guess," he admitted.

She relaxed, one hand on the desk. "Can I assume you're not going to arrest me?"

"Yes, you can. We don't have a law against just entering."

"Fine, but I still have an earring to find."

"I guess I could help you."

She started to protest, imagining a large, polished boot crunching the delicate gold mounting. "No need..."

"It's okay. Firemen get cats out of trees. I suppose I can do jewelry recovery." He started to bend in front of the desk when they heard a beeping sound from outside.

Evie spun around to the window and stared at a small vehicle racing toward the school at perhaps a wicked fifteen miles per hour. She turned back to the officer. "What's that?"

"Oh, shi—shoot. I forgot to cancel Lou." He pressed a button on a radio attached to his shoulder, and the device crackled to life. "Lou, it's Billy. Never mind. False alarm. Everything's under control."

Too late. Whoever Lou was, he was arriving amid a blaze of flashing lights attached to the top of his vehicle. "Are you kidding me?" Evie asked. "Your backup is arriving in a golf cart?"

The man who had just identified himself as Billy joined her at the window. "He had to. I have the squad car."

"*The* squad car? As in, there's only one?"

"It's all we need. You can see how fast Lou got here in the golf cart."

At this moment Heron Point and her hometown seemed more than thirteen hundred miles apart. They could have existed in different galaxies. Imagine golf carts fighting crime in the Motor City!

She looked over at Billy who was intent on watching the battery vehicle purr to a stop at the school's entrance. An older, decidedly well-nourished officer in the cart lifted a radio from the dashboard. His voice emerged from the radio at Billy's shoulder. "Ah, Roger that, Billy. But I'm already here."

Evie got down on her knees. "I've got to find my earring, while you tell your crime-fighting partner about the potentially volatile situation here."

Billy returned to the desk and stood a couple of feet from where she was searching. He didn't say anything, but Evie could hardly ignore his presence towering above her. She looked up at him and sighed. "Is something else wrong, Officer?"

He was staring disapprovingly. "Maybe there is. I think you're having a bit of fun at the expense of our town's law-enforcement division. We take our jobs seriously here, Madam Principal, and if you ever find yourself in real trouble, you'll be thankful for our commitment to keeping order on this island."

Oh, dear. She'd hurt his feelings. She hadn't intended to. All she wanted was to find her precious earring and crawl between clean, pink sheets. "I'm sorry, Officer…?"

"Muldoone. Billy Muldoone."

"Officer Muldoone." She stuck her hand up to him. "I'm Evie Gaynor."

He took her hand. His lips curved into a sort of conciliatory smile, but she sensed he was a long way from becoming a friend.

"I apologize if it seemed I demeaned your position and authority. I assure you I have the utmost respect for the law and police officers." She felt rather silly looking up at him from all fours, while he stood like one of the pine trees outside, tall, unyielding and, in his cop way, even more impressive. "I meant no offense, really."

"Then none taken." He pointed to her left foot. "Look there. I think that's your earring."

She scooted around, spotted the glimmer of a diamond and exhaled a sigh of relief. "That's it. Thank you, Officer." The small gold post backing was next to the gemstone, and she palmed both pieces.

"No thanks necessary. And call me Billy. Everybody does."

"Okay, Billy. You can't imagine what this means to me. My father was never much for shopping, so when he actually went to a jeweler for this and wrapped it…" She cleared her throat. "Well, enough about that. I'll just be on my way so you can return to whatever it was you were doing before—"

A knock at the front door cut her off. "That's Lou," Billy said, heading out. "Maybe we can get to the bottom of who left the door unlocked."

While Evie wiped off the earring and reinserted it, Billy returned with Lou. He explained that she was the new principal and introduced her to the man he iden-

tified as a service aide. Lou, while not exactly the
ideal image of first responder, was jovial and probably
competent enough to deal with problems that could be
investigated from a golf cart.

"Lou thinks one of the maintenance crew left the
door unlocked," Billy said. "I'm sure it was a mistake.
It would have gone unnoticed if I hadn't seen someone
moving behind this corner window."

"Yes, I'm sure it was." She twirled the diamond
stud, relieved to have it back where it belonged. Billy
had removed his cap, revealing an abundance of wavy
hair. When he ran his fingers through it, spiky strands
fell onto his forehead nearly reaching his straight black
eyebrows. Evie reaffirmed her first impression that he
was decidedly well-proportioned at better than six
feet. She didn't doubt his ability to maintain the upper
hand over most any law-breaker.

But Officer Muldoone wasn't all brawn. His facial
features gentled him in a way his build and that deep
baritone voice never could. His eyes were a soft
brown, the color of wet sand. His lips were full and
framed by fine crescent-shaped creases. Something
Lou said made him chuckle, and the low, rumbling
sound seemed to vibrate into Evie's chest. The tough
cop had a nice laugh.

Lou flipped a notebook closed and stuck a pen in
his pocket. "I've got some time, Billy. We'll secure the
building and then you go home to your family. I'll
write up the report."

Go home to your family... Evie turned away from
the men and fiddled with the zipper on her purse. She
didn't even know Billy Muldoone, so how could she
be disappointed to learn he had a family? He appeared
to be in his mid-thirties, and he was a decent-looking
guy. Of course he would have a wife and kids. Most
men did at his age. Most women at thirty-four did, too,
but Evie had learned to live with being the exception.

Settling the strap of her purse over her shoulder,
Evie headed for the door. "Thanks again, Billy," she
said, "and I'm sorry for any misunderstanding."

"No problem." He wiggled his cap into the groove
around his hairline. "We'll follow you to the back door
and make sure the lock is secure."

It was dark when Evie got into her car. She pulled
out of her spot and took one last look at the men
checking the mechanism on the door. Billy gave a
wave and hollered at her to drive safely. She exited the
parking lot in the direction of Gulfview Road and the
Pink Ladies.

She planned to take a shower and ask her landlady
about the nearest place to grab dinner. Then she'd call
her father and spend the rest of the evening curled up
in bed thinking about plans for Heron Point Elementary. Her mind raced with opportunities for the school
year. That was a good thing. Because she couldn't
allow her mind to dwell on any possibilities as far as
family man Billy Muldoone was concerned.

CHAPTER TWO

BILLY WATCHED THE Malibu turn the corner. Behind him, Lou rattled the doorknob. "She's locked now," he said.

The last splash of red from Evie's taillights faded behind a stand of cedars. Still Billy stared at the road until Lou jostled his arm and asked if he'd heard him.

Billy focused his attention on his partner. "Sure I heard you."

Lou smiled. "You could have fooled me. I figured the way you were watching that girl drive off, you'd forgotten about the school."

"*Woman,* Lou," he said. "I don't think the new principal would appreciate being called a girl."

"All business, is she?"

"Pretty much."

Billy fell into step beside Lou when he started around the side of the building. "She doesn't look like a principal," Lou said. "At least not any I remember. I could be happy going back to school myself if the woman in charge of spankings looked like her."

Lou was as committed to his forty-year marriage as anybody Billy had ever known, so he didn't respond to the older man's attempt at humor with more than a shake of his head. Then he rubbed the back of his neck and tried to dispel the notion of Evie Gaynor standing in front of the student body in that sexy little shirt-thing, her pink-painted toenails peeking out from an equally sexy pair of sandals. "She was kind of attractive, I guess," he admitted.

Lou snickered. "Kind of? Come on, Billy, you can't kid me." He locked the front entrance, did his knob-jerking routine again, and faced Billy squarely. "You going to ask her out?"

"What? No. At least, I hadn't thought about it. I don't even know if she's married."

"She's not. I heard Claire talking about her the other day. As far as I know, she's come to Heron Point all alone. So maybe you should ask her out. New gals don't come into town too often, at least with the intention of living here, and you've pretty much worn out your welcome with the ones who've been around a while."

Billy frowned. "Thanks for pointing that out, but our artsy-type gallery owners haven't proved a good match for a cop." He pictured Evie again. Shoulder-length, light brown hair, green eyes the color of the Gulf at dawn, a smile that could be killer if she'd stop trying to hide it. "I don't know," he said. "My dating has changed a lot in the last few years."

"Don't think too long," Lou said. "You don't want your second meeting with the principal to be official school business."

"What's that supposed to mean?"

Lou chuckled. "You know darned well. The first week of school won't be marked off the calendar before you're in that principal's office, and it won't be to ask her for a date."

Billy sighed as he walked to the cruiser. Lou was right. The last principal had left Heron Point for a number of reasons, not the least of which was Billy's daughter, Gemma Scarlett Muldoone.

THE NEXT MORNING Evie woke in a cloud of pink sheets and down-filled pink comforter. The air conditioner hummed across the room, and she cuddled deeper into the covers and let the soothing sound leisurely stir her to life.

She'd been assigned the first cottage in a row that stretched to the Gulf. Hester Poole, the owner of the Pink Ladies, had greeted Evie looking like a fairy-tale godmother, complete with floral apron and a crockery bowl full of sugary cookie dough. She'd said she'd saved the cottage nearest the office for Evie so she could come to Hester with any questions she might have about Heron Point and its citizens.

So far, the only question Evie had concerned her landlady's obsession with pink. She wasn't complaining though. The room was clean, comfortable and, if one ignored the Barbie-doll ambience, charming. She had nothing planned for the day. Perhaps she'd return to her office to unpack some personal possessions.

"Yoo-hoo, Miss Gaynor."

She glanced at her travel clock: five past nine. Evie hadn't slept this well or this long in ages. She swung her legs over the side of the mattress and reached for her robe. "Just a moment, Mrs. Poole."

She opened the door to her landlady's welcoming smile and a muffin nestled in a cloth napkin. "Just made these this morning," Hester said. "Blueberry."

Evie took the muffin. "Thanks. It smells delicious."

"And that's not all, dear," Hester said, thrusting a vellum envelope at Evie's chest. "This was just delivered for you."

Evie's name was scripted across the front. "Who is it from?"

"Our handsome chief of police, Jack Hogan, dropped it off, so I assume it's from his wife, our mayor."

"Oh? That would be Claire."

Hester nodded. "Hope I didn't wake you, dear, but you've already missed our famous sunrise. I didn't think you'd want to sleep through the spectacle of the dolphins swimming just off shore."

"No. Absolutely not."

"Sister and I are outside now. Why don't you bring your muffin and join us?"

"I will. Just give me a moment."

Evie shut the door, opened the envelope and unfolded a note in clear, precise handwriting. It was signed, "Claire Hogan," the woman Evie had spoken with on several occasions.

She read the note while she filled the teakettle. Claire was welcoming her to the island and asking her to meet her and some friends for lunch at the Heron Point Hotel. Evie wondered how Claire knew she had arrived, but then she realized that in a town this size, her escapades at the school last evening might have become a topic for local gossip. Or, more likely, Jack Hogan had read a report of the incident when he'd come to work this morning and told his wife.

She filled a mug with tea, took the portable phone to the dinette set and dialed the number on the invitation. The mayor answered on the first ring. "Hello? Claire Hogan."

Evie identified herself and confirmed that she would be delighted to meet at the hotel at noon. The prospect of making female friends cheered her. She dressed in shorts and a T-shirt and went outside to watch the dolphins, the first of many experiences she never could have had if she'd stayed in Detroit. She'd work on those educational goals later.

CLAIRE HOGAN LOOKED pretty much as Evie had pictured her—a combination of sophistication and small-town charm. She was tall and slim, with blond hair pulled back in a smooth style. She'd been the mayor of Heron Point for two years and, Evie decided, the town couldn't have a better representative.

Her two friends were quite different from Claire, but it was obvious the three were bound by a deep emotional connection. Petula Sweeney, Claire's aunt, readily admitted to being a "sexy sixty" and newly married to fishing charter captain, Finn Sweeney, who just happened to be the father of the third woman in Claire's luncheon group. Helen Sweeney-Anderson, a new mother, was blond, wiry and outspoken. Evie liked them all right away.

Helen took a sip of Coke, while rocking a baby stroller gently with her toe and complaining that she couldn't wait to be done with breast-feeding so she could have a beer once in a while. "So what do you think of Heron Point so far?" she asked.

"It's great," Evie said. "This morning I saw my first dolphins not in an aquarium."

"That's the best thing about the Pink Ladies," Pet said. "The dolphin show. Every morning like clock-work. It's almost as if the dolphins know they're supposed to entertain Hester's guests."

Claire leaned forward. "There's a lot to like about this quirky little town, Evie. The longer you stay, the more you realize our island is quite unique."

Evie smiled. "I think I already know that. I looked for an office supply store and a supermarket on my way in this morning. I didn't see either one."

"The Island Market has fresh produce and meat," Helen said, "and you can get pens and paper at the Island Drug Store. For anything else, you have to go to Office Max in Micopee."

"What about a beauty salon?"

"We have a lady who cuts hair in her kitchen," Claire offered. "I go to her for trims, but at least four times a year my daughter, Jane, and I get the royal treatment at a spa in Gainesville. You'll have to come with us next time."

The conversation switched to each woman's occupation. Petula worked as a waitress at the Green Door Café and said she wouldn't quit no matter how much Finn pleaded with her to stay at home. "I get to be first to learn all the gossip," she said. "I can usually just look at our customers and tell what's going on in their lives."

Helen laughed. "Pet is our resident psychic—or at least that's what she wants you to believe." She looked at the baby sleeping in the stroller. "But she was wrong about this one. Until the last moment she thought this baby would be a girl. I never even asked the doctor the sex since Ethan and I were so confident of Pet's prediction. And yet here he lies, Thomas Finn Anderson in the flesh."

Pet shook her head and chuckled. "I don't know how I missed this one. I was so sure." She laid her hand on top of the baby's. "But I've changed enough diapers since Thomas was born to know without a doubt that he's male."

"So you're a stay-at-home mom?" Evie asked Helen.

"Actually, I'm a college student. I've just earned enough credits to be an official sophomore." Helen laughed. "I know what you're thinking. I'm a bit old for keggers and sorority rushes, but better late than never, I always say."

"Absolutely. What are you studying?"

"I'm going to be a teacher."

"Really? You'll have to apply at Heron Point Elementary when you get your degree," Evie said. "I have a sixth sense about people, and I can tell you'd make a great teacher."

"Thanks, but I'm kind of an English freak. I'm going for my secondary certificate."

The waiter brought a tray of scones and filled each woman's cup with tea. Evie took a sip, savoring the hint of orange flavor. "This morning when I was dolphin-watching, I never thought I'd be enjoying real English tea three hours later," she said.

Claire gave her a coy smile. "Like I said, there's a lot about Heron Point that will surprise you. Have you met anyone besides us, and Hester Poole, of course?"

Figuring that Claire knew about her encounter with one of her police officers the night before, Evie spooned a generous helping of jelly onto her scone and thought about her answer. The words describing Billy Muldoone caught in her throat, however, when she glanced up and saw the man himself standing at the entrance, all neat, pressed, decidedly official and every bit as handsome as he'd looked the day before. She swallowed, nodded toward the doorway and said, "As a matter of fact…"

All three women followed her gaze. "You've met Billy?" Helen said.

"I did. He caught me red-footed, prowling around the school last night before dark. The back door was unlocked, so I just walked in for a quick look-around." She smiled. "He didn't seem to like it much."

Helen laughed. "That's our Billy. And I bet he didn't believe a word of your story, either."

"Something like that. For a minute I thought he was going to—" she lowered her voice in her best imitation of Billy's growl "—take me downtown for questioning."

"I know what that's like," Helen said. "I've had my share of run-ins with Heron Point's finest." She licked jelly off her finger and whispered, "Don't look now, but he spotted us and he's headed this way."

Evie quickly buried her face in her teacup, afraid the flush in her cheeks would be evident to everyone at the table. Good grief, she shouldn't be having a physical reaction like this. She hardly knew the man, and he was married.

Billy ambled over. Out of the corner of her eye, Evie watched him take off his cap and stick it under his arm. "Afternoon, ladies."

"Hi, Billy," Claire said, her tone bright. "I understand you've met our new school principal."

"Sure have."

Evie felt his full attention on her, and her heartbeat kicked up a notch. She returned her teacup to its saucer and risked looking up at him.

"So you survived your first night in town, I see," he said.

Relieved when her voice was calm and even, she said, "I did. No problems."

"Good. You've got a fine group of tour guides here. They'll tell you how it really is."

"Oh, yeah, she can count on us," Helen said. "We'll tell Evie what she needs to know."

The waiter returned to the table with a brown bag in his hand. "Hey, Billy, your take-out is ready."

"Okay, thanks." He stared at Evie a moment longer. "Nice seeing you again."

"Same here."

He left the dining room, and Evie watched out the front window as he crossed the street toward the Heron Point City Hall. When she looked back at her companions, they were all smiling. "What?"

"He likes you," Helen said.

Evie's mouth dropped open before she said, "No, I don't think so." She was about to explain that she knew Billy had a family, but Helen interrupted.

"Of course he does. He didn't come over here to check out the kind of tea we were having. His interest was all on you."

Pet flipped her long platinum braid over her shoulder. "Be fair, Helen. Maybe Billy was just being friendly. His days as a womanizer are pretty much behind him now. And he's a good person. He's just been unlucky in love."

"That's right," Claire agreed. "And he's hardworking. He's eating his lunch in the squad car. That shows dedication."

Helen snickered. "More likely he's avoiding that control freak of a mother who lives with him. I wouldn't go home to lunch with her, either."

Evie leaned back, trying to catch a glimpse of the cruiser through the window. "He lives with his mother?"

"Yes, he does," Claire said. "And his daughter."

So this was Billy's family? His mother and daughter?

"By the way, Evie," Helen said, "you'll get to know Billy's daughter, Gemma. She'll be in the fourth grade this year."

"Oh, really? I look forward to meeting her."

Helen sent a devious glance to her friends.

"Okay, Helen," Evie said, "is there something you're not telling me?"

"Do not influence this woman one way or the other," Claire said. "It wouldn't be right."

The baby woke and started to fuss. Helen picked him up. "I guess you'll draw your own conclusions soon enough," she said. "Just remember that name— Gemma Scarlett Muldoone." Settling the baby against her shoulder, she added, "And you might want to put Billy's cell phone number on your speed dial."

CHAPTER THREE

SATURDAY NIGHT YAWNED ahead of Evie like the flat Florida landscape she'd driven through two days before. She'd spent the day at the school organizing her work space and adding personal touches. The small office was beginning to feel like home.

She wished she could say the same for Hester Poole's frilly little haven. But Evie didn't think she could stand sipping another iced tea from a flowery pink tumbler or bathing with another of the rose-shaped, quarter-size soaps Hester provided with a ruffled shower cap. And surfing the eight channels the outdoor antenna picked up wasn't any more appealing.

If she were in Detroit, Evie would be spending Saturday night with one of her few remaining friends who still lived in the city, or going on a don't-get-your-hopes-up date, or hitting one of the local cineplexes. A movie wasn't an option in Heron Point. There wasn't a single theater in town.

She supposed she could wander down Hester's brick-paved walkway to the Gulf and watch the tide roll in, but she was starving. She decided to go into town to the Green Door Café for supper. Maybe she'd run into Pet Sweeney.

What Evie hadn't counted on was the volume of traffic in town on a Saturday night. After two slow passes down Island Avenue, she finally spotted a car pulling out of a space. She did what she always criticized other drivers for doing—she sat in the street with her blinker on to nab the spot before anyone else could. And she did her best to ignore the drivers in the line behind her.

When she got out of her car, she noticed she was close to Wear It Again, the clothing store owned by her new friend, Claire. Evie walked up to the display window and looked inside. Claire had said she ran a vintage shop. All the selections Evie could see through the glass were elegant and unusual, and according to the tags within sight, some once belonged to Hollywood celebrities.

The store was crowded, but Evie ventured in anyway. She wouldn't stay long, just say hi to Claire. A young woman signaled to her when she came inside. "Be right with you," she said.

"Hi, I'm Sue Ellen," she said a few minutes later, unnecessarily. She wore a name tag on the lapel of her shabby chic jacket. "Can I help you?"

"I stopped by to see Claire," Evie explained.

"Oh, she's not here. She's hardly ever here on a Saturday night." She nodded toward another girl who had pinned her name tag to a wide band around her hair. "We handle things on weekend nights."

Evie thanked her and left the shop. Imagine not being present for what must be the biggest sales night of the week. Claire must have a lot of confidence in her employees or, more likely, she wasn't as concerned about the income as many of the island's shopkeepers appeared to be.

Evie walked the three blocks to the Green Door, dodging couples holding hands or families with strollers. She hoped she wouldn't have to wait long for a table since it was nearly eight o'clock. The restaurant was busy, but Evie managed to grab a small table by the window. She asked the mature waitress if Pet Sweeney was working.

"Oh, honey," the woman said, "Pet only works in the daytime. She vowed when she got married she'd never volunteer for a Friday or Saturday night again." The waitress flipped open her order pad and pulled a pencil from behind her ear. "A lot of the local employees avoid the Avenue on weekends, which is fine with me. It gives us Micopee gals a chance at the biggest tips."

Evie ordered a hamburger and a raspberry iced tea. So that's it, she thought, when the waitress had walked away. The locals prefer Heron Point during the week when the tourists weren't invading.

Since Claire and Pet weren't in town, and since Helen lived more than an hour's drive away in Gainesville, Evie had exhausted her supply of new friends who could teach her the fine art of livin' easy. She bit into a juicy burger and smiled to herself. Unless I count Officer Billy Muldoone, she thought. He must be around town tonight. And I suppose I could call him my friend. She swallowed a sweet gulp of tea. He did find my earring.

She was still thinking about Billy after she left the Green Door and had resumed window-shopping. When she was opposite the largest building in town, the hotel where she'd had lunch yesterday, a commotion near the sidewalk café stopped her. In the middle of it was the tall, broad-shouldered Muldoone.

He saw her at the same time and greeted her in that booming baritone that muted every other sound on the street. "Hey, there, Evie. Come on over."

She approached slowly since it was obvious Billy was on duty and, in fact, was performing one of his legal responsibilities at that very moment. She stopped a few feet from the entrance to the café. Billy propped his foot on a bench next to a man who was slouched forward with his hands behind his back. Billy rested his elbow on his bent knee. "What are you doing out tonight?" he asked Evie.

She couldn't resist staring at the man she assumed was Billy's captive. He was a scruffy-looking character perhaps in his mid-thirties. Though his head was down, she could see a scowl on his face. She noticed, too, a strand of white plastic sticking out from behind his waist. The new type of restraining device used by police forces.

"I'm, uh, just wandering."

Billy smiled. "Nice night for it."

She blinked a couple of times. This was the first apprehended criminal she'd seen that wasn't on the eleven o'clock news. "So what are you doing?"

"Had to grab this guy," Billy said. "And a couple others earlier. Been a busy night."

The man looked up at Billy and barked an expletive.

"Watch it," Billy said. "We've got ladies all around us. Maybe if I tighten those restraints, it'll encourage you to mind your manners."

The man stared at the sidewalk.

The knee of Billy's uniform was ripped through, showing bruised flesh beneath. And when she looked more closely at him, she realized that his elbow had been scraped raw, too. "What happened to you?" she asked.

He shrugged one well-rounded shoulder. "It's nothing. I had to use a Pensacola High School tackling move to get this fella to slow up." He pointed down, and for the first time Evie noticed his criminal wore a pair of ragged socks on his feet and no shoes.

"Look under there," Billy said, and Evie bent to see under the bench. "He was wearing those Rollerblade skates, which meant he had a good head start on me."

"You caught him when he was on inline skates?" she asked, amazed that a man Billy's size could churn up that much speed.

"The crowd slowed him down some," Billy

admitted. "That's the thing about these weekend pick-pockets. They don't take into account that there are disadvantages to stealing in a mob." He grinned at her. "Or the fact that my mother had a willow tree in her backyard, and avoiding her switch taught me a good deal about hauling a—" he paused "—running fast."

He looked over her shoulder toward the street and nudged the man beside him. "Time to go, Eugene," he said. "Our ride's here."

The glossy-white porch railings around the café reflected the blue and red cruiser lights, and Evie stepped out of the way with the rest of the crowd. When the car stopped, a young female officer got out. She walked up and grabbed the pickpocket by the elbow while Billy tugged him off the bench.

"Hey, Gail, say hello to Evie," Billy said as he pushed the top of his captive's head to lower the guy into the back seat. "She's our new principal."

Gail, a cute yet officious-looking brunette about Evie's height, stuck out her hand. "Heard about you. Welcome to town."

"Thanks."

Billy called to a civilian on the porch. "You mind tossing me those skates and that pocketbook?"

The unsuccessful getaway wheels and a Louis Vuitton bag came sailing over to Billy. "Much obliged," Billy said to the tourist. He handed the purse to Gail. "You'll see that lady gets this back?"

She nodded.

"Tell her not to let this spoil her impression of Heron Point. The only reason this guy was able to grab her purse without somebody stopping him was because he was wearing those damn wheels. I'm going to suggest a new code at the next town council meeting. No skates after 8:00 p.m. on weekends."

"Good idea," Gail said. "You sure you don't want me to ride into Micopee with you? I can call Jack to come in and spell me."

"No. Don't bother him. I'll pick up Lou, and he can help me escort Eugene as well as those other two guys at city hall. We've just got one holding cell on the island," he explained to Evie, "and that's only because Jack insisted on having it built when he became chief of police. So when we've got more than one perp, we've got to take them to the county jail in Micopee."

Raised in an area where the jails were generally larger than high schools, Evie simply said, "Oh."

Billy winked at her. "I'd ask you to ride along, but the front seat next to me will be occupied."

She smiled uncertainly back at him. "That's quite all right. I understand completely."

He slid into the driver's seat of the cruiser. "I hear you're staying out at the Pink Ladies."

"That's right."

"Maybe I'll give you a call sometime, see how you're doing. I've lived in Heron Point a good long while, and I can tell you about the area."

From the backseat, a nasal voice mimicked,

"Maybe I'll give you a call sometime." Billy glared over his shoulder through a protective screen. "You watch yourself back there. It's a dark, lonely ride to Micopee. One more missing person along that stretch of roadway wouldn't even raise an eyebrow around here." He nodded to Gail. "You see Evie gets back to her car okay, will you? We've got some smart mouths in town tonight."

"You got it, Billy."

The two women watched him drive away, and Evie realized she hadn't responded to his offer. Maybe it was just as well. She heard Gail sigh beside her and turned to look at her. "Is something wrong?" she asked.

"Isn't he wonderful?"

Evie didn't quite know how to answer that. She hadn't decided if Billy Muldoone was any part of wonderful, though she now knew that at least one woman in town thought he was all that and more. "He seems to be an excellent police officer," she said, confident that the man she'd just seen in action would have no trouble with the criminals he was hauling off to jail.

AT FIVE O'CLOCK Sunday afternoon Billy drove down Island Avenue in the squad car and convinced himself that it was quiet enough to go home. Most of the tourists had left, and the shopkeepers had pulled their merchandise in from the sidewalks. It had been a busy couple of days, even for an August weekend. The

weather had been balmy with no rain, no doubt attract-
ing last-minute visitors.

He rolled down the window and rested his arm on
the car door, enjoying the warm refreshing air that
flowed through the cruiser and erased the sour smell
of cheap alcohol from the inebriated petty thieves he'd
picked up. He didn't know exactly when he'd become
the unofficial second-in-command on the police force,
but he was proud that Jack trusted him so much.

Thankfully they had a good crew. Gail was a competent cop even if she was sweet on him. Billy admired
Gail, but he would never date anyone on the force.
Personal relations didn't mix with official responsibilities, especially for cops. Ricky, the transplant
from the Orlando P.D. Jack had hired when he took
over, was working out great. Lou was a willing and sat-
isfactory service aide, and among the five permanent
members of the Heron Point department and the
couple of extras they hired on particularly busy
weekends, the town was enjoying low crime and de-
pendable service.

But now, as he was most times at the end of the
tourist rush, Billy was tired and ready to settle back into
his recliner and sniff whatever his ma was preparing
for dinner. Mulligan stew probably, since it was Sunday
and she never let her family forget they were Irish.

Beginning to sweat, Billy jacked the A/C another
notch, taking advantage of the salty air outside and the
cool, recycled air coming from the vents. He took off

his hat and tossed it next to him on the bench seat. He could practically smell the roast beef simmering now. He may have some complaints about living with his mother after so many years of independence, but no one would ever catch him bad-mouthing her cooking.

As he approached the turn to Gulfview Road he considered detouring away from the middle of town, where he lived in a hundred-year-old clapboard house on what his mother called one of the prettiest little streets she'd ever seen. Billy would have much preferred the unobstructed view of the water from a property on Gulfview Road. Heck, with the price of real estate escalating in Heron Point, he doubted he'd ever own a piece of the Gulf shore now.

But Claire and Jack did. And so did Hester, whose fancy Pink Ladies cut a flowery trail all the way to the water. Where Evie Gaynor was renting.

Billy turned onto Gulfview Road. Maybe he'd stop and pay Evie a visit. On the other hand, he'd told her he'd call, so that's probably what he should do.

Since he'd already made the turn and since the water looked so blue and endless and since dinner wouldn't be ready for at least an hour at the Muldoone house, Billy veered into Claire and Jack's driveway. He'd give Jack an informal report, maybe have a beer and talk for a few minutes—who knows? Maybe the conversation would lead to the new principal.

He pressed the button on his cell phone that connected him home. "Hey, Daddy," his daughter answered.

"Hi there, Gemma, what's goin' on?"

"Nothing much. Nana's making me fold my laundry. She says I have to have all my clothes in order by tomorrow morning so she can take me shopping for new school things."

Clearly detecting the irritation in his daughter's voice, Billy said, "That's a good thing, isn't it? You want new clothes, don't you?"

"Don't care one way or the other," Gemma said. "New clothes just get to be old clothes soon enough, and you end up starting all over again anyway."

Billy shook his head. Sometimes there was no point arguing his daughter's logic. "I'm over at Jack's," he said. "Tell Nana I'll be home in time for supper."

"I'll tell her. Don't be late or you'll be in trouble."

He could picture Gemma's finger shaking at the phone—the same sassy gesture Brenda Muldoone had perfected raising Billy and his two brothers. No one should ever underestimate the value of a good finger-shaking. "I won't be late."

He stuck the cell phone in his pocket and walked up the few steps to the Hogan's front porch. Tapping lightly on the door, he hollered, "Anybody home?"

He heard a youthful squeal and a voice calling out that she'd get it. In a few seconds, the door swung open and Billy stared down at Jane, Claire's daughter. The girl's deep brown eyes smiled right along with her mouth as she announced over her shoulder, "Billy's here." She opened the door wider. "Come on in."

Jane was cute as a button. All sweet-smelling and sparkly in pink shorts with ribbons in her long dark hair. She was only a year older than Gemma, and Billy often regretted that the two girls had never seemed to hit it off.

"How are you, Jane?" When she assured him that everything was rosy in her life, he asked where Jack was.

"He's outside." She pointed through the rear of the house. "Go on out."

Billy entered the kitchen where Claire and Pet Sweeney were concocting something that smelled delicious. "Ladies," he said. "Hope I didn't interrupt anything."

Claire motioned to a tray of raw steaks on the counter. "You're not going to be in our way, Billy. At least not until I can actually get Jack to put these things on the grill." She paused and then said, "Why don't you stay for dinner? We have an extra. I thought we were going to have company, but she turned me down."

"She?"

"Yes. You met her—our new principal, Evie Gaynor."

Billy leaned against the counter. "Evie was coming here?"

"Well, she never agreed to. But I invited her. She said she had some work to do before the teachers arrived for planning sessions tomorrow." Claire glanced at Pet. "Actually, she didn't say so, but I think Evie was afraid she'd be intruding. What do you think, Aunt Pet?"

"Maybe." Pet delivered a mischievous look to Billy. "What do you think? You know her as well as anyone."

"Me? I just met her…"

Pet continued as if he hadn't spoken. "Surely you've formed an opinion about our Miss Gaynor."

Normally, Billy could ramble for ten or fifteen minutes on most any subject. But in this case, he simply said, "She seems real nice."

Pet smiled. "She does, doesn't she?"

Billy stood straight, suddenly uncomfortable under Pet's scrutiny.

Claire sprinkled seasoning on the steaks. "So what do you say, Billy? Will you stay?"

"Thanks anyway, but I promised Gemma I'd be home. She's got my evening all planned out with video game challenges. But I'd like to have a word with Jack, if that's okay?"

"He's in the gazebo, avoiding the grill," Claire said. "I'm pretty sure he and Finn have had enough girl chatter for one afternoon." She pointed her spoon at the back door. "They'll welcome another male."

"Thanks." Billy left and headed down the pathway to the gazebo, which stood near the shore. He hadn't been pleased to hear that Jack wasn't alone and, worse, that his company was Finn Sweeney. "That's just great," he grumbled to himself as he meandered through the herb garden Pet had maintained while she'd lived in the smaller cottage behind Claire's bungalow. He never looked forward to seeing the gruff old fisherman.

Billy and Finn had never gotten along, especially since Billy had once pursued his daughter Helen. Finn had always criticized any guy Helen went out with, and yet she'd ended up with the son of the one man the old grouch had sworn never to forgive. Yet Finn had gotten over his grudge with his decades-old enemy, proving again that life could take some odd turns.

"Look at you," Billy said to himself. "Who'd have ever thought you'd actually ask your mother to move in with you?" But when Gemma had shown up on his doorstep four years ago, and Billy hadn't known the first thing about kids, he'd seen Brenda as the answer to his prayers.

Widowed and with no family members who needed her anymore, Brenda Muldoone had willingly come to help her eldest son. Now she strived to keep all of them on the straight and narrow. Though no longer one of her weapons, that now-legendary willow switch reminded Billy every day that she was the woman who could do it.

Jack looked up when Billy stepped on a dry twig. "Hey, look who's here."

Finn frowned. "You write your quota of speeding tickets for one day, Muldoone?"

Billy stepped into the gazebo and shook his head. "I'm not getting into an argument with you, Sweeney."

"It'd be the first time."

Apparently, Finn was never going to get past all those reckless driving tickets Billy had given Helen, even though the old man knew darned well she'd deserved every one of them. At least motherhood had turned Helen into a conservative driver—something half a dozen fines hadn't been able to do.

"I've come to talk to Jack," Billy said, sending a pleading glance to the man who was both his boss and his friend.

"I'd like to give you some privacy and take a hike, Billy," Finn said, tapping the arms of his wheelchair. "Unfortunately my hiking days have been somewhat limited the last forty-odd years."

Jack motioned for Billy to sit on the bench built into the wall of the gazebo. "What's on your mind? Is this something you can't discuss in front of Finn?"

Billy studied the old man's face for a moment. "I suppose he can hear."

"Then go ahead and spill it," Finn said. "Since there's no way I'm going to end up with you as a son-in-law, I don't dislike you half as much as I used to."

"That's a relief," Billy mumbled. He clasped his hands between his knees and looked at Jack. "I'm just wondering what you know about the new principal, Evie Gaynor. Have you met her?"

"Not much, but Claire likes her. She was going to suggest Evie move into Pet's old cottage. It's been sitting vacant since Pet and Finn got married."

"That's a great idea," Billy said.

"So what's your interest in her?"

Billy shrugged. "I was just thinking of being friendly."

Finn snickered. "So that's what they call it these days."

Jack scowled at Finn. "Never mind," he said and gave Billy his full attention. "That's a good plan. If you like this lady, take things a bit more slowly. She's new in town. She'll need friends, and, speaking from experience, I don't know of a better one than you."

"So you don't think I might be reaching too high?"

Jack draped his arm around Billy's shoulder. "Buddy, I don't think the Queen of England is beyond your reach. I feel about you like I would a brother, but that doesn't mean I'd marry you."

"Well, thank God for that," Billy muttered.

Jack laughed. "Evie's not going anywhere. I have it on good authority from the mayor that she signed a two-year contract to stick it out down here. That gives you plenty of time to sweep her off her feet."

"Right. If I don't step on her toes in the process."

Claire hollered at them from the house.

"Oh, Lord," Finn said. "She's waving that spatula like it was a battle ax. I'd suggest you take the hint."

Jack went behind the wheelchair and pushed it toward the ramp he'd installed when Finn and Pet married. "Stay for dinner, Billy?"

"Can't. Ma's got stew cooking." He went down the steps, walked briskly toward the house but called back to the other two, "Thanks for the advice. I know what I'm going to do." And he did. He'd wait until tomorrow to call Evie and let her know how good a friend he could be.

CHAPTER FOUR

So FAR Evie's first official day had gone extraordinarily well. She'd arrived at Heron Point Elementary a few minutes before eight o'clock, just ahead of her administrative assistant, Mary Alice Jones, a middle-aged whirlwind of energy.

The eight teachers and auxiliary staff assembled in the cafeteria, a portable metal structure next to the main building, at eight thirty, where Evie introduced herself. Since most of the staff had been at the school for three years or more, they knew the procedures and made Evie feel welcome.

The third-grade teacher, a man in his mid-fifties, had lived in Heron Point since the school opened ten years earlier. He treated everyone by bringing in doughnuts from the town's bakery, which happened to be owned by his wife. When he offered to bring coffee cake the next morning, Evie knew the figure she'd worked so hard for at her gym was in serious jeopardy.

After meetings all morning and a lunch of lasagna and green beans prepared by the cafeteria staff, Evie settled down at her desk with a stack of one hundred and twenty-five student folders that reached nearly to her chin. She'd gotten to know the teachers, now it was time to familiarize herself with the students. She pulled the first one off the top and opened it.

Johnny Adler. Evie studied the third-grader's features from last year's school picture, scanned the teacher's comments about Johnny's progress and behavior, and tried to place his face with his name.

Two hours had flown by when Evie reached the middle of the alphabet. She opened the folder containing records for Gemma Scarlett Muldoone and looked into mischievous brown eyes that immediately made Evie think of the girl's father. Her hair was lighter than Billy's, more the tan of a coconut and streaked with highlights the color of a new penny. The long waves were gathered into a neat ponytail with a bright green ribbon.

Smiling at the girl's photo, Evie said, "Is this the child Helen Sweeney hinted was the terror of Heron Point? She looks so sweet."

Evie flipped to the page containing Gemma's vital information and gasped. Gemma's record resembled a daily diary rather than a recap of educational milestones. Evie counted a dozen sheets of paper filled with comments from teachers and counselors and the previous principal.

When she'd reached the end of Gemma's profile, Evie stuffed all the pages back into the folder and slammed it closed.

If a child is believed to be bad, or rumored to be bad, or expected to be bad, he will behave badly.

"I refuse to read a single word of this," she said. "I will not be prejudiced by past opinions about this girl. It's a new year, and every child deserves a clean slate."

She couldn't imagine the easy-going, self-assured cop she'd met raising a child who had a problem following rules. Evie didn't know what had happened to Gemma's mother—if she had died or if Billy and she were divorced—but she did know that Billy's mother lived with them. Gemma had the input of both her father and grandmother.

Evie shoved the folder aside, picked up a pencil and began tapping it on her desk. Just because Billy was a capable cop, didn't mean he was a competent father. She'd encountered many parents who, in her opinion, weren't qualified for the job. Plus there were those who'd been willing and interested parents but not necessarily good ones. From this perspective, Evie was able to rationalize her growing desire to know more about Billy.

Her tapping grew more insistent as she recalled his announcement that he would call her sometime. He'd said it in front of Gail, so she assumed they didn't have a relationship. And he wouldn't have mentioned calling her at all if he hadn't intended to do it, would he?

She spun her chair around to stare out the corner window. "Of course he would," she said. "It was a casual comment, nothing more. Billy probably had no intention of calling despite what you let yourself believe and despite what Helen said about the over-zealous cop." Evie had to take Billy's comment as just what it was—a local guy's good-humored welcome to a newcomer. And that was just as well. Evie's focus should be on Gemma, not the girl's father.

Billy's ruggedly handsome face evaporated from Evie's mind at a knock on her door. "Come in," she said, turning away from her view of the outside world.

Mary Alice stuck her head inside. "Sorry to bother you, Miss Gaynor, but we have a problem."

"Oh?"

"One of our mothers is outside with her son and an-other student. It seems there was an incident on the playground before she came to pick up her child."

"What? School hasn't even started yet."

Mary Alice shrugged. "We let the kids use the fa-cilities all year long. These two were playing on the equipment. Shall I send them in?"

"Of course." Evie rose. A girl entered first, and Evie's gaze traveled from her pretty, pixie face and sun-streaked dark hair to the folder she'd just finished perusing. The girl's familiar brown eyes glittered with indignation.

"This is Gemma Muldoone," Mary Alice said, nudging the student farther into the room so the others could enter. The secretary introduced a slightly taller, husky boy as Bernard Hutchinson. "And this is Bernard's mother," she said. "Missy Hutchinson."

Once everyone was inside, Mary Alice quickly

slipped out and closed the door behind her. Evie faced three scowling faces. "What's happened?"

"I'll tell you what happened," Missy declared. She pushed her son forward. "Look at him."

Once she got a good look at Bernard's shirt, Evie jumped back a step. "Good heavens. He's covered with bugs!"

"You're telling me," Missy said. "They're glued on."

Regaining her composure, Evie advanced toward Bernard. She reached out and tentatively touched a lifelike roach, half expecting it to dart from under her finger. It didn't. It remained immobile as one would expect from glued plastic. "They're not real."

"Thank heavens for that!" Missy said. "But they've ruined his shirt just the same." She jabbed a finger toward Gemma's head. "And her father can darned well replace it. I don't care if he does only make a policeman's salary. This shirt cost thirty dollars."

Thirty dollars? For a kid's play shirt? Evie refrained from commenting. "Did you do this?" she asked Gemma Muldoone.

"Why are you asking her?" Missy practically squealed. "I just told you she did. This child would lie about anything."

Evie held up a hand. "Excuse me, Mrs. Hutchinson, but will you let me handle this?"

Missy released a pent-up breath and tugged at a caterpillar on Bernard's collar. "See? They don't come off."

Evie pulled a chair next to Gemma. "Sit down, please."

The girl's chin thrust forward. "I don't want to."

"But I would like you to, so please do it."

Gemma sat, appearing more like a wooden statue than a flesh-and-blood child.

"Now, I'd like you to tell me if you glued bugs to Bernard's shirt and, if so, why you did it."

Gemma's eyes narrowed to slits. "I'm not saying I did, but *if* I did, it was because Bernard said I wasn't going on any field trips this year."

"Why would Bernard say that?"

"Because he's mean and stupid."

Missy fisted her hands on her hips. "There, you see? That's what you're dealing with, Miss Gaynor. A vandal and a name-caller."

Evie sighed. "Please, Mrs. Hutchinson. There's no need to resort to more name-calling." She leaned over to be closer to Bernard's height. "Did you tell Gemma that she wasn't going on any field trips?"

"Sure. She's not. She didn't go on any last year— after the first one."

Missy nodded dramatically. "Gemma's not allowed near a public school bus," she declared.

Evie didn't intend to discuss that matter. Not when she still had the plastic bug caper to deal with. "This is a new year," she said. "I think we'll let Gemma's teacher and I make field trip decisions."

Missy smirked. "Don't say I didn't warn you."

Evie perched on the edge of her desk and stared at Gemma, whose expression remained stoic. "You do realize, Gemma, that you can't react to something someone said with a physical attack. That behavior is unacceptable. In this school we will respect each other's personal property."

Gemma huffed. "School hasn't started yet. We were just playing. And besides, I didn't say I did it."

"No, but I believe you did. And you're going to have to tell your father that if those bugs don't come off, you owe Bernard a new shirt."

"*You're* not going to tell him?"

"I haven't decided yet. I'm going to ask Bernard to give me his shirt, and you and I are going to stay in this office for as long as it takes for you to remove those bugs. And if Mrs. Hutchinson isn't satisfied with the result, then we'll see about involving your father."

Gemma crossed her arms over her chest and slouched. "That's not fair. He started it."

"And it will end here, today. Do you need to call someone at home to say you'll be delayed at school?"

"No."

"Fine." Evie wiggled her fingers at Bernard. "The shirt please."

He took it off, handed it to her, and stood there in an Abercrombie T-shirt.

"I'm curious about one thing," Evie said. "Did you try to stop Gemma from gluing bugs to your clothes?"

The considerably larger Bernard refused to look in

Gemma's direction. "Not after she said she'd punch my stomach."

A smile lurked at the corners of Evie's mouth. "I see. So you pretty much let her glue the bugs on?"

Bernard shrugged.

"Well, I hope you'll remember from now on that you are not in charge of school policy, and that includes making decisions about who will and will not go on field trips."

The boy hung his head. "Yes, ma'am."

Evie turned to Gemma. "Is there something you'd like to say to Bernard?"

Gemma glared at him. "Yes, but then you'd call my dad."

"Gemma!"

"Okay." She squinted her eyes so tightly her face looked like a piece of overripe fruit. "I'm sorry, Bernard."

Missy Hutchinson wasn't satisfied. "That's it? You're not going to punish this child? You're not even going to call her father?"

Evie was losing patience with Missy about as quickly as she was losing it with Gemma. "I'll take care of matters from this point, Mrs. Hutchinson. You and Bernard may go. I'll see that the shirt is returned for your inspection."

Missy spun toward the door, pushing Bernard ahead of her. Evie tossed the shirt to Gemma. "You'd better get started."

Gemma plucked a couple of bugs free before

looking up at Evie with soulful dark eyes. "Thanks for not calling my dad."

"Don't thank me yet. It's still a possibility."

"Excuse me." A gray-haired man appeared in the doorway.

"Yes?"

"Are you the new principal?"

Evie nodded. "And you are?"

"I'm Malcolm VanFleet, the maintenance man."

Evie walked over and shook his hand. "It's nice to meet you, Malcolm. Did you need me?"

He stepped into her office. "Yes, ma'am." Holding up a clear plastic bag, he said, "It's about these things."

Evie recognized the contents immediately. Dozens of bugs just like the ones on Bernard's shirt. And a tube of quick-drying cement. She looked at Gemma who remained remarkably intent upon her task. "Where did you find these?" Evie asked Malcolm.

"Oh, they're all over the playground. Bugs are stuck to the swings, the slide, the monkey bars, everywhere. I don't know how long it'll take me to get them all off, but I expect you should plan on paying me overtime since school starts in two days."

Evie took the bag. She almost didn't recognize her own voice when she said through clenched teeth, "Thank you, Malcolm." Then she stuck her head out the door. "Mary Alice!"

The secretary jumped up from her chair. "Yes, Miss Gaynor?"

"Do you have Officer Muldoone's phone number?"

Mary Alice smiled. "Oh, yes. I believe his cell number was left on the Rolodex on top of your desk. Would you like me to call him for you?"

Evie whirled around and went back into her office. "Never mind. I'll do it myself."

BILLY ALWAYS CARRIED a couple of small animal cages in the trunk of the cruiser. Living this close to water, you never knew when something would find its way onto a resident's property. This afternoon's creature was the belly-crawling kind.

He picked up the wire mesh box to show Mrs. Blake. "It's just a harmless rat snake, ma'am," he said. "I guarantee it was more afraid of you than you were of it."

The elderly woman fluttered a handkerchief in front of her face. "You're wrong about that, Billy. When a lady sees something like that coiled around the commode, well, I tell you, she's plenty scared. It could have been a moccasin or some other poisonous snake."

Billy smiled. "That would be *venomous,* Mrs. Blake. Snakes have venom in their bites, not poison. And this guy doesn't have any venom at all."

"I'm glad to hear that," she said. "And I do thank you for coming to my rescue."

Billy refrained from telling her that he more likely came to the rat snake's rescue. Mrs. Blake hadn't dropped her shovel since he'd arrived. When he got off work, he'd take the harmless creature out to the Indian burial grounds on the other side of the bridge and release it. He couldn't see any justification in killing something that just happened to wander out of its element. "You're welcome," he said. "You call me anytime."

He set the cage on the back seat. "Here you go, buddy. Unfortunately this is where most snakes in Heron Point end up eventually, usually the human kind." After rechecking the box latch, Billy got behind the wheel. One more pass around town and he'd head back to city hall to write up a mostly uneventful report. He dreaded that job. Jack was a great boss and certainly a qualified chief of police, but he was a stickler for paperwork.

As Billy backed out of Mrs. Blake's driveway, his cell phone rang. He pulled it out of his pocket and checked the caller. "Heron Point Elementary," he said. "Well, I'll be." A smile broke across his face. He could only think of one person at the school who might be trying to reach him—Evie.

He pressed the connect button. "Muldoone here."

"Billy, it's Evie Gaynor at the elementary school."

His smile widened at the sound of her voice. Brisk, official-sounding even, but music to his ears. "Hey, Evie, I was just thinking about—"

"Billy, we have a problem."

"We do?" His smile began to fade.

"I have Gemma in my office."

Oh, boy. "What's she doing there? School doesn't start for two days yet."

"Maybe so, but your daughter made her presence known a little early. Can you come by?"

Billy sighed. "I'll be right there…. What did she do?"

"I think you should see this for yourself. A description doesn't do this particular situation justice."

The line went dead. And unless he could smooth this over, so would his hopes for developing any kind of relationship with Evie.

EVIE HEARD HIS VOICE the moment he entered the outer office. Billy Muldoone had a way of making his presence known.

"I'm here to see Miss Gaynor," he said to Mary Alice.

Mary Alice's answer crooned with sympathy, as if she were used to this scenario. "Oh, hi, Billy. Yeah, I know. She and Gemma are in there."

He stood on the threshold and looked into the office. Evie stood and came around the desk, her hands clenched at her waist. Meetings with parents under these circumstances was never pleasant, and this particular meeting was already topping the tension meter. Billy had been popping into Evie's head with alarming regularity all day. But any relationship she'd envisioned had just moved to the principal's office. It was a shame, really. Billy looked so crisp and competent…and, with his face shadowed with a day's end beard, even sexy. But when the little creases at his mouth deepened, Evie realized he also looked uncharacteristically vulnerable.

He closed the door and removed his ball cap. His

gaze held Evie's for a moment before he looked to his left and saw Gemma. She stared up at him through wispy bangs that needed a trim. She struggled to pull a bug from a shirt and finally dropped it into a pile on the floor beside her chair. "Hi, Daddy."

His mouth twisted into a frown. "Hi, yourself. What'd you do?" He stared at the plastic items by her feet. "What are those?"

"Bugs. They're not real."

"How'd they get on that shirt?"

"They got glued there."

He took a few steps closer and wiggled a stuck bug. "They sure did."

Evie motioned to a chair. "Why don't you sit down, Officer Muldoone?"

He sat stiffly, as if he were the one in trouble, and ran long fingers through his hair. "What happened?"

Evie briefed him, ending with the clean-up necessary to the playground. "Naturally we want all plastic insect infestation gone before Wednesday."

"I saw Malcolm working out there when I drove up," Billy said. "I couldn't figure out what he was doing picking at the monkey bars like he was."

"Well, now you know. He says he has a solvent that will loosen the glue, but it will take time."

"Time the taxpayers of Heron Point will have to pay for," he said, staring at his daughter. "Where did you get the bugs, Gemma?"

"At the Dollar Mart in Micopee. Nana had to go

there for something and she gave me five dollars to spend. Somebody was putting out the Halloween stuff, and I saw these." She held up a rubbery spider. "There were fifty in a bag. I bought five bags." She paused before anticipating his next question. "I got the glue from Nana's kitchen drawer."

"*One* bag of bugs didn't do it for you?"

"Not once I got started. It was fun putting them places."

Billy pointed to the shirt on her lap. "Like that."

"Specially here."

"Whose shirt is it?"

She mumbled the answer.

Billy's face blanched. "Whose did you say?"

"Bernard Hutchinson's."

He looked at the ceiling. "That's just great. Why did you pick Bernard's shirt?"

"He was saying stuff I didn't like and that wasn't true." She blinked at Evie. "Isn't that so, Miss Gaynor? He can't say whether I go on field trips."

Evie leaned against the desk. "You know that's not the point, Gemma. There are more appropriate ways of handling problems. We don't damage anyone else's property. In this school we will respect one another's belongings."

Gemma raised a supplicating gaze to her father. "You would have done the same thing, Daddy."

"Me? I don't think I would have put bugs on Bernard's shirt."

"Maybe not Bernard's, but you would his mother's. You don't like Missy Hutchinson. Didn't you say she was stuck-up and con-de…" She pulled her lower lip between her teeth. "What's that word?"

"Never mind. And that's not the point, either. No matter how I feel about Missy—and quit listening in to adult conversations, by the way—I wouldn't glue bugs to one of her hundred-dollar blouses!"

Gemma wiggled a centipede loose. "Oh. Well, we owe Bernard another shirt if this one is ruined."

"That ought to set you back about a dozen weeks of allowances."

Evie raised her eyebrows. "How much allowance does Gemma get, if I may ask?"

"Fifty cents a week…not counting the windfalls my mother obviously drops in her lap for no reason."

"That would be more like sixty allowances," Evie said. "Missy told me what the shirt cost."

Billy shook his head. "Wonderful. *I* don't have a shirt that costs thirty dollars."

Evie sympathized with Billy's situation. Thirty dollars was probably a lot of money to a small-town cop. "You can see why I called you," she said. "This wasn't just a harmless incident. When other students are victimized—"

His eyes rounded, and he interrupted her. "I'd hardly call Bernard victimized. That's an exaggeration."

"I don't think so. His rights were definitely violated.

And there is the matter of financial restitution." Evie folded her arms across her chest. "I don't think we can minimize this."

Billy glared at his daughter. This time she actually squirmed. "You're grounded until you're twenty. You know that, don't you?"

Gemma started to speak, but a commotion in the outer office stopped her.

"I'm going in there right now, Mary Alice." The woman's voice coming through the closed door was intended to dissuade all argument. "You can't stop me."

Gemma's hands stilled. The shirt slipped between her knees to the floor. "Daddy, I think Nana's here."

The door flew open and a deceptively small, wiry dynamo in yellow sneakers, flowered shorts and a sweat-dampened crimson T-shirt burst into the room. Her tomato-red hair was loosely bound in a scrunchy, leaving coarse strands sticking out like sun-dried pampas grass. Her eyes, under bright lavender shadow glittered as she surveyed the scene. She looked first at Evie, then Gemma, then Billy. "What's going on here? I saw the cruiser in the parking lot as I was jogging past."

Billy's face flushed as he turned from the huffing jogger to look at Evie. He stood. "Miss Gaynor, apparently it's time for you to meet my mother, Brenda Muldoone. Ma, this is the new principal."

Brenda nodded once. "What's going on? You going to tell me, Billy?"

He frowned at her. "It seems that five dollars you

gave Gemma at the Dollar Mart was not a particularly wise investment."

"What are you talking about?"

"She bought a few hundred plastic bugs and has been sticking them on everything inside school property."

"Oh." Brenda's perpetual motion ground to a stop as she considered her son's statement. "So that's where my glue went. I tried to seal the crack in a vase earlier and couldn't find the tube of cement." She stuck her hand out at Gemma. "Give it back, young lady, and the rest of those bugs, too."

"I can't, Nana. It's all been con...confis..." She looked at Billy. "What's the word?"

Evie answered for him. "Confiscated, Gemma. Not to be returned."

"She glued plastic bugs on Bernard Hutchinson's shirt." Billy filled Brenda in. "It's probably ruined."

A sound inappropriately like a bark of laughter came from Brenda's cherry-red lips. "I'll bet the little heir to the Hutchinson fortune just stood there and let her do it."

"Ma..."

Brenda quickly recovered and said, for Evie's benefit, "Oh, Gemma, what a naughty thing to do." Then, under her breath she added to Billy, "Guess she couldn't find any live ones."

"Mrs. Muldoone..." Evie said.

"I know, I know." Brenda stared at the shirt. "What

are the damages, Miss Gaynor? We Muldoones pay our bills." She slipped her hand into the pocket of her shorts. "I've got a few bucks on me."

"I don't know yet," Evie said. "If we can remove the bugs without damaging the shirt, then I'll give it back to Mrs. Hutchinson for her approval."

Brenda waved her hand in a dismissive gesture. "That's no problem. I'll have that shirt looking like new."

Billy took hold of his mother's arm. "Ma, you're not helping Gemma realize what she's done."

Brenda's brows came together in a scowl. "I'm not finished with her yet. We haven't started talking punishment. Now, what else?"

"The schoolyard has to be cleaned up. Those bugs are everywhere."

Brenda strode to within a few feet of Gemma's chair. "You really did it this time, didn't you? Got yourself in a peck of trouble."

Gemma shrugged. "Looks like it."

"No dessert for you tonight." She tugged at the tangled bangs on Gemma's forehead. "Well, come on. You look a mess. I've got you an appointment to get your hair trimmed over at Ida's. Then I'll come back with you later and we'll unstick all those bugs." She turned to Billy. "With three of us working, we'll have the place exterminated in no time." She looked at Evie. "I'm going to go ahead and take my granddaughter and the shirt now, Miss Gaynor. We'll fix up the schoolyard."

"But wait…"

Gemma had already taken her grandmother's words as her release from custody. She bolted to the door.

"Stop right there, Gemma," Evie said.

Brenda grabbed her granddaughter's arm and held her still. "We'll see that Gemma learns her lesson."

"I wish you could also assure me this type of behavior won't be repeated."

Staring at the top of Gemma's head, Brenda said, "My granddaughter is a bit high-strung. But this was just a childish prank, a stupid one to be sure, but still a prank." She curved her hand over Gemma's hair. "I think we can assure Miss Gaynor that you won't do this again, can't we, Gemma Scarlett?"

The girl nodded. "I won't do this again."

"There, you see? So I'll take Gemma and we'll come back later for clean-up duty." Brenda's lips widened in a calculated grin. "You tell Missy Hutchinson that Brenda Muldoone is taking charge of Bernard's shirt. I don't think you'll have any more trouble from her."

"I'll take you at your word, Mrs. Muldoone."

"Call me Brenda. Everybody does." She turned Gemma around and nudged her out the door. "You coming, Billy?"

"Not quite yet, Ma. If you need to use my truck to go to Ida's, the keys are in the ignition."

"Never mind," she said. "I'll use the Minnie Winnie. See you at home." She flicked a wave at Evie and left.

Evie walked around her desk and sat. "Minnie Winnie?"

"Winnebago. My mother drives a motor home."

"Is she always like this?" Evie asked.

Billy scratched the back of his neck. "Who? Ma or Gemma?"

Evie laughed. "I was talking about Brenda this time."

"Yes. Pretty much. She's kind of hard to ignore. But she takes good care of Gemma. And she means what she says. We'll see that Gem doesn't act out in this way ever again." He gave her a sympathetic smile. "I know this wasn't how you hoped to start the school year."

"No, but with kids you can never be certain of anything. I'm aware that you're a single father, and raising a child isn't easy under the best of situations. I'm sorry I had to call you."

"Don't apologize," he said. "I'm not sorry I'm here." He passed his hand over the start of a grin. "Well, I'm sorry about the circumstances that brought me, but now that we're alone, I'm kind of glad."

He was glad? That wasn't the response Evie had expected. "What do you mean?"

"I was hoping we could get to know each other a little better."

CHAPTER FIVE

EVIE STARED AT Billy while she caught her breath. He would never win an award for impeccable timing.

After her silence became uncomfortable, she folded her hands in her lap and said, "Billy, are you asking me out?"

He walked over to the pile of litter Gemma had left on the floor, scooped up the bugs and deposited them into the trash can. Then he pulled his chair to the opposite side of Evie's desk, sat and leaned back. "I'm not sure. But you have this look on your face that tells me you wouldn't say yes."

She sat forward. "No, I wouldn't. We just had an incident with your daughter. I've had to appease Missy Hutchinson, who, I'm starting to believe, is not the town's most understanding and forgiving citizen. And I'm still somewhat breathless over encountering your mother."

She shook her head. "And to top it off, I've spent the day adjusting to a new job, new staff and the responsibility that comes with preparing for the arrival of one hundred and twenty-five youngsters the day after tomorrow."

"Looks to me like you could use a night out," he said. "With a friend."

She pointed at him, then pointed at herself. "You and I? Friends?"

Billy shrugged one shoulder. "Sure, why not?"

"But we're here as parent and school administrator. I was just about to discuss your daughter's behavioral problems."

"Okay. I know Gemma can be a handful. She's going through a stubborn phase right now. Why don't you and I talk about it over a couple of seafood dinners at the Tail and Claw restaurant?"

"I don't know that we should—"

Mary Alice opened the door. "Sorry to bother you again, Evie," she said.

Evie was beginning to think of the secretary's sudden appearances as precursors of trouble. "What is it, Mary Alice?"

"There's a UPS truck outside. The driver has a delivery for you."

Evie groaned. "Already? I didn't expect such prompt service."

Mary Alice jutted her thumb at the window. "See for yourself."

Leaning over the back edge of a van, a man dressed in trademark brown shorts and shirt lowered a hand truck laden with boxes to the ground. A half dozen other cartons already sat in the school yard.

"He needs to know where you want it," Mary Alice said.

Evie pressed her hand against her forehead. "I never dreamed… I thought it would be days yet."

Billy strode to the window and stared at the growing pile of boxes. "What is all that?"

Evie sighed. "Oh, books, reference materials, clothes, knickknacks…" A burst of near hysterical laughter escaped her. "…ice skates."

Billy turned. "Ice skates?"

"I thought there might be an indoor rink. We have them up north…" She waved her hand in front of her face. "Never mind. It's a total of fifteen boxes of all the things I thought I couldn't live without."

He chuckled. "You can live without ice skates in Heron Point."

"I know that now," she said. "I was hoping my things would arrive after I found a place to live." She stared at the stack in the yard. "I can't fit even half of this at the Pink Ladies."

Mary Alice tapped her foot on the wood floor. "So what should I tell him?"

Evie looked around. "In here, I guess. Temporarily at least."

Mary Alice made a clucking sound with her tongue. "It's going to be crowded."

Grimacing at the woman's obvious and unnecessary observation, Evie said, "I've got to find a place. Now!"

The phone in the outer office rang and Mary Alice hurried to answer it. She called to Evie a moment later. "It's for you. It's the mayor."

Evie grabbed the phone. "Claire?"

At the sound of her new friend's calm voice, Evie's breathing returned to normal. With each sentence from Claire's mouth, she relaxed more. She finished the conversation by thanking Claire, hung up and looked at Billy.

He raised his eyebrows. "Good news?"

"Yes. What did I just say five minutes ago?"

"That we were heading to the Tail and Claw."

She scowled at him.

"Okay, second guess. That you need a place to live."

"Right. You won't believe this. Claire just offered me the cottage behind her house. She said it would be ready by Friday." As the first load of boxes was wheeled into her office, Evie exhaled a deep sigh. "I said yes. I'm moving in Friday."

"I should have told you Claire was going to do that," Billy said.

"You knew?"

His response was matter-of-fact. "It's Heron Point. Of course I knew." He began stacking the cartons against the only spare wall in the office. "I have Friday night off and I own a pickup." The mischievous look over his shoulder was disturbingly similar to Gemma's. "So, do you want my help?"

She watched him squeeze a box into a space between the stack and the ceiling. "Sure. And I'll buy the pizza."

THE NEXT AFTERNOON after school, Evie went by Claire's bungalow, which she'd learned was called Tansy Hill by local residents. Interested in the history of the century-old home, which sat on a rise with a stunning view to the Gulf, Evie discovered that the original owner had raised herbs in the backyard, tansy being one of the principal varieties. Since then, everyone in town, even the postman, knew the property as Tansy Hill.

Claire took Evie through the kitchen, out the back door and down a brick pathway to a charming cottage that could have been out of the pages of a child's book. It had a peaked roof with scalloped shingles over the eaves, small casement windows with flower boxes at the sills and a leaded-glass front door with a brass knocker shaped like a crescent moon. The entire structure was painted yellow and white to match the main house.

Claire opened the door and stepped aside. "I just had the cleaning lady here today," she said as Evie went in. "If there's anything you want to change, feel free. Aunt Pet packed up her personal belongings when she moved into Finn's place, and what's left is just the furniture that's been here for a while. It's still serviceable I guess, but I have no great love for any of it. You can bring in your own things."

Evie quickly appraised the cozy parlor. "Oh, no, I wouldn't change anything. Besides, I'm not moving the furniture from my apartment down here. It's all in storage in Detroit."

She was more than pleased with the bright chintz sofa, overstuffed wicker chairs and glass-topped wrought-iron tables covered with magazines dedicated to herb growing and the celestial arts. It was Evie's taste with a touch of the unconventional Pet, and once she filled up the empty bookshelves along one wall and set out a few precious treasures, she knew she'd be comfortable here for as long as Claire allowed her to stay.

The kitchen was simple and tidy with a white porcelain sink, small stove, refrigerator and rustic pine table with four chairs. There was no dishwasher, but a brass rack next to the sink held an assortment of brightly colored linen towels. An open hutch with shelves built into the wall would be perfect for Evie's rose-patterned Royal Doulton dishes.

One bedroom and bath completed the floor plan. A pair of antique bureaus provided ample storage, one with a large tilt mirror reflecting an artificial arrangement of wildflowers and eucalyptus on top of the polished surface. Evie imagined her crystal perfume bottle collection lined up on a delicate lace dresser scarf. The narrow closet might be a problem since Evie had always been something of a clothes fanatic, but she would make do.

"It's wonderful, Claire," she said, sitting on the

pastel quilt covering the plump double bed. "We haven't discussed rent yet. What did you have in mind?"

Claire blushed as if uncomfortable discussing money with a friend. "I don't know. I haven't really thought about it. I suppose I should though."

"Absolutely." Evie was already calculating what she could afford. A place this nice with a view of the water and a fragrant garden just outside the bedroom's French doors would command a high price up north, and probably in Florida, as well. She'd taken a pay cut to come to Heron Point but if she watched her expenditures, she could afford as much as fifteen hundred a month.

Claire paused, chewed on her fingernail a moment. "I don't want you to feel burdened by your living expenses. This place has its own electric meter, so you'll be responsible for that bill, and for your telephone." She suggested a figure tentatively, as if she would consider a counter offer. "What do you think of five hundred a month?"

Evie smiled. "I think I can manage that."

Claire relaxed. "Good. It's settled then. You'll probably be glad when all your things are moved in. If you need any help besides Billy's, just let me know."

Evie was stunned by Claire's innocent remark. "You know that Billy is helping me move?"

"I heard him confirm with Jack that he would have Friday night off. He said he was bringing your boxes over from the school."

"I'm sure we'll be able to handle everything," Evie said. "But thanks for the offer."

Claire headed back to the parlor, but stopped in the doorway and turned around. "You know, Evie, I pretty much mind my own business. I won't be watching out my kitchen window to see what's going on here. I thought you should know that."

Now it was Evie's turn to feel a flush of embarrassment. "Oh, well, I wasn't worried about that at all. As for Friday night, it's only Billy coming over. We're just friends."

Claire grinned. "I know."

"He's just doing me a favor."

"Billy Muldoone is very good at doing favors," Claire said as she continued through the cottage to the front door. "But I imagine you'll find that out for yourself."

THE OPENING OF SCHOOL on Wednesday went fairly smoothly. Though she was a bit concerned about Gemma's antics, Evie was pleased when the girl came up to her in the hall during a break in morning classes. Gemma looked pretty in a pair of plaid cotton pants and a lime-green shirt. Her newly trimmed hair was brushed to a shine and held back from her face with glittery butterfly barrettes.

"How is everything going today, Gemma?"

"Great. My dad told me to tell you that Nana washed Bernard's shirt."

"Oh, good. How did it look?"

"I thought it was fine. Daddy said not to get my hopes up, though. The shirt still had to pass Mrs. Hutchinson's inspection. He dropped it off at her house yesterday."

That was good news. Evie hadn't had an urgent call from Missy in the past twenty-four hours, so maybe she'd decided to make do with Brenda Muldoone's laundering expertise. Or maybe the thought of tangling with Brenda made her more cooperative. At any rate, perhaps this was a sign that the school year would run smoothly for Gemma.

Unfortunately, Thursday matters took a turn for the worse, and Evie's hopes for Gemma's improved behavior faded. The girl's teacher, Betsy Haggerty, a fifteen-year veteran with elementary-age students, came to Evie's office during her class recess period. "I felt I should tell you that Gemma isn't cooperating with my policies," she said.

Evie paused over the amended school budget and braced herself. "What's happened?"

"She didn't have the list of supplies I gave the students yesterday. They were supposed to have everything by today."

"What items were missing?"

Betsy began enumerating on her fingers. "Number two pencils, wide-ruled paper, an eraser, colored pencils…" The teacher's voice droned on as if the list was infinitely long.

Evie took a more expedient route to get the information she wanted. "What *did* Gemma have?" she asked.

"A box of eight crayons. I didn't even have that on the list. And she kept trying to borrow the missing items from other students, preventing them from doing their work. She caused a disruption several times."

Evie considered the island's location, far from a major office-supply store, and wondered if this explained it. Perhaps no one was able to take Gemma to get what she needed. "Are these things only available in Micopee?"

"Oh, no. I make sure everything is available at the Island Drug Store. All the other students had filled the requirements."

Great. "If she doesn't have her things by tomorrow, I'll speak to her," Evie said.

"She'll have them," Betsy assured her. "I have her father's cell phone number in my address book. I called him, and he said he'd pick everything up."

"Fine. Then there's really no reason for me to be involved at this point."

"I guess not. But I thought you would want to keep a record of the step I took to correct the misbehavior." The teacher frowned. "Last year we documented each and every problem with Gemma, and since this is only the first that I know of…"

Evie twisted her diamond earring. "Thank you, Betsy. I'll make a note of it."

On Friday, a cafeteria worker popped her head inside Evie's office. Gemma had tried to take two pieces of chocolate cake instead of the allotted single serving.

"Did this result in a situation?" Evie asked.

"No." The woman smiled. "If it was up to me, I'd have given it to her, but we have rules. I just told her no. She groused a bit, held up the line a minute or two and went on when the other kids started hollering at her."

Evie glanced at Gemma's burgeoning folder still on her desk. "I guess I'm supposed to make a note of this?"

"That's up to you. I was just told to tell you whenever that child causes a ruckus."

"Well, thanks then."

After the woman left, Evie swiveled in her chair to look out the window. Each day she grew more fond of the view. The sweeping pine trees and flowering bushes were a respite from the complications of her new position. "What's going on here?" she said to herself. "It's as if this entire school is made up of spies against this one child."

Later that day, she had plans to meet up with Billy. Her hands trembled and she clutched them in her lap. Was she anxious about spending the evening with him? That would be understandable considering her problems with Gemma. Yet it wasn't an unpleasant feeling. Just different, exciting, stimulating in a way Evie hadn't felt in a long time. Maybe she was just looking forward to moving into her fairy-tale cottage. Yes, that was very possible.

She smiled, imagining Billy lifting her boxes and carrying them effortlessly into the cottage. In her mind she saw his easy smile, heard his low rumbling chuckle, felt his warm gaze on her as he watched her unpack.

"For heaven's sake," she said. "That's enough, Evelyn. You're starting to think of this as a date, which it clearly isn't." She gripped the arms of her chair and shook her head.

Then she spun the chair around, reached for Gemma's folder and opened it. "Maybe I'm just anxious knowing that the subject of his daughter will come up. Maybe I should know as much about Gemma as I can before tonight."

She flipped through the pages, ones she'd already read, and stopped when she came to a psychological evaluation she hadn't noticed before. "Gemma has seen a psychologist?" Evie leaned back and began to read.

BILLY DROVE a late-model tan pickup truck around Tansy Hill to Evie's cottage at six that evening. Evie watched him get out. This was the first time she'd seen him out of uniform. He wore a pair of neat denim shorts and a pale blue T-shirt with the words Marina Tavern sculpted across his chest.

He ran his fingers through his hair as he approached the front door. Was he as nervous as she was? Evie doubted it. Billy didn't seem like the type.

She opened the door before he knocked. "Hi. Come on in."

He had to lower his head to clear the frame, and once in the parlor, his presence filled the small area with that unmistakable energy that seemed to emanate from him wherever he went. "This is nice," he said. "I don't think I've ever been inside this place."

"It is nice," she agreed. "Just perfect for what I need. Although I don't know how I'm going to fit fifteen boxes of stuff in here."

He smiled. "I guess we'll find out. You can ride with me in the truck. I'm figuring it will take two trips."

She grabbed her purse and walked into the late-afternoon warmth. "I really appreciate this, Billy."

"No problem."

He had guessed right. When they returned with the second load, Evie's office was back to normal. Half of her possessions were stacked in the cottage parlor, and Billy was reaching for the first carton still in the back of the truck. Evie offered to help.

"I can get them," he said. "You go ahead and start opening boxes if you want." He reached into the back seat and pulled a bottle of wine out of a cooler. "I figure you must have a couple of glasses packed in there somewhere, and you still owe me a pizza."

She took the wine and went inside where she'd scribbled the number of the pizza delivery restaurant on a scrap of paper. By the time she'd ordered, found the carton marked Dishes, and set the table with plates and napkins, he was finished unloading and watching her from the kitchen door.

"The pizza will be here in thirty minutes," she said.

He came into the room and picked up the bottle of

wine. "Great. I'm starved." Pulling a small corkscrew out of his pocket, he peeled the foil from the neck of the bottle. "Did you find those glasses?"

She set them on the counter and he poured. "Do you want to go outside and wait?" he suggested. "The view of the Gulf is pretty spectacular from the gazebo and, now that the sun is almost set, it's cooled down enough to be comfortable out there."

He followed her outside and down the herb-lined pathway to the gazebo. They sat on a bench under the slat roof, and Evie sipped her wine. It was cool and fruity and delicious. She was a little surprised to see Billy enjoy the drink as much as she was. She'd figured him for a Budweiser guy.

He angled his body so he faced her. "Have you ever been out on the Gulf?"

"No. I've never been on a boat anywhere," she admitted.

"No kidding? Well, we have to change that."

"You have a boat?"

He snickered. "Look around you, Evie. We're surrounded by water and I'm a guy. What do you think?" He stared at the Gulf view. "So, as far as boats go, what's your pleasure? Speed or leisure?"

"Definitely the second." She smiled. "And then, if all goes well, maybe the first."

He nodded. "Just what I thought. I figured you for a canoe girl. How about this Sunday afternoon? I should finish my shift about five. That still gives us

enough daylight to take the canoe down the Sassahatchee River a couple of miles. It's mainly brackish
water, a mixture of spring-fed and salt. You can see a
lot of the native wildlife in two miles of drifting."

She peered at him over her glass. "Wildlife? What
kind?"

"Birds. Turtles. Otters." He grinned. "Maybe a
gator or two."

"Gators? I don't know. In Detroit wildlife means a
stray tomcat or maybe a family of squirrels."

He chuckled. "Don't worry. We won't see one that's
longer than the canoe, and I can paddle faster than he
can swim. So what do you say?"

She wanted to say yes. At this moment, with a
glass of wine taking the edge off her anxiety, pre-
dictable, hardworking city girl Evelyn Gaynor definitely wanted to float down a river with a tall, strong
island guy.

But how could she agree to go when she hadn't
talked to him about Gemma yet? She was still waiting
for the right time—maybe after they'd had pizza. She
was, above all else, the principal of his daughter's
school, and according to everyone she'd met, Gemma
had a problem. And according to a child psychologist
whose report was in Gemma's folder, that problem
could be a serious one.

Billy gave her a quizzical look. "You're always
thinking too much," he said. "And this time I don't
figure it's because you're afraid of alligators."

"I'm not really. But I probably should say no. I don't know if it would be appropriate."

"Appropriate? This is Heron Point. Everything's appropriate." He smiled back at her. It was an engaging boyish grin, and her gaze locked onto his wide mouth and held for several seconds. He had full lips, and Evie could imagine…well, she had to stop doing that. She was imagining far too much lately where Billy was concerned.

"I hope you don't mind, but I thought we might go into town later," he said. "I told Gemma I'd take her for ice cream. I'd like it if you'd come, too…if that's not inappropriate."

She hadn't planned on extending the evening beyond sharing a pizza, but the weekend was just beginning and ice cream sounded good. "Maybe," she said.

"I'll take that as a yes. Now, what about Sunday?"

The principal took charge, straightened her spine, inhaled a deep breath. "I'll let you know," she said. "But first, I have to talk to you about Gemma."

He blinked hard, pulled back a few inches. "What about her?"

"Will you tell me about her? About your family situation? Her mother?"

He leaned back farther, narrowed his eyes. "How did we get around to this topic?"

"I'd really like to know. I think I can help…"

He stood. "Help with what? Who needs help?"

She started to speak, though she was not at all sure which words to use to put him at ease. He cut her off, looking over his shoulder and announcing with gritty clarity, "Pizza's here." Picking up the wineglasses, he headed back to the cottage.

CHAPTER SIX

BILLY SCOWLED over a wedge of pizza. "It's cold. I don't know why that delivery guy can't get the order here while it's still hot. It's not over a couple of miles to anywhere on this island." He looked around Evie's kitchen. "Don't suppose you've unpacked a micro-wave?"

She shook her head. "No. I have one, but I don't know which box it's in. I can heat up the oven for you."

"Never mind." He took another bite. "It's not like I haven't eaten cold pizza before."

Evie nibbled on her slice. The pizza wasn't the only thing that was cool in her cozy new cottage right now. She had effectively dumped ice water on the sunset mood at the gazebo and, even though she told herself it had been the right thing to do, she wasn't happy about it. "Billy, I think we should discuss this…"

He poured more wine into his glass. "What the heck is Oppositional Defiant Disorder anyway? What kid isn't defiant from time to time?"

At least he was willing to talk about the problem.

"Of course they are. Defiance is a normal part of development. It's how children express their fears, desires and independence. But when that defiance becomes consistently uncooperative or hostile, then it becomes a concern."

"And just who judges when the behavior has reached the *concerned* level?"

"Several people can. Parents. Teachers or..." She held up the psychologist's report. "An expert in the field of childhood development, like this man, Dr. Hugh Grey."

He hadn't looked at the test results, and didn't now. Billy had a stubborn streak. "When was this evaluation made?"

"At the end of the last school year," Evie said. "It's current, although there could be changes in his analysis since then."

Billy's brow wrinkled. "You make it sound like my daughter has some kind of mental illness."

"It's not like that. At least not in the traditional sense. But Oppositional Defiant Disorder can lead to a more serious emotional problem..." Billy's eyes narrowed, and Evie knew she'd chosen a hot-button expression. But she had to be honest. "That could develop in the teen years," she continued. "Something called Conduct Disorder."

He snatched the test results from her hand. "Why didn't I know about this so-called evaluation?"

"I don't know," she admitted. "You should have

been informed. Parental or guardian consent is needed before the evaluation can go ahead. The previous principal or Dr. Grey would have known that."

Since he wasn't doing anything other than frowning at the papers, she reached across the table. "May I?"

He handed the test back. She flipped to the last page. "There is no consent form attached," she said. A possible explanation occurred to her and she flinched. "Is it possible that someone else in your home signed the papers?"

Billy's eyebrows came together in a threatening V, and he raked his fingers through his hair. "It's possible."

She spoke softly. "Billy, I don't want you to be too anxious about this. ODD is a condition that requires attention, but it isn't serious yet. It may not even be necessary to seek outside treatment. Often this disorder can be addressed at home and in the school." She tried to give him an encouraging smile. "Sometimes a child outgrows it. And there is good news."

He stared at her as if he didn't expect to be placated by whatever supposed good news she had.

"Gemma shows no signs of other conditions that often accompany ODD. No learning disabilities, no verifiable symptoms of depression—"

He shot forward in his chair. "Depression? She's the happiest kid I've ever seen."

"Is she?"

"Of course."

"Who are her friends, Billy?"

"Different ones."

"Bernard Hutchinson? How about Jane Hogan? You're friends with Jack. Is she friends with Jane?"

He looked away, his voice low. "Not so much."

Evie raised her hand. "We're getting off track here. I don't think depression is a problem yet. That's good."

Mollified, he sat back.

"There's no evidence of anxiety disorder, bipolarism—"

"Good grief! When did the world get so complex that these words you're using even applied to kids? She's nine years old. She gets angry. She refuses to make her bed. Sometimes she hates me. But that's all part of growing up. She's not sick. She's like every kid."

"No, she's not sick. But something's going on. She's repressing something and it's affecting her socially and academically. A bad memory, instability in her life, a death, an abandonment—"

His hand shot up between them. "Whoa. You've been at your job for a whole week. You don't know my daughter."

"No, I don't, but I'd like to. I have some expertise in dealing with children like Gemma."

"Yeah? Well, so do I. I have four years' worth of expertise in dealing with her."

"*Four* years?"

He clamped his mouth shut as if he'd said too much.

After a moment he shrugged. "What the hell. It's no secret. Gemma's only been with me since she was five."

This was a significant revelation. "I had no idea," Evie said. "Why is that, Billy? Did she live with her mother before that? What happened to her mother?"

He scoffed. "'Fraid you'll have to get a crystal ball to answer that."

"What do you mean?"

He rubbed his hand over his mouth, breathed heavily. "Look, Evie, I've done some things in my life that weren't particularly responsible."

She nodded, urging him on. "Haven't we all?"

He responded with a cynical burst of laughter. "I'll bet you haven't."

She was grateful he didn't ask her to come up with a specific example from her own life. Evie had always been a look-before-you-leap type.

He sighed. "Okay, here's the story. Four years ago, Gemma arrived to remind me of one transgression that obviously was meant to affect the rest of my life." He closed his eyes, opened them again after a moment. "Astrid Moonflower. How's that for a name?"

Evie shrugged.

"Moonflower wasn't her real name. I found that out the hard way. It's the *professional* name she used when she came to Heron Point ten years ago. She was a palm reader, fortune-teller, all-around con, if you know what I mean."

Evie nodded.

"She had this long silvery hair, kind of like a veil that went all the way to her waist," he said, wiggling his fingers around his head. "She had a soft voice, like she was singing all the time. Her fingers were covered in rings. Some of them even moved when she fluttered her hands. And even though I'd been a cop in Heron Point for over five years and had run into all kinds of quirky people, I'd never met anyone quite like Astrid."

"She sounds striking," Evie said.

"Yeah. If you don't mind being struck by a bowling ball in the forehead. That's the effect she had on me. I don't know how else to explain my total inability to think and reason."

Evie smiled.

"Anyway, Astrid and I hit it off for a while. Opposites attract, I suppose. It only lasted a few weeks, but I was crazy about her. I thought the relationship would go somewhere."

"And it didn't?"

He chuckled self-consciously. "*Astrid* went somewhere. One morning she was just gone, crystal ball, tea leaves and all." He shook his head sadly. "I should warn you about Heron Point, Evie. Don't get involved with some of the crackpots that breeze in and out of town. Ask Helen. She'll tell you about our transient population. But good for her. After her heart was broken, she got lucky with Ethan Anderson. I guess it can happen."

"Thanks for the advice," Evie said, feeling a burst of sympathy for this unlucky cop. *If I get involved with anyone, I'll make sure it's someone who's been around for a while.*

"So, that's the last I saw of Astrid…for six years."

"And then she came back?"

"I'd almost forgotten about her, but one day there she was on my doorstep. Hair short, brown and straggly. She was bone-skinny, didn't wear jewelry anymore. And she had a little kid hanging on to her hand for dear life."

"Gemma?" Evie knew the answer.

"Gemma. And Astrid told her I was her father, and that was the first time I knew I had a kid. As you can imagine, it was an awkward introduction. Gemma just stood there, quiet, not moving, the saddest eyes I'd ever seen."

"Did you question Astrid?"

"Well, sure. You don't drop a bomb like that on a guy without expecting to be grilled. But Astrid was a pro at evading questions. She was here a total of ten minutes, said she'd prepared Gemma for this and the kid understood." Billy snorted. "Yeah, right. Astrid also said she couldn't afford to keep Gemma any longer, handed me a bag with a few pitiful clothes—not even any toys—and said I had to take over."

"And you did? With no proof, no substantiation?"

"Like I said, there was no time for any of that. There was a guy in a car waiting at the curb, and Astrid just leaned over, gave her five-year-old daughter a kiss on the cheek and left without giving me a forwarding address—or her real name." Billy threaded his hands on the table. "To tell you the truth, I would have probably kept that child either way that day. I'm no saint, but a guy would have to have had a heart of stone to send that little girl back to that car."

A slow buzzing began in Evie's head and she realized she was close to tears. She knew she was violating Billy's privacy, but she had to know. "Since then," she said cautiously, "did you ever find out for sure that you're Gemma's father?"

"I thought it might be important to know," he said, "so, yeah, I did." He laughed softly. "That girl is Muldoone, through and through. And I guess she's proving it to everybody now."

Evie reached across the table and covered his hand. "We'll work this out, Billy. I'll help her…"

Her attempt at kindness was met with unexpected resistance. "Wait a minute. She's my kid, my responsibility, and I won't have her tested and poked and made to feel like she's different. She's not, and I won't have you or anybody else make her feel like she's some kind of laboratory subject."

Evie withdrew her hand. "No, I would never—"

"No, you won't. You're a nice woman, Evie, but I'll be responsible for Gemma. You just teach her. I'll raise her."

His chair scraped along the wood planks of the kitchen floor as he rose. "I've got to go. I'm going to swing into town and make sure everything's okay." He paused on the way to the parlor. "Thanks for the pizza."

She spoke to his back. "I should be thanking you."

"You did. It's enough."

The front door closed behind him. Evie heard the truck engine roar to life and wondered what had gone wrong. All she'd done was try to do her job. Maybe he didn't want to admit Gemma had a problem. So if he was the irrational one, why did she feel so bad about not going into town to have ice cream?

BILLY DIDN'T DRIVE through town as he'd told Evie. He went straight home, pulled into his driveway and stormed into the kitchen. His mother was emptying the dishwasher. She looked up when the door slammed. "You're home early," she said. "Date didn't go well?"

"It wasn't a date. I told you that. Where's Gemma?"

"Upstairs watching TV. She's waiting for you to take her to the soda shop."

"I will later, but I don't want her to hear this."

Brenda closed the cupboard she'd been filling and gave Billy her full attention. "Hear what?"

"You and I are going to have words, Ma."

Brenda fetched a kettle from the stove. "Do you want tea?"

He glared. "No. I want to know how you could have done what you did."

She filled the kettle anyway and set it on a burner.

"Look, William, do you want to talk in riddles all night? Why don't you just come out with it."

"Okay. You gave consent for Gemma's psychological tests last year."

She might have tried to deny it, but to her credit, she didn't. The guilt in her eyes gave her away anyhow. She took off her apron and hung it on a hook by the refrigerator. "How did you know about that?"

"Evie Gaynor told me."

"Oh. The last principal said if I signed the forms, there'd be no reason to tell you. That's why I did it."

Billy was fuming. He'd had no idea his mother and Heron Point Elementary had been involved in some sort of conspiracy against him. "But I'm her parent!"

"Of course you are. And I'm also her legal guardian. You wanted it that way, William, so one of us would always be able to make decisions in case of an emergency. Your job is dangerous. You never know…"

Giving her legal power had seemed the right thing to do at the time. "So you just signed consent without asking me?"

The kettle whistled and Brenda poured hot water over a tea bag. She sat at the table and slowly stirred it. "I didn't ask you because I know how hard you work. That was before Jack hired the extra help from Orlando. I've always tried to handle the little details of raising Gemma without putting pressure on you. I figured, why bother you with something I could take care of."

He yanked a chair away from the table, turned it around and sat on it backward. "This isn't a little detail, Ma. Gemma's my daughter. I should know if a head shrink is taking a tour through her brain!"

Brenda smirked; an expression he remembered well from his childhood. She could say more with a subtle twist of her lips than most people could with a lecture. "This was insignificant, believe me," she said. "I let them do their stupid test because those people at the school kept badgering me. Bah! No test is going to tell me something I don't already know about my granddaughter."

"But you took away my right to decide this for myself. And the administrator or that doctor... somebody, let you do it."

She took a long sip of tea. "The truth is, everybody thought it was better if you didn't know."

"What?"

"You're known as a guy who doesn't hide his emotions very well."

He almost had to laugh at that one. Brenda Muldoone could rail at a fly for five minutes for just landing on her apple pie. "Did you see the results of that test?" he asked.

"I listened to what they said, and then I promptly ignored it. A crock of manure if you ask me." She pointed her finger at Billy's nose. "There's nothing wrong with our girl, and I don't want you to believe for a minute that there is."

"I don't believe it, but that's not what the test says.

The doctor determined that she's got something called ODD. Oppositional Defiant Disorder."

"Nonsense. She's independent."

"And because of that, she breaks the rules."

"She's got a mind of her own."

"That you must admit can sometimes be annoying."

"She's high-strung. And highly intelligent." Brenda laughed out loud. "That thing she did with those bugs the other day… I didn't tell her, of course—we have to live in this town—but that was the funniest thing I've ever heard. Imagine that prissy eejit of a boy standing there and *letting* our Gemma stick those bugs to his shirt." She thrust her finger at Billy again. "You tell me which kid has the problem."

"What Gemma did was wrong."

"And I told her that. And as cheesed off as I was, I washed the boy's shirt, didn't I? We haven't heard a word from Missy."

"Only because she's scared to death of you."

Brenda smiled. "It doesn't hurt to have a reputation, now does it, William?"

Billy stood, began pacing. "We've got to take this seriously, Ma. Gemma's nine years old."

"Exactly. She's still a child. Let her have some fun. We can keep her in bounds like we always have."

"I don't know if that's true anymore. I told Evie that Gemma was fine, just like every other little girl. But what if she's not?"

"Of course she is. I just told you she was."

"But I don't know enough to agree with you. Maybe Gemma is different. Maybe we should be doing something about this ODD."

Brenda smiled with aggravating confidence. "I know what this is really about. You didn't hit it off with the principal like you wanted to."

"Actually, you're wrong. We were getting along fine, for a while. But then she brought the conversation around to Gemma and everything went downhill."

Brenda started to grin again, and Billy's anger spiked. "Don't push me, Ma. This isn't about me and Evie. It's about you and how you overstepped your boundaries with Gemma."

Brenda lay her palms flat on the table. "Look, William, you asked me to come here to help you with the child. And I was happy to do it. Since your father died, I've not had anything to set my mind on. I was floundering, and you gave me a purpose again. And now my heart's full of that girl. But if you don't want me here… If you don't approve…"

Here we go again, Billy thought, half admiring his mother's knack to shift the burden of guilt. "Come on, Ma."

"If you think it's easy running a household…"

"I don't."

"I have to tell you every day to pick up your dirty socks. And have your uniforms ever been cleaner than they are now?"

"No, Ma, never."

"I don't believe you can manage without me, but if you want to try…"

He sat again and covered her hand with his. "I don't want you to go. I appreciate all you do for us. But you've got to tell me what's going on with my daughter. You can't keep secrets."

She appeared to agree, but with Brenda, you never really knew for sure. "I won't," she said. "But you can't take the word of every so-called educated person who tries to fill your mind with theories about disorders and complexes, and all manner of poppycock. You've got to believe in Gemma. Like I do."

Maybe his mother was right. Gemma was just a normal girl with good days and bad days.

"Hi, Daddy. You're home."

He snapped his attention to the doorway where Gemma stood, eyes bright, looking like the angel every parent imagines their kid to be. Her hair, clean and shiny, was pulled into a ponytail. Her bare foot tapped lightly on the floor. "Hey, kiddo. You ready for some ice cream?"

"Thanks, but I've changed my mind. I'm going to bed now."

He checked his watch. "At nine o'clock on a Friday? You feeling all right?"

"Sure. Fine. I just want to get up early." She went to the sink and poured a glass of water. "You should get to bed, too, Daddy. You've been looking tired lately."

"I have?" He watched her chug the water and

waited while she planted a moist kiss on his cheek. He didn't have a reason *not* to go to bed early. "I guess I'll go on up," he said.

"I'm right behind you," Brenda said. "Weighty discussions like the one we had take the starch right out of me."

BILLY STOPPED at his daughter's door and listened. Not a sound.

He continued to his room, stripped to his skivvies and pulled down the covers on the double bed, which, thanks to his mother, was always meticulously neat. Picking up the remote control, he switched on the TV, channel-surfed for a couple of minutes and decided there was nothing he wanted to watch. A good night's sleep might be just what he needed anyway, so he turned off the light, punched his pillow into head-hugging submission and closed his eyes. He tried not to think of Gemma or Evie or any woman from his past or present. Instead he thought of the reports he still had to fill out for Jack. It was a sure way of nodding off quickly.

And then he heard sounds coming from downstairs.

"What the…?"

He couldn't be certain, but it sounded like the clicking of the front door latch. Hadn't he locked up? Was someone coming in?

He threw back the covers, bounded from bed and went into the hallway. His mother's and Gemma's doors were both closed.

Standing at the top of the stairs, he looked down at the entryway. The front door, half open, was drawn closed by an unseen hand. Someone had obviously just gone out. He ran down the stairs, jerked open the door and saw the last person he'd expected to find mounting a bicycle on the sidewalk. "Gemma! What the heck do you think you're doing?"

There was no way she hadn't heard him, but she pretended she hadn't. Without a backward glance, she began pedaling. Billy looked down, gave a brief thought to his tank top and boxer shorts, and darted after her. "Stop right there, young lady!"

Her legs churned with ferocity, and Billy started running. "You'd better put those brakes on right now, Gemma. You know darned well I can catch you!"

She risked a glance over her shoulder and must have realized the futility of her escape. Her heel jammed down on the pedal and the bicycle came to a sudden halt. She straddled the bike with her feet on the street, her eyes straight ahead. "Go back in the house, Daddy. This is none of your business."

Her declaration knocked the wind out of him even more than the unexpected exercise. He grabbed hold of the back of her bicycle seat. "None of my business? You're out after ten o'clock, going who knows where—" a further inspection only added to the mystery "—with a backpack that's obviously stuffed full with something…and it's *none of my business?*"

Her lips pursed, she breathed heavily. "It's personal."

"You're damn right it is, and I'm the person who's going to hear about it."

"Let me go. You can't stop me!" she hollered in a tone he'd never heard come from her before.

"Oh, no?" He lifted her off the bicycle, set her on the pavement and turned the bike around. "Let's go. You first, and don't try anything that's going to get you in bigger trouble than you are already."

They walked in silence back to the house, but Billy could tell his daughter was steaming. Her sneakers pounded on the cement. Her breath came in ragged gasps. Her back was straight as a broom handle. Oh, yeah, she was, as Brenda would say, super cheesed off.

Brenda met them at the door. "What's going on?"

Billy leaned the bike against the front steps. "When you find out, we'll both know."

"What were you doing, Gemma?"

The girl stood there, still as a statue.

"Go into the kitchen, Gemma," Billy said. "And, Ma, you wait in the living room."

Brenda's eyes rounded. "But I want to know—"

"Please, just go."

She sauntered off, her robe swishing behind her in a wake of indignant fury. Gemma headed for the kitchen. "Wait a minute," Billy said, pointing at the backpack. "Give me that."

"No. It's mine."

He slipped it from her shoulders.

"Hey, give it back. That's private."

"Not anymore it isn't. Remember that word you learned the other day? Well, this backpack has just become confiscated property."

Her hands balled into fists. "That's not fair."

He nudged her toward the kitchen. "Who said I have to be fair?"

He pulled a chair out for her and she dropped down as though the seat of her jeans was filled with concrete. "I want water," she said.

He brought her a full glass. She ignored it.

"Where were you going?"

Silence.

He stood against the counter, his arms folded across his chest. He didn't move, hoping he looked as intimidating as any force this child had ever encountered. "Look, we can do this your way…stay in this room and stare at each other for hours. Because if you don't answer me, that's exactly what we're going to do. Or you can spill the beans right now, take your punishment, and we can get back to bed. Me between my comfy sheets, and you handcuffed to the bathroom sink with a pillow and a towel. Which is it going to be?"

She considered her options, and Billy prayed she'd choose the right one.

After a moment she said, "I was going to Whitney Broadmoor's house."

"At this hour? What the heck for?"

"She's having a sleep-over party."

"You're telling me this party starts at ten o'clock?"

"No. It started at seven."

"Then why didn't you go at seven? Nana would have taken you."

Her bottom lip trembled. "Because I didn't, that's all."

"Why not?"

"Just because, okay?"

"No, it's not okay. I want to know why you didn't go at seven, and why I didn't know anything about this party—" He stopped, realization hitting him like a gale-force wind. He pulled out a chair and sat. "Gemma, were you invited to this party?"

"Shit, no."

"Gemma—"

"I didn't want to be invited. They're all dumb girls. All they talk about is stupid clothes and boy movie stars and stuff nobody cares about."

He sat for a moment, not knowing which direction to take. Emotions were involved now. Sensitive female emotions, and Billy was suddenly out of his parenting league. So he switched to cop mode and reached for the backpack between them on the table. "I'm probably not going to like what's in here," he said, unzipping it.

He pulled out three cans of black spray paint. "Where did you get these?"

"From our shed."

"You can't take things from the shed without checking with me."

"Why not? I live here, don't I?"

"Yeah, but would you take my pickup truck and drive it around just because you live here?"

"Probably not."

That wasn't as decisive an answer as he'd hoped for. "Then you can't take my spray paint. But now that you have, I want to know what you were going to do with it."

"I don't know. I hadn't decided yet."

"Gemma…"

She rolled her eyes. "Fine." The word sounded like the cork exploding from a pop gun. "I was going to paint some words on Whitney's house. Nothing she didn't deserve to see in the morning."

Suddenly very tired, he picked up a can and pointed it at her. "Gemma, vandalizing property is a crime."

The lip started to quiver again. "How 'bout being mean to somebody? Isn't that a crime, too?"

"Not in the same way. What you were going to do is a legal crime. You could get in a lot of trouble."

"I don't care! I'm the only girl in the class who wasn't invited to that stupid party. And I wanted them to know that I came anyway."

He rolled the can in his hand. "They would have known, all right. And we would have spent the next few days painting the Broadmoors' house. Believe me, that's a lot harder than unsticking a few bugs."

She remained silent, not giving anything away. Finally she picked up the glass and took a swallow of water. "Can I go to bed now? I told you everything."

Not sure of what more he could accomplish, Billy gave in. "I suppose. But this isn't over. You know that. Tomorrow we talk about your punishment. What you did tonight can't happen again. It's not just the destruction of property, though that would have been bad enough. You left the house after dark. What if I'd looked in your room and found you missing? Can you imagine how I would have felt? How worried I would have been?"

Her lips twisted into sarcastic denial. "You don't care about me."

"What?" Billy was at a loss. Part of him wanted to hug her, though he wasn't much of a hugger. Part of him wanted to stoke up the head of steam he'd had a few minutes ago. What she'd done, what she'd almost done… This parenting stuff wasn't easy. After four years of trying, he still wasn't very good at it.

"Go on to bed," he said. She got up and started to walk away. "And, Gemma?"

She stopped, turned around.

"I'm sorry you weren't invited to the party. There will be other parties, you know that, don't you?"

She looked at the floor. "I won't care about those any more than I did this one."

BRENDA CAME INTO the kitchen as soon as Gemma's footsteps faded on the stairs. "What happened?"

He told her, watching her expression change from anger to pity. "Why that stuck-up little Broadmoor girl."

"Ma, don't. This isn't Whitney's fault. We've got to admit that Gemma has a problem."

"Well, of course she does. Her feelings were hurt. She lashed out. Anybody would—"

"No, anybody wouldn't."

Brenda put her hands on her hips. "What are you going to do about it?"

"About her punishment? I don't know. I'm glad I've got the rest of the night to think about it."

"You'll do the right thing, once you calm down."

"I don't know what the right thing is anymore." He rubbed the nape of his neck. "Get some sleep, Ma. I'll be up awhile."

She smiled. "I've got so much energy all of a sudden. I was actually thinking of going jogging."

"Now? It's after eleven."

"I know." She picked up a can of spray paint. "I was thinking of taking one of these along with me. Maybe running past the Broadmoor place."

He stared at her. "Good night, Ma."

She patted his hand. "Good night, William."

When she'd left and he was alone, Billy came to one conclusion. He didn't know what he was going to do about Gemma, but he'd definitely decided to show up at Evie's house with the canoe on Sunday afternoon. Maybe she'd go with him. Maybe she wouldn't. But he had to at least admit to her that she might have a point about his daughter.

CHAPTER SEVEN

EVIE PUT THE LAST neatly crushed box into the trunk of her car to take to the island recycling center. In two days she'd unpacked all her belongings, and the cottage was beginning to feel like home.

Satisfied, she picked up her portable phone and walked through the French doors to a small patio just outside the bedroom. It was nearly five o'clock, a good time to reach her father before he left for his regular Sunday night bowling league. Sitting on a plump cushion in the patio lounger, she punched in Harry's number.

He answered right away. "Hey, Evie, I knew it was you. Good to hear from you."

She smiled. He'd objected when she'd insisted he get Caller ID, though he'd been complaining since his retirement six months ago that he was being bombarded with calls from telemarketers at dinnertime.

"How are you, Dad?"

"I'm fine. Just fixing dinner for me and Muffler."

She heard the sizzle of hot oil in the background and grimaced. "Not fried food again, Dad?"

The sound faded. He'd no doubt removed the skillet from the hot burner. "Pork chops. Muffler likes them."

She pictured the tiger-striped cat her dad had picked up outside the General Motors Assembly plant three years ago. When Harry had decided to keep the feline, they'd taken him to a vet. The cat was somewhere between ten and twelve years old, and Evie had cautioned her father about feeding him the same fried diet Harry ate.

She couldn't help frowning into the phone. Even though her father was in good health, he still ate like a twenty-year-old lumberjack. "Now, Dad…"

"Don't start, Evelyn. Muffler and I have few enough pleasures these days. Besides, I'll work off this meal at the bowling alley in a couple of hours."

She reserved further comment for a later time. There wasn't much she could do about her father's lifestyle choices from Florida. "So how has your weekend been?"

"Oh, fine. I tidied up the garage some. Helped Mrs. Ingram prune her tomato plants. Too bad you weren't here. She cut some beautiful beefsteaks and offered them to me. But you know me and rabbit food. My stomach wants good old-fashioned protein."

Evie didn't want to think about her father having nothing constructive or interesting to do but putter around the old two-story brick home where he'd lived for thirty years. She wished he would go out more, maybe even find a nice woman to date once in a while.

As far as Evie knew, he hadn't had a relationship since her mother died twenty-seven years ago. That was a shame. Harry was a decent, giving man. And he had the calmest disposition of anyone she knew. She couldn't remember him ever getting really angry or, now that she thought about it, even passionate about anything. Perhaps the emotional highs and lows of his life died with her mother, but Evie wanted more for him. And that was why leaving Harry had been the hardest part about coming to Florida.

"You didn't go out at all this weekend?"

"Sure I did. Went to the market for these pork chops." Without waiting for more questions, he steered the conversation in her direction. "So, what about you, Ev? What did you do this weekend?"

Since Friday night her life hadn't been any more stimulating than Harry's, and she hated admitting it. "I unpacked," she said. "I'm very pleased with the way my place looks now."

"Good. Anything else happen?"

She closed her eyes remembering Friday evening and the disappointing way it had ended. "I've been doing some research," she said. "I have a student who appears to have emotional problems, and I read through a few sources on child development to see if I can help."

"And can you?"

She rubbed her fingers over her tired eyes. Actually she'd spent hours poring over material on Oppositional Defiant Disorder. "I have a pretty good idea about what needs to be done. But it's basically up to her father. Problem is, I don't know if he'll cooperate."

"You'll get him to," Harry said. "You've perfected your nagging skills with me over the past couple of decades. This girl's dad won't stand a chance."

She smiled, not sharing his confidence. "I hope you're right."

"I'm going to hang up now, Ev. Long distance costs money."

"And your pork chops are done," she added.

"That, too. I miss you, and so does Muffler. We old bachelors liked having a woman's touch around the place once in a while."

"I miss you, too, Dad. You take care now, and I'll call you in a few days."

She hung up and stared past the palm trees bordering the garden at the Gulf. It was peaceful here on the patio. Fragrant breezes wafted from Pet's garden, scents of lilacs and delicately spiced herbs. Tiny creatures buzzed and hummed, preparing to settle in for the close of day. Nice sounds, comforting ones.

All except for the roar of a powerful engine. Evie stood. "What's that? It sounds like…"

Billy's pickup?

She walked around the side of the cottage to the pebbled drive. Billy was just getting out of his truck. She couldn't help noticing the canoe stuck out of the cargo bed, an orange flag fluttering from the pointed end.

He leaned his elbow on the roof of the vehicle and smiled at her. "Hi. Ready to go?"

"What?"

"The river trip. Remember? I just got off work and hurried over here so we'd still have a few hours of daylight."

"But…I never said I'd go," she stammered.

He stood straight and took a few steps toward her. "You didn't? I could have sworn you did."

She knew she hadn't. If she'd been expecting Billy she would have fixed her hair, put on something other than faded denim cutoffs and a jersey tank top. Applied a bit of body splash. Some makeup. "But…I thought you were angry with me."

"Oh, that. Maybe I was. It doesn't matter now. If I were you, I wouldn't let that little disagreement spoil your opportunity to see one of our rivers."

She couldn't go, could she? She'd rented a movie that had to be returned tomorrow. A frozen dinner was thawing on her counter. She had more reading to do. And the superintendent from Micopee County was coming the next morning. She had to prepare. But Billy looked so cool and sexy in shorts that showed off his long, lean legs and a cotton knit shirt that hugged his biceps in the most flattering way. "I don't know, Billy…."

He came closer and the woodsy pine scent he wore mingled with the fragrances of Pet's garden. And made Evie just a bit dizzy.

"You're worried about the bugs, aren't you?" Billy said.

"What? No."

"I brought repellent, so even though the sun will be setting soon, insects won't be a problem."

"I was thinking about all the work I have to do."

"What work?"

She couldn't honestly answer because nothing she had to do sounded nearly as interesting or fun as going with Billy. So she used her typical Evie excuse. "If I'd known. If I'd had notice…"

"Okay. I'll give you some notice. Go inside and get a hat. Grab anything you want to bring, but not food. I brought that. I'll wait here for five minutes."

She drew her bottom lip between her teeth and tried to ignore the rush of adrenaline. She wanted to go. After an indecisive period of maybe ten seconds, she said, "And a camera. I'll need that."

"Sure. Bring a camera."

Evie turned toward the cottage and glanced up at the sky. The sun was warm and bright, the fluffy clouds moving leisurely across the blue expanse. No chance of rain. She could leave her umbrella behind.

AFTER A FORTY-MINUTE drive that took them over the Heron Point bridge, across the thirty-mile stretch to the four-lane, and a mile or two south, Billy turned into a densely wooded campground. He braked in front of a log cabin office with signs pointing in all directions to facilities on the property. Evie stopped reading when she realized that most of the signs, like the one pointing to the opera house, were just for fun.

"Be right back," Billy said, and disappeared inside. He returned with a stooped old gent wearing overalls and a plaid shirt. The man talked a streak and laughed at everything Billy said, when he could get a word in, obviously glad to see an old friend.

They approached Evie's window. "This is Walter," Billy said. "He and his wife own this place."

Introductions complete, Walter climbed in the back of the truck. Billy drove down a shady pathway bordered by an eclectic array of campground living, from tents to pop-ups to travel trailers in various conditions and sizes.

When they reached the end, Billy turned the truck around so the rear was facing a cement ramp leading into murky water. He backed the truck up until Evie thought he might roll the vehicle into the river. He didn't. He stopped when the water was just inches from Evie's door. Smiling across the seat at her, he said, "Time to get out."

The two men lowered the canoe into the water. Walter held the rope, keeping the boat near the concrete embankment while Billy got out a cooler and two life jackets. "Put this on," he said, tossing a jacket to Evie. He chuckled when he saw the look on her face. "We won't need it, but Walt won't let us go unless we're buckled up."

Billy stowed the supplies, including Evie's camera bag, and offered her his hand. The boat wobbled under her shifting weight until she managed to sit on a bench at the front. She knew her expression must have conveyed her discomfort when she looked up at Billy. "This isn't going to tip over, right?"

Billy shook his head. "Hasn't yet. Once she's on the river, she steadies up real well." Apparently realizing he hadn't convinced her, he added, "Evie, the Seminoles were traveling this river in dug-out logs long before white men came along with their picnic baskets and fiberglass canoes."

"Right." She held on as Billy stepped down from the embankment and took a position at the rear of the boat.

He tossed his truck keys to Walter. "Cast her off," he said. The old man waded down the ramp, set the sole of his rubber boot on the back edge of the canoe and pushed. They shot forward before floating awkwardly away from land. And then the boat miraculously leveled itself in the middle of the river. Billy picked up a paddle and began to stroke through the water. Soon the campground, Billy's truck and all semblance of civilization were lost in the deep green shadows of overhanging tree limbs burdened with thick foliage.

After a moment Billy said, "You doing okay?"

"Yes, fine." Since she hadn't pried her fingers from the sides of the canoe, she wasn't surprised when he laughed.

She soon forgot her unease in an effort to keep up with Billy's chatter. He explained about the river, where it originated and how it emptied into the Gulf twenty miles south of Heron Point. The river was one hundred miles long, but they were only going to travel a few miles of that today. She listened intently when he described the flora and fauna around the salt water to their west, fresh water to their east, and the blended brackish current they followed now, a mixture of the two.

Evie looked into the gently flowing river. They'd left the murkiness at the ramp behind. She trailed her hand in the cool, clear water, watching the minuscule wake left by her fingers. They'd only journeyed a few minutes when she saw her first wildlife. A family of turtles sunbathing on rocks. Billy pointed them out or Evie might have missed them, they blended so well with their surroundings. She removed her camera from its bag and snapped a picture.

They navigated a narrow bend in the river, and Evie nearly lost her breath when a huge bird Billy identified as a great blue heron spread its giant wings, squawking his displeasure at being disturbed. The bird rose effortlessly from a gnarled branch suspended above the river. He then swooped rather than flew across to the other side.

They traveled a few hundred yards in silence except for the ripple of the water against the paddle. And then civilization appeared once more. Houses began dotting the banks of the Sassahatchee, their foundations built into the lush landscape several feet above the river.

Some of the dwellings were magnificent multilevel, terraced structures built so residents could enjoy the scenic view from various angles. Others were nothing more than simple shacks, stubbornly surviving sun, humidity, hurricanes—and the encroaching wealthy neighbors.

As Billy paddled by one such humble place, a middle-aged man in an old lawn chair lifted his hat and raised a fishing pole from the water. "Hey, Billy. How you doing?"

"Pretty good, Isaac."

The man leaned forward, peered intently into the canoe. "If that's Gemma with you, I gotta say, that girl's grown up some. Looks like she's got all the right fittings to be a looker, too."

Evie's face flushed. Billy snickered. "Sometimes, Isaac, I manage to actually convince a female other than my daughter to come down here."

The man's chuckles followed them around a bend. "I see you have friends here," Evie said.

"A few. Isaac's a good guy. He told me the last time I went by that a fella from Miami offered him two hundred thousand for his property. Wants to tear down the shack and put a vacation home in its place."

Evie whistled. "Is Isaac going to sell?"

"He's thinking about it. But when I see him sitting on his dock with that fishing pole, I figure he won't budge."

Billy turned the canoe into a small tributary that

ended where the branches of a tall Cypress tree stretched over the water. He angled the boat under one of them and tied the rope around a limb.

"Why are we stopping?" Evie asked.

"This is as good a place as any."

"For what?"

He smiled. "I was thinking of eating. But if you have something else in mind, I'm willing to consider it."

GETTING EVIE TO BLUSH was about the easiest thing Billy had ever done. And more fun than he'd had in a long time. "Food," he said, taking a plate loaded with ham slices from the cooler. "Bought at the Buy and Fly Take-out in Heron Point just before I picked you up. Interested?"

She laughed. "I'm starved."

He removed a bowl of potato salad, sliced cheese, a loaf of French bread, plates and plastic utensils. "Dig in."

After wiping her hands on her shorts, she daintily scooped portions onto her plate. Then she surprised him by eating with gusto. "This is delicious."

Billy agreed. In fact, he found the setting, the company and the prospects for the immediate future pretty favorable. Unfortunately nature has a way of encroaching on the most idyllic situations. Evie started swatting.

Billy reached in his pocket and pulled out a tube of insect repellent. "Here. This is the lotion kind. They say it works better and it's good for the skin."

She opened the cap.

He grinned. "Need any help? I'd be glad to slather it on."

The look she sent him was a warning, but only half-hearted. She squeezed a puddle of thick white gel into her palm. "Thanks, anyway, but I can manage."

After rinsing her hands off, they ate in silence for a few moments, giving Evie the chance to enjoy their surroundings and Billy the chance to enjoy her. He'd never been with anyone like Evie. He generally didn't gravitate to reserved women. And Evie wasn't what he'd call a knock-'em-dead beauty. She was certainly easy to look at with her flawless skin and intelligent eyes the color of the Gulf.

But she couldn't be summed up by her outward appearance. Evie was smart, accomplished, even aloof, and, to a guy like Billy, probably unattainable. Of course, Billy was stubborn. More than one woman had told him so. If Evie was unreachable, that only made him want to reach out all the more.

She wiped her hands on a napkin. "What are you thinking about?"

He took a swallow of soda. "I was thinking how cute you look in that baseball cap. You a hockey fan?"

She flattened her hand over the embroidery on her hat. "I've been to a few Redwings games."

"I'll have to take you to a Tampa Bay Lightning game this season," he said.

Without commenting on his offer, she picked up the

remains of dinner and tucked everything away in the cooler. "Maybe we should start back. I don't think we have much sunlight left."

"Whatever the lady wants." Billy untied the rope from the tree.

The trip back took a little longer since the current was against them. It was nearly dark when Billy maneuvered the canoe next to the embankment at Walter's campground. The old man was waiting. Within ten minutes the boat was loaded onto the truck and they were headed back to Hcron Point.

"How'd you like the Sassahatchee?" Billy asked when they turned onto the two-lane road.

"Very much. It was a beautiful trip."

"Wait until you see what I have planned next." He shouldn't have said it, but too often words came out of Billy's mouth before he had the good sense to stop them.

She stared down at her hands clasped in her lap. "Billy, how's Gemma?"

Okay. The inevitable had happened. He'd known she'd bring up their conversation from the other night. "She's fine."

Evie glanced over at him. "Really?"

He'd been prepared to admit a few concerns about Gemma, but now that he had the opportunity, he wasn't as willing. Somehow an admission of flaws in Gemma seemed to be an admission of flaws in his ability as a parent. He took a deep breath, blew it out. "Look, Evie, I know Gemma's not the perfect student. It's no secret she's had some discipline problems at school."

He risked a glance at Evie. Though the truck interior was dark, he thought he saw sympathy in her eyes. "But I've got it under control," he added. "I had a talk with Gemma the other night. We came to an understanding of sorts."

"You did? That's great."

"I don't think she'll give you any more trouble." He meant what he said but realized Evie was probably skeptical. "But if she does, you call me. I'll handle it."

They rode in silence for a few minutes. "Do you mind telling me what you said to Gemma?"

He tightened his grip on the steering wheel. Evie might be reserved, but she had steel under the surface. And he did mind. His discipline often involved exaggeration, like when he'd threatened to handcuff his daughter to the bathroom sink. He wouldn't have done it. Gemma knew that.

The next morning, when he was calmer, he'd told Gemma she had to stay in her room for most of the day. But at least he'd gotten her solemn vow she wouldn't plan to do anything stupid like spray someone's house with graffiti ever again. And he'd rewarded her by stealing an hour off work and taking her for burgers at the Green Door on Saturday night.

But was it enough? Hell, he didn't know. Brenda claimed Saturday had been as peaceful a day as she'd ever known in his house.

"I'd rather not," he said.

"Okay."

The silence that followed grated on his nerves. "Look, Evie," he began, "I don't know how to be a parent. Until four years ago, I'd never even *thought* about being one. So I more or less discipline from my gut. You may think my tactics are lame. I don't know, but I've got to do what feels right to me and hope it works."

"Sometimes parenting from the gut is best," she said, laying her hand on his bare arm. "And if it suits you and Gemma, I'm all for it." Billy flinched at the unexpected touch, and then something ignited deep inside him. Evie's hand was warm and gentle. Nice.

"But if you ever need any advice," she said softly in the quiet of the cab, "or want any help…"

He covered her hand, resisting the urge to wrap his fingers around hers and hold on. "I'll ask."

When he pulled in front of Evie's cottage, Billy had convinced himself his conversation about Gemma had gone reasonably well. He turned off the engine, shut down the lights. When he stretched his arm across the back seat, Evie didn't move away. Encouraged, he inched over, brought his lips near hers. "I'd kind of like to move on to another topic," he said.

Her smile emboldened him further. "You would? What?"

"I'd like to talk about kicking this friendship of ours up a notch."

"Really."

He reached up, removed her hat. Her hair, gathered in an elastic band, tumbled down past her nape. He slid the band past the end of the ponytail and slipped it over her wrist. "Wouldn't want this to get lost."

"No, we wouldn't want that."

He spread her hair over her shoulders, enjoying the silken feel of it, the tawny strands bronzed by the moonlight through the window. Dropping his hands to her shoulders, he pulled her to him. She came willingly. When his lips covered hers, she sighed, allowing him to deepen the kiss. His fingers flexed on her bare skin as he leaned over her. She bent back, accepting, inviting. He moved his mouth on hers, tasting, relishing the warmth of the contact. When the sweetest sound came from her throat, he gently pushed her against the seat and twisted his body to cover hers.

It was as perfect a kiss as Billy could remember. He probed the line of her mouth with his tongue until she opened to him. The nearly perfect kiss got better, hotter, moister. And to a guy who thought all kisses were women's gifts to men, Billy suddenly realized that this one was special because she was.

He pulled back and whispered hoarsely, "I don't have to be back any time soon."

She grew rigid. Just a little, but it was probably a sign that she was going to send him away. He kissed her again. She moaned with frustration or desire. He didn't know which, but hoped it was the latter.

And then her camera bag vibrated between them. Billy jerked back. "What the…?"

"It's my phone. I put it in the camera bag."

He reached for her again. "Oh, well, forget it then."

"No, I can't." She pushed him away and unzipped the bag. Wiping her mouth, she stared at the number and pressed the connect button. "Dad? What's wrong?"

Her shoulders sagged. "Really? Two games over 200? It's been quite a night for you." She talked a minute more and ended the call. "My dad bowled two games over 200. Top scorer in his league tonight."

Billy reached for her again. "Good scores. Now, where were we?"

She pressed her hand on his chest. "I'm going in, Billy. Thanks for a wonderful evening."

He'd figured his hopes for the rest of the night had been dashed the second her phone rang. But he didn't have to like it. "Sure, anytime."

She got out and walked a few steps before returning to the truck. He rolled down the window. "Can you come for dinner Wednesday night?" Evie asked. "I'm not much of a cook, but…"

His heartbeat sounded like a pinball game in his head. "I'll be here."

She smiled. "Good. See you about seven."

IF BILLY HAD been walking, his feet wouldn't have touched the pavement. And then he got home and discovered that Gemma had refused to wash her hair and, when Brenda reprimanded her, she'd locked herself in the bathroom and cut it all off. It didn't help when Brenda said, "Don't worry, Billy. I can fix her hair. I can make a ball gown out of a burlap sack."

CHAPTER EIGHT

EVIE MADE IT a point to be in the school yard every morning when the children arrived. She always singled out a half dozen or so, asked their names and initiated conversations, committing them to memory.

On Monday morning, while commenting to one student that his Harry Potter backpack was way cool, she noticed a familiar pickup parked half a block away. Billy and Gemma seemed to be having an animated discussion that ended when Billy pointed his finger toward the school. Gemma got out of the truck and slammed the door.

She stomped up the sidewalk, her head lowered, her arms swinging at her sides. Evie didn't need a child development textbook to tell her the girl was angry. *Oh, dear.*

As the child drew closer to the school, some of the youngsters whispered behind their hands. Others taunted. Some laughed. Evie came to her rescue.

"Good morning, Ge—" The rest of the name caught in Evie's throat. Billy's daughter was neat and clean and nicely dressed as usual, but something horrible had happened to her hair! A floral elastic headband covered much of her forehead and ears, but there was no hiding the springy patches of auburn fluff.

Gemma stopped in front of Evie, looked up and glared, daring her to comment.

Evie smiled. "I see you have a new hairdo."

Gemma's face pinched in a frown. "So what?"

"Nothing. I'm sure you had a reason for cutting it and, if you like it, then that's all that matters."

She tugged the headband over her earlobes. "I do like it. I love it!"

"Good. But it is a change. I hope you won't let your hair create a distraction in the classroom. I suggest you take your seat as soon as you're inside and think about your schoolwork. If you don't bring attention to the new look, I'm sure everyone will soon forget about it."

If Gemma did this to herself, then attention was exactly what she'd hoped for. But since she'd apparently been reluctant to get out of her father's truck, perhaps she was having second thoughts now. It was a tough lesson, but children had to learn that one impulsive act can result in a mountain of regret.

Evie stepped aside. "Have a nice day." She watched the child proceed amid snickers and stares. Evie urged all the children inside and warned them with a stern look to mind their manners. When she looked back down the street, the pickup was gone.

On Tuesday, Gemma had refused to do any work at

all. She claimed her right hand was sore from doing chores at home and she couldn't write. She could, however, climb the monkey bars with remarkable agility and hurl a bullet of a pitch in dodge ball. Mrs. Haggerty called Billy.

On Wednesday, Gemma came to class without having done her homework. She insisted her grandmother accidentally burned it making oatmeal that morning. The comment drew a laugh from her classmates who eventually got irritated when Gemma spent the morning trying to copy answers from everyone. Mrs. Haggerty called Billy.

By the close of day on Wednesday, Evie was anxious about the dinner she'd planned with Billy for that night. She absolutely had to discuss Gemma's problems with him. Billy called her at three-thirty. She knew from his tone he was aware of Gemma's behavior. His call was brief and to the point. "I'm still planning to come," he said. "You still want me?"

"Of course. If you're still brave enough to try my cooking."

But she wasn't a bit confident about how the evening would turn out.

BILLY ARRIVED right at seven o'clock. He looked handsome in chino pants and a short-sleeved shirt with a muted print of sea shells. He had a bottle of wine in his hand. Evie decided there would be plenty of time to talk about Gemma after they ate. She'd taken extra pains with her appearance and simply wanted to enjoy herself without pressure for as long as possible.

She hardly ever cooked, so Evie was glad when Billy complimented her chicken and rice. Even if he did it more than was necessary. She commented more than once on the quality of the wine. And she was thankful that two glasses had mellowed her out so she could relax. She even told Billy about her life in Detroit.

Once the dishes were picked up, Billy carried their glasses into the parlor and sat next to Evie on the sofa in front of the unused fireplace. Neither spoke for a few minutes. Unexpectedly, it was Billy who broke the ice. He set his glass on the coffee table and said, "I don't suppose we should ignore the third person in this cottage with us."

Evie fortified herself with another sip. "No, I don't suppose we should."

Billy clasped his hands, let them dangle between his knees. "I figure you've seen her hair."

"Yes."

"Moral to the story—never let a nine-year-old near scissors. Especially if she doesn't feel like taking a bath and washing her hair."

Typical oppositional child's reaction to being told to do something. It was the ODD kid's way of holding on to the power she thought adults were trying to take away from her. "I'm glad she didn't hurt herself," Evie said. "But I have to admit, I was shocked to see what she'd done."

"I know. Ma said she'd only been in the bathroom alone for a couple of minutes." He sat against the back of the sofa. "I asked Gemma if she was teased about it at school. Her answer was typical. She couldn't remember and didn't care."

"There was a little teasing," Evie said, "but some-one—I'm guessing Brenda—did a good job fixing what was left of Gemma's hair. No one commented after the first few minutes."

"One thing you'll learn about Ma, if you get to know her any better, she never admits there's something she can't do. She trimmed and rolled until those cowering strands didn't have the nerve to defy her."

Evie stared at his stern profile. A muscle worked in his jaw. "There's more, you know. There were other problems."

"Oh, yeah. Her teacher called me twice this week." His gaze snapped to Evie's face, took on a defensive mask. "Gemma knows she's in trouble. Ma's making her do her homework in the kitchen, where she can watch her. I've taken away her allowance. She'll learn she has to behave."

Unknowingly, Billy had given her the perfect opportunity to say what he needed to hear. She lay a hand on his arm, felt the muscles retract. "That's a start, but, Billy, Gemma's not the only one who needs to learn."

His expression sharpened, became wary. "What do you mean?"

"Parents of oppositional children need to be trained almost as much as their kids, maybe more." She watched the lines around his mouth deepen, but went on. "Billy, you've got to learn how to be a parent to Gemma. Now, before it's too late."

He fixed his narrowed gaze on a spot across the room. "You mean, I've got to learn how to parent according to your rules, don't you? You want me to change the way I've been doing things for four years."

"Some people practice parenting a lifetime and never get it right. And with ODD kids, it's especially important to do what has been proven effective when there's an act of defiance. You're going to have to invest some time to understand and implement the steps you should take, the concepts you need to be familiar with."

He stood abruptly and stared down at her from his height advantage. "And you're going to teach me?"

"I'd like to try. What you're doing now isn't working. Gemma appears to be getting worse, more confrontational. I can give you coping mechanisms, reinforcement procedures proven in other cases—"

His hand shot up. "Stop right there. I don't need to hear psychobabble."

"It's not psychobabble. I'm talking about sound parenting techniques, things that work—"

"Yeah? And how do you know they work?"

"I've taken courses. I've studied child development. It's my field, Billy."

"Tell me, Evie, how many kids do you have?"

She took in a quick breath, feeling as if she'd plunged her face into ice water. If there was one great disappointment Evie had suffered from too many failed relationships with men, it was the agony of watching her biological clock tick away her opportunities. Determined that Billy wouldn't see how his callous statement had affected her, she struggled to control her emotions. "A hundred and twenty-five, at the moment."

"You know what I mean."

"Now who's being confrontational?"

"I'm a cop. It's my field." He had the decency to at least look away from her when he added, "Besides, like father, like daughter."

She stood to face him on a more equal level. "I don't know why you're being so unreasonable. I'm just trying to help. For heaven's sake, Billy, I *can* help."

He walked to the fireplace, turned and glared at her. "What are you? Super Teacher? You just want to teach everybody, don't you? What do you want? Every apple grown in the state of Washington on your desk?"

She couldn't help smiling. "Well, I do like apples."

"Fine. I'll send you a bushel." He blew out a frustrated breath. "I know you mean well—"

"No, Billy. Church ladies and philanthropists mean well. I mean business."

"Fine. But education isn't mine. I work forty-eight

hour weeks. I support a household of three people on my salary. Up until four years ago I had a nearly perfect life." He frowned. "I mean, I love my daughter... My point is that I don't have room on my plate for anything else right now. I know Gemma is being a little stinker these days. But I'm still head of the house. I still have control over what she does."

Evie gave him a doubtful look. "All the time?"

"Most of it. She listens when I talk to her. I just have to threaten her within an inch of her life and she'll straighten up. I don't need a lot of psychological mumbo jumbo to raise one nine-year-old."

Evie went to her bookshelf and pulled out the copy of a child development book she'd been studying the past few nights. "You don't even have to read this. I'll be happy—"

"I can read."

"Of course you can. I was only trying to—"

"I know. Trying to help. I don't want your help on this matter. I don't need it. What I want from you, *friend*...what I tried to tell you with that kiss the other night, just in case I have to spell it out, is something entirely different."

She dropped the book to the coffee table and stared at him. "You're being narrow-minded."

"You're being interfering. If you don't want a personal relationship with me, fine. Just say so."

He was giving her an ultimatum? Love me, ignore my daughter? Be a fun date and forget you're a principal? How dare he? They'd only just met. She threw him her frostiest glare.

He cocked his head to the side. "I guess that's my answer, then."

He headed to the door and, quite unexpectedly, Evie experienced a moment of uncertainty that was frighteningly near panic. She didn't want him to go. She'd made chicken and rice for heaven's sake. She'd had hopes for tonight. And now it was all going up in smoke.

Do something, Evie. Good grief. This ridiculous standoff is like the macho posturing of two bullies on a playground.

You can stop him, she thought. You have the power.

He grasped the front doorknob, began to twist.

"No, wait." She came up behind him, stopping within touching distance, but she kept her trembling hands to her sides. "Don't go."

He turned around.

"I want you to stay. This is silly." His expression was unreadable. "I have dessert."

The wariness in his expression became guarded interest. "What kind of dessert?"

She wished she'd baked something homemade, something at least as good as his mother probably gave him every night. "Ice cream. Ben & Jerry's."

He pondered a moment. "I like ice cream."

"Great. I'll get two bowls."

She went into the kitchen and pressed her forehead

against the cool door of the refrigerator. Every cell in her body had suddenly come alive. What was she thinking? The Evelyn Gaynor of even a week ago didn't act so rashly. But she'd definitely asked him to stay, practically begged him. So now Billy, tall, handsome and extraordinarily male, waited in her living room for something she knew darned well she wasn't ready to give him…yet. She gripped the smooth chrome handle of the fridge and just held on. "Now what are you going to do?" she mumbled.

"Get the ice cream, I expect." His voice rumbled low and seductively across the room.

She spun around, saw him in the doorway. She told herself the sudden movement was making her dizzy. Nothing else. She flattened her back against the metal door. "Right," she breathed. "The ice cream."

He walked toward her. "Can I help?"

Stop. Don't come any closer. I don't know what I'll do. I don't know who I am. "No. I can manage," she said.

He halted within inches of her and placed his hands on her waist. His thumbs gently massaged the base of her rib cage through her blouse. Silk had never felt so good. He smiled down at her. "Pact?"

She nodded. "Uh-huh."

He leaned over. A woodsy scent teased her nostrils as he spoke into her ear. "We won't talk about anything more serious than the flavor of the Ben & Jerry's for the rest of the night."

The voice that came from her throat sounded like

a stranger's. And the words were equally alien. She put her palms on each side of his face and said, "The truth is, right now I don't care to talk at all."

Evie knew that days from now, perhaps years from now, she would remember this kiss. And when she thought of it, there would be no doubt that she had been the one to make it happen. She wrapped her arms around his neck, raised herself on her toes and, as boldly as she'd ever done anything in her life, she pulled him down to meet her mouth.

Billy enclosed her in his strong arms and pressed her against his chest. His mouth devoured hers, releasing their pent-up emotions in a blending of mouths and passions. Evie's knees went weak. With a rumbling growl, he probed his tongue against her lips. She opened to his thrust, welcomed it.

His hands caressed her hair, smoothing it back from her temples. He kissed her eyelids, the crest of her cheekbones. His warm breath fanned her neck below her jawline. She leaned back, raised her face to give him access to her throat. His voice vibrated in her ear. "I've never made love against a refrigerator," he said, "but I'm about to unless you put a stop to this or suggest someplace more comfortable."

"The sofa."

He grinned. "It's a start."

Billy somehow maneuvered them through the door and around the coffee table. He fell back on the soft cushions, pulling her on top of his hard body. His hands firmly on her back, he tugged her closer until her breasts pressed against his chest. She felt his heart beat in a crazy rhythm with hers. His fingers clawed at her blouse, pulling the ends from her skirt. And then his hands were at her back, kneading, riding the sensitive ridge of her backbone.

This isn't you, Evelyn. Stop this madness now.

But with Billy, now, tonight, madness was what she wanted.

But she couldn't ignore the pounding on her front door.

Billy's head snapped up. "Who's that?"

Evie cleared her throat. "I don't know. It's not like I have many friends in this town."

"It could be Claire or Jack."

"No, it wouldn't be. Claire told me the other day…" She stopped before revealing Claire's pledge to mind her own business as far as activities in the cottage were concerned.

They heard the knock again. Billy, ever the cop, rolled Evie to the side and stood. "Wait here. I'll check it out."

He started for the door just as a voice called, "Evelyn? Are you in there?"

Evie's stomach plunged. She jumped up, frantically smoothed her hair into place, tucked her blouse back in her waistband. "Wait, Billy. I'll get it."

He turned toward her, frowning.

"It's my father."

CHAPTER NINE

BILLY, who normally considered himself cool under the most adverse conditions, stared dumbfounded at the front door. "Your father? I thought he was in Detroit."

"That makes two of us."

He stood by and watched as Evie hastily repaired her appearance while hurrying across the room. She took a deep breath and opened the door. "Dad! What a surprise."

The older gentleman who stood beaming on the threshold didn't look a bit like Evie. He was tall, gray-haired, square-jawed, and carried at least an extra twenty pounds around his waistline. The other noticeable feature about him was the plastic animal cage hanging from his left hand. The man leaned in for Evie's quick kiss to his cheek. "Hello, Ev. I knew you'd be surprised."

"I just talked to you on Sunday," she said.

"Right. And I got up Monday morning and thought, Why the heck don't I just put ol' Muffler in the car and run down to Florida to be with my daughter?"

Evie's smile was only a hint of the real thing. "And so that's just what you did," she said.

"You glad to see me?"

"Of course." She paused a moment and then stepped aside. "Come in."

He closed the door behind him, set down the cage and bent to release the latch. "I've got to let Muffler out. We did an eight-hour stretch without any exercise."

A large striped cat lumbered out and paused before stretching first one hind leg and then the other. He cast a haughty gold-eyed look at the man. Evie bent to scratch behind his ear. "Nice to see you, Muff."

Mr. Gaynor scooted the cage out of the way and took a long look around the room. "Nice place you have here, Ev." His gaze settled on Billy and his eyes widened. "Am I interrupting?"

Evie grabbed her father's arm and began chattering nonstop. "Of course not, Dad. This is Billy Muldoone, a...friend of mine. We were discussing his daughter, one of my students." She finally took a breath. "Billy, meet my father, Harry Gaynor."

Billy shook the man's hand. "Nice to meet you, sir."

"Call me Harry."

"Okay. Harry." He pointed to himself. "Billy."

Harry smiled. "Oh, say, I'll bet you're that fella Evelyn mentioned to me. The one that's the single father with the daughter who..."

Billy cast a sideways look at Evie. "That's me. Your daughter's latest project."

Harry's expression reflected his fatherly pride. "She can help you, I guarantee that. When Ev's got her mind on something, she's like a dog with a bone. Won't quit till she gets it right."

Evie froze, mortified.

"Well, never mind," Harry said. "It's my daughter's business, certainly not mine." He scooped the cat off the floor. "I've got to feed Muffler. You got any scraps, Ev?"

"There's some chicken and rice in a plastic bowl in the refrigerator."

"And some ice cream in the freezer," Billy added. "In case Muffler has a sweet tooth."

Harry laughed and patted his stomach. "Oh, we both do. That's why we've got more girth than we need." He headed for the kitchen with Muffler tucked in the crook of his elbow.

Once they were alone, Evie let the plastic smile fade from her lips. She reached for Billy's arm. "I'm so sorry."

He kept his voice calm. "For what?"

"That thing my father said. Don't jump to the wrong conclusion."

Billy frowned. "You didn't discuss Gemma and me with him?"

"No. Of course not. He asked what I'd been doing over the weekend. I just mentioned I'd been reading up, hoping I could advise one of the parents. I never gave him details. I wouldn't do that."

"I suppose it was a lucky guess, then, that he knew I was a single father with a daughter."

She wrapped her hand around his wrist. "That's all I told him—well, mostly all. And I had no idea he was driving to Florida. He never said anything."

"He's a man of action," Billy said. "Now I see where you get your impulsive nature."

That brought a flush to her cheeks.

"I think it's my cue to leave."

She nodded. "I'm sorry."

He shrugged, though the casual gesture in no way mirrored the tumult of emotions he felt. "Stuff happens."

She walked him to the door. "I'll see you."

"Yeah. See you around."

She shut the door behind him and Billy walked alone to his truck. Cramming his nerve-taut body behind the steering wheel, he started the engine. Hearing that Gemma's problems, to Evie, were like a bone in a fierce canine's jaws was not the image he'd hoped to take to bed tonight.

EVIE LEANED AGAINST the door, covered her face with her hands and exhaled a deep breath. Two images came to mind. In the first one, she pictured herself shutting the door on her father and Muffler with a stern warning to come back later. In the other, she saw herself on her knees thanking Harry that he'd shown up when he had.

Billy's hands had felt so good on her skin, and Evie

had been as primed for his caresses as…well, as the love-starved woman she now realized she had been for much too long. Two years, to be precise.

She pushed away from the door at the sound of Billy's tires grinding on the drive. Grabbing the two wineglasses still on the coffee table, she ran her fingertip lightly over the rim of Billy's glass. Damn it. She liked him. A lot. Too much. He was funny and interesting. Spontaneous yet grounded. Committed to his job, his town, his friends. And the fact that she found him incredibly handsome was just a bonus.

She walked toward the kitchen and reminded herself that Billy was also stubborn, proud and impatient. And his fragile ego was certainly wounded too easily. "Think about those traits the next time you're about to jump off a cliff with that man," she said to herself.

Her father turned from the sink. "What's that, Ev?"

She nearly dropped a glass. Oh, blast. She'd completely forgotten about Harry. "Nothing. What are you doing?"

"Washing your dishes. Two of everything. Did Billy have dinner here?"

She picked up a dish towel and began to dry. "Yes. I invited him. I hadn't used the oven since I moved in. I figured he would be as good a test subject as anyone." She laid a hand on Harry's arm. "Of course I didn't know that my all-time favorite guinea pig was coming to see me."

"I guess a big strapping guy like him appreciates your healthy cooking." He nodded toward the cat, hunched over a crockery bowl. "Muffler's eating it up. But as far as diet's concerned, he's easy to please."

She returned the dry plates to the hutch. "So how long are you going to be around to complain about my cooking?"

"Not long. I've got things to do back in Detroit. I only hired the kid down the street to cut the grass one time. Probably after a couple of weeks I'll start to miss the guys at the lodge. And you know how I am about the *Detroit Free Press*. I like my hometown newspaper."

A couple of weeks? "I only have one bedroom," she said.

"I can make do with the sofa," Harry said. "My needs are simple."

Evie sighed. *I wish I could say the same thing.*

HARRY CALLED EVIE at school the next afternoon. "I'm treating you to dinner tonight, Ev."

She wasn't surprised. To avoid her cooking, Harry would gladly pick up the tab. "Sounds good. Where are we going?"

"I found a great place while I was out exploring today. You're going to love it."

Evie smiled. She and her father hadn't agreed on a restaurant in years. What was the chance they would find one to suit both their tastes in Heron Point?

That question was answered at seven o'clock when

Harry pulled into the parking lot of a wood-sided road-house. The Marina Tavern. He shut off the engine and killed the lights of his six-year-old Buick. "What'd I tell you? Looks great, eh?"

Evie got out of the car hoping that looks could be deceiving. Then she got a whiff of overfried beer batter.

"The locals eat here," Harry told her. "That's how you know a restaurant is a good one."

A neon light above the door zapped an electrical hiccup. "And since I'm an islander now," she said, "it stands to reason that I will like this place."

Harry chuckled and held the door for her. "You probably won't, but since this is my first day in Heron Point, you have to indulge me."

She smiled over her shoulder. "I've got antacids in my purse."

A sign by the front door made it clear customers should seat themselves, so Evie and Harry found a vacant booth in the main dining area. Through the entrance to an adjacent room, Evie caught a glimpse of a bar and a pool table. The place was crowded. Evidently her father's rule for choosing restaurants had some validity.

At the deep rumble of a familiar laugh, she leaned to look into the game room. Sure enough, Billy and Gemma Muldoone were playing air hockey, and if Gemma's smile was any indication, she was winning.

Gemma saw Evie at the same time and waved over

her head. "Hey, Daddy, look who's here! It's Miss Gaynor."

Evie wiggled her fingers in return. "Hello, Gemma."

The girl headed for their booth with Billy trailing behind. "Isn't that the fella from last night?" Harry asked.

"Yes."

"That's his kid?"

Evie nodded.

"Cute little thing. Got a weird hairdo though."

Evie whispered, "It's the latest fad."

"Oh. The weedeater look, I guess."

Gemma skidded to a stop by the booth, placed both hands on the table and grinned. "I didn't know you liked to come here."

Evie glanced up at Billy whose five-o'clock shadow had a rugged earthiness that made her heart race. He took a drag from a Bud Light bottle and wiped his hand across his mouth. Evie stared at a hint of moisture on his bottom lip. "I'm just full of surprises," she said, and introduced Gemma to her father.

Billy acknowledged that it was nice seeing Harry again, and then he spoke to Gemma. "Your drink is on the table. Why don't you go sit with Nana now?"

Gemma stomped one foot on the floor. "I don't want to. I want to play more air hockey."

"Too bad. I just told you to—"

Harry scooted out of the booth. "I'll play a game with you, kid. I haven't played air hockey in years."

Gemma debated the invitation a moment and apparently decided it was the best deal she was going to get. "Okay. You got a quarter? That's what it costs."

Harry dug in his pocket as he followed her toward the other room. "I guess I can scrounge one up."

Billy slid into the empty seat. "I never expected to see you here."

"And that's why you came?"

"No. That's not what I meant. I'm glad to see you. I'm just surprised, that's all."

"I haven't had a decent onion ring since I left Detroit."

A waitress dropped two menus on the table. Evie grabbed one, opened it and held it in front of her face. "They must have a salad on here somewhere."

Billy's finger curled over the top of the menu and he slowly pulled it down. "You're driving me crazy, but you know that, don't you?"

"No. I had no idea."

"I can't stop thinking about you."

"In a good way or a bad way?"

"I haven't decided yet. I figure I've got to see you about a hundred more times before I'll know for sure. When can we get together again?"

"I don't know. Maybe we shouldn't. We almost crossed a line last night."

"What line?"

"You know darned well. I'm your daughter's principal. You're her father. We both recognize she has issues. We both want to help…"

His expression sobered. "I think we're about to cross another line right now."

"Exactly. That's my point. We can't be together for five minutes without arguing."

He raised his eyebrows and smiled. "*I* wasn't arguing. You're the one who keeps bringing up the same subject. I've thought of more creative ways to spend our time together. Last night I was just beginning to explore one of those."

She folded her hands over the forgotten menu and looked directly at the game room where Gemma had just raised her hands in triumph. "Besides our obvious difference of opinion, our lives are a little complicated now, don't you think?"

"Only a little."

She shook her head. "No matter how you try to spin this, Billy, we have three factors that can't be ignored. My job. Your daughter. And now, my father."

He stood and pulled her to her feet. Before she could resist, he led her to the rear of the restaurant.

"What are you doing?"

"Hiding." He tucked their bodies into a narrow alcove by the restrooms. When a man tried to squeeze by them, Billy told him to come back later.

Evie started to protest, but Billy put his finger over her lips. "Let's think about this logically," he said. "We can eliminate the first two problems if you get another job."

She jerked his finger away. "Are you crazy?"

He smiled. "I heard today that Hester Poole over at the Pink Ladies is looking for a gardener."

"Billy…"

He turned her around so she was facing the dining area. "And don't look now, but I think the problem of your father is about to be solved. In about ten minutes he ought to be laying rubber on his way back to Detroit."

"What are you talking about?" She'd no sooner asked the question than she saw Brenda Muldoone making a beeline across the tavern floor for Harry, and there was an unmistakable sway in her hips.

HARRY CONGRATULATED his young opponent in the competitive hockey game and watched her saunter away from the table with the dignified demeanor of the victorious. All he wanted now was a large platter of hot wings, blue cheese dressing and French fries smothered in ketchup. He inhaled deeply, hoping for the mouthwatering smell of grease. But all he got was the cloying odor of flowers. He wrinkled his nose. "What the heck?"

And then, out of the corner of his eye he glimpsed something small, imposing and very, very red churning toward him. A woman to be sure, and one who didn't try to hide the fact behind demure clothing and accessories.

Gemma walked past the woman. "Hi, Nana. I won." They exchanged smiles, and Gemma kept going. The woman advanced—right up to Harry. She stopped and peered closely at him. "You came in with the new principal, didn't you?"

Harry stared at her purple-shaded green eyes, ruby-ringed mouth and cheeks the color of overripe watermelon before he took in her mass of curly red hair held back with rhinestone clips. Reminding himself it wasn't polite to stare, he mumbled, "Yes. I'm her father. Name's Harry Gaynor."

She stuck a diminutive hand out. When he grasped it, she pumped a greeting like she was wringing out wet laundry. "You met my son," she said. "William Muldoone."

His brain didn't recognize the name immediately. "Oh, Billy."

"Right." She stopped pumping. "I'm Brenda Muldoone. I've raised three sons. One's in the navy. One rides a Harley. And William's the best of the lot. I've buried one husband, and this is my real hair color—almost. What's your story?"

Story? Harry didn't have a story. What woman would be interested in hearing that he'd worked forty-odd years at the General Motors Assembly plant and now lived with an imperious cat? He pointed to his thick gray hair. "These aren't plugs."

Brenda threw back her bird's nest of a head and laughed, a deep, full-throttle laugh. She scared the living daylights out of Harry.

"Come on, let's eat," she said. "We'll pull our tables

together. The kids already know each other, so we might as well take advantage of the connection."

At a loss, he followed her.

"What are you having?" she asked as she scooted a table next to Harry's booth.

That was an easy question, at least. "Wings. I love 'em."

Brenda dropped down into a chair, opened a menu and pointed. "I'd suggest the trout. Wings'll send you to an early grave. I ought to know. Fried food is what killed my husband. Clogged his arteries like he'd eaten glue soup. I never touch anything greasy now." She chuckled. "'Course it might have been the whiskey, too."

Harry didn't know how anyone could possibly respond to a stranger about such intimate details, so he simply narrowed his eyes. "I'm having wings."

She reached over, patted his hand. "Suit yourself, honey. It's not my place to tell a man what to put in his stomach. At least not when I first meet him."

Harry pondered the long-range significance of that statement.

"Now then, Harry, buy me a Guinness?"

EVIE DARTED from the alcove. Billy grabbed her arm and pulled her back. "What's your hurry?"

"Don't you see the look on my father's face? It's like he's lost in a fog."

"He's a grown man. He'll find his way."

"I'm not so sure. I've seen your mother in action. She can be…well, intimidating."

Billy smiled. "She's not brandishing a willow branch. I think Pops will come out unscathed."

Evie peered over her shoulder. Harry's color seemed to be returning to normal. But he'd clasped his hands on the table and was looking around the restaurant. Evie figured he was praying for the cavalry to rescue him. "I've got to go."

"Okay. But first, this." He lowered his mouth to hers.

She tried to push him away, but the moist softness of his lips stopped her. A moan of capitulation came from her throat and she gave herself up to the kiss, which was too short and too potent. She pulled away and sent him her best how-dare-you look. "Can I go now?"

"Was it so horrible?"

"Yes." She lowered her voice. "No."

He leaned against the wall. "Good. We agree on something."

She ran damp hands down her jeans. "We can't change the facts, Billy."

"Right, and I'm beginning to see the downside of that." He held up his hand. "Here are the facts I have to deal with every day, and these are just the ones concerning the women in my life." He bent his index finger. "One. I've got a nine-year-old female in my house who challenges me at every turn." Next finger. "Another one who tells me what to do every minute I'm home." Third finger. "And now a know-it-all educator who wants to teach me a whole new set of rules."

He ran one of those long fingers over her jawline and down her throat. "You can see that this thing between us is not making my life any easier."

When he traced a seductive line down the V of her top, she grabbed his hand. "It's no picnic for me, either. We should have remained just friends."

He smiled. "I wouldn't go that far."

She felt her heart pounding through their clasped hands and realized she was a beat away from dragging his mouth back to hers. "Let's eat."

He turned her around and nudged her forward. "After you." She'd only taken one step when his hand slipped around her waist and his breath warmed her earlobe. "Why don't you bring your father into town tomorrow night," he whispered. "It's Friday, lots going on."

"I'll think about it."

"I'm off at eleven. I'll bring Brenda to entertain Pops and you can meet me under the boardwalk."

She pushed his hand down. "You're hopeless. I've got to rescue my father."

But she was too late. When she walked up to their table, she heard Harry agree to meet Brenda at another restaurant the next evening. Harry looked up at her and shrugged his bewilderment as if to say he had no idea how any of this had happened.

These Muldoones knew how to work their way around a Gaynor. And it certainly wasn't a fair fight.

CHAPTER TEN

THE NEXT EVENING at six o'clock, Harry came out to the porch where Evie was reading a book and waited for her to notice him. "I guess I'm going now," he said when she looked up.

"Very spiffy, Dad." She appraised his slicked-back hair, which had been tamed into a neat part, his crisp plaid shirt and creased trousers. "Are you meeting Brenda at the restaurant?"

"No. I said I'd pick her up."

"Oh. So it's a real date, then?"

Harry squinted into the fading sunlight. "No, it isn't. It's just that she drives a motor home and she said the parking in town is bad on Friday nights. She thought it would be easier if I just picked her up. I don't mind, of course. It's the gentlemanly thing to do, but darned if she isn't a hard woman to say no to."

"I see." Evie set her book on the wicker end table. "Are you looking forward to the evening?"

"I suppose. I haven't done anything like this in a long time, you know. It's just a meal, but it feels strange all the same. Kind of exciting in a way, too."

He patted his pockets. "Can't forget my wallet. I suppose I'll have to pay."

Evie smiled. "It's the gentlemanly thing to do even if this isn't a date."

Harry gave her a sheepish grin. "Can't be a date. I wasn't the one that did the asking." He went down the three steps to the driveway. "But I'm ordering what I want to eat," he said. "She's not going to order for me."

Evie lightly punched her fist into her palm. "You tell her, Dad. Be your own man."

"Sure you don't want to come along?"

"Oh, yeah. I'm sure. Have fun. And if you run into any trouble, call me. I don't care how late it is. I'll come get you."

"That's what I used to tell you."

She waved as he got into the Buick. A few minutes later, Harry was gone and Evie reached for her book. Who would have thought she'd be the one sitting alone reading on a Friday night while her stay-at-home father was having a night on the town? The pathetic irony of her situation made her reluctant to return to her novel. All she really wanted to do was to wallow in self-pity for a while and blame Billy Muldoone.

Here she was, half nuts over a guy who didn't respect her advice. What sort of future could there be with a man like Billy? "None," she said out loud. "But if you're so smart, Evelyn, you should cut your losses."

Unfortunately, Evie's wallowing ended when she saw Claire coming up the drive.

"Hi, neighbor," Claire said when she reached the porch.

"Hi, yourself. You're not going into town tonight?"

"Never do. Not on weekends. Too crowded." She sat on the top step. "Which is why I've come to see you. Jack is working tonight. Jane is going into town with a friend's family, and I have absolutely nothing to do. It seemed like the perfect opportunity to invite you for a gourmet meal of tomato soup and grilled-cheese sandwiches. Followed by a giant bowl of popcorn and wine with a good tear-jerker movie." When Evie didn't immediately respond, Claire added, "I don't think I'm going to take no for an answer."

Evie laughed. "I wasn't going to say no." She looked down at her tank top and shorts. "I was just wondering if I'd be admitted to Tansy Hill for a gourmet meal dressed like this."

Claire stood. "Evening wear not required."

Two HOURS LATER, Evie and Claire sat on the veranda of Tansy Hill listening to faint strains of pop music coming from Island Avenue. Evie sipped at her wine and sighed. "Sounds like they're having fun."

"I suppose. You sorry you didn't go in?"

"No. This evening has been perfect. And I wouldn't want to miss that popcorn and the movie."

Claire poured another inch into Evie's glass. "So

how are you getting along? We haven't had much chance to talk."

"Very well. I love the school and my job. Everyone has been friendly and helpful. You have a great staff at Heron Point Elementary."

Claire swirled the wine in her glass and smiled. "And how about our law-enforcement division? What do you think of our police officers?"

"Of course I like Jack."

"Just Jack?" Claire asked.

Evie hid a smile behind her glass. "There's one other guy who's kind of interesting."

"I've seen Billy's truck at your place a couple of times," Claire said. "Tell me I'm out of bounds and I'll mind my own business."

"No, it's all right. Billy has been over. We went on a canoe trip, and he came to dinner."

"That's great. I'm very fond of Billy. And Jack thinks the world of him. You may have heard that at one time he had a reputation as a woman chaser. But he's not like that anymore." Claire smiled. "Unless maybe he's chasing you."

Yeah. One minute he makes me want to run for cover. And the next all I can think about is running into his arms. He's still pretty adept at the chase. "He's hinted that his life has changed over the past few years," she said.

Claire's expression became somber. "I wasn't here when Astrid dropped Gemma at his door, but I can only imagine what a shock it must have been. Here's a guy who answered to no one but himself for years, and suddenly he's raising a five-year-old and asking his mother to move in with him. I have to admire Billy for the way he's managed the responsibility."

"I admire him, too, for the most part. But something about Billy puzzles me."

"Oh, what's that?"

"From the conversation you and I had at the hotel that day with Helen and Pet, I assume everyone knows that Gemma can be a handful."

"Her misdeeds are legend. She wasn't always such a terror, just for the past year or so." Claire leaned forward, looked over the quiet street in front of her house. "While I can't condone her behavior, I can understand it. She was literally dumped by her mother. Gemma was too young when it happened to realize what that meant, but she's older now, and somewhere, deep inside her, resentment must be an emotional wound that's only now festering. I'm sure Billy has been as delicate as he can be about Astrid's actions four years ago, but the bottom line is, Gemma's mother abandoned her. There's no gentle way of saying that, and I think Gemma's suffering for it now."

Evie nodded. "Billy seems like a caring father."

"Oh, he is. And Brenda loves Gemma, too." Claire swatted at a tiny bug circling her chair. "I hate to say this since I heard your father stepped out with Brenda tonight, but Billy puts up with a lot from his mother.

She's about as controlling as anyone I've ever met, except for maybe Missy Hutchinson. But Brenda can even manage her."

Evie sighed. "Oddly, someone like Brenda may be just what my father needs. Though I'm sure he would never admit it."

Claire agreed. "Some men do need that, but not Billy. He's got an enormous well of patience with his mother. And that's because he really loves Gemma and wants what's best for her. Unfortunately he doesn't have a clue how to deal with her."

Evie frowned. Everything Claire had said mirrored her own opinions. "And Brenda defends the girl no matter what she does."

"True. I believe Brenda spent her married life defending three rowdy sons and a drunkard of a husband, and she can't stop now. Gemma is getting a ton of assurance that she's loved, but zero discipline, I suspect. And she's taking full advantage of it."

"Exactly," Evie said. "If you and I both see this, why can't I get Billy to listen to me? Believe it or not, I really like Gemma. She's got spunk and heart. I can help Billy with her if he'd only give me a chance."

Claire reached over and patted Evie's arm. "What can you expect? He's wounded, too, in a way. Billy's had some disappointments in his life. He's given his heart to all the wrong women. When Gemma came into his life, he saw a chance to do the right thing, to make up for past mistakes. But if you, or anyone else, tries to point out that he's not making a success of fatherhood, I'm afraid he'll view it as another in a long line of failures."

She held up the wine bottle. Evie declined. "It's a pride thing," Claire continued.

"I suppose you're right," Evie said. "Childhood development is my specialty. Being stubborn is his."

Claire nodded. "My guess is that he'll wise up and figure out that you're too good a resource to waste."

Evie laughed. "But will that happen before Gemma does something serious enough to affect the rest of her life?"

"Who knows? I hope so."

The trill of a cell phone interrupted their conversation. "That's my ring," Evie said, digging in her pocket. She glanced at the digital screen. "It's my father. I told him he could call if he ran into trouble."

Claire sputtered a chuckle. "No surprise there."

Evie connected. "Hi, Dad. Everything okay?"

"Sure. I just thought you might want to join us. It's really hopping down here tonight."

Evie covered the mouthpiece to speak to Claire. "He wants me to join him downtown."

"You should go. Don't worry about keeping me company."

Evie couldn't deny that she wanted to join the festivities on Island Avenue. Maybe she'd run into someone she knew…not under the boardwalk of course, but all this talk about Billy made her want to see him again. "You sure?" she said to Claire. "We haven't watched the movie."

"It's part of my collection. We'll watch it another time. Go."

"Okay, Dad," she said into the phone. "But can you pick me up in front of Claire's? I've had some wine."

"I'll swing by now."

Evie disconnected. "Should I change?"

"You look fine. This is Heron Point, remember?"

"Okay. I'll just run home and do something with my hair." Evie bounded down the steps. "Thanks so much for dinner, and your advice."

"You're welcome," Claire called. "And tell Billy I said hello. And if you see Jack, tell him to bring home a pint of Rocky Road."

EVIE WAS WAITING when Harry pulled up in front of Claire's cottage. She started to climb in the back, but stopped when she noticed the front passenger seat was empty. "Where's Brenda?"

"She's still in town. She left Gemma with a neighbor tonight, and for some reason the lady brought the kid to the restaurant a while ago. Said she couldn't keep her any longer. I don't know what the problem was."

"Hmm. That's strange, all right." Actually it wasn't strange at all. Evie could imagine a number of problems that might have prompted the neighbor to bring Gemma to her grandmother.

"Anyhow, I dropped the two of them off near a park at the end of Island Avenue."

"Point Park?"

"I guess so. We're going to meet them there and then walk back up for a drink or ice cream. That sound okay?"

"Sure, fine." Evie studied her father's strong profile in the glow of the dashboard. "So how has the date or, as you prefer to call it, 'meal appointment' been going?"

"Pretty well." He propped his arm on the open window. "Gotta tell you, Ev, there's no conversational lull when you're with Brenda. She could talk a dead man back to life." He chuckled. "Or the other way around. And there isn't a question she won't ask, either."

"So she's delved into your fascinating personal life?"

"More than I'm comfortable with ordinarily. And whenever I balk at answering her, she just smiles and says, 'We'll talk about it later, Harry.'" He frowned. "I wonder how much *later* she thinks we're going to have. I'm headed back to Detroit before long."

"Right. Of course you are." Evie stared out the front window. Foot traffic increased once they turned onto Island Avenue. She wondered if she would see Billy among the tourists. Maybe he was busy chasing purse snatchers. Remembering the scrapes and bruises Billy had suffered, Evie felt anxious for his safety.

Harry found a parking place close to Point Park. They got out and began walking the block to where kids were playing games on the sandy beach. Evie looked at her watch. It wasn't yet ten o'clock, and the night air was invigorating. She wasn't surprised parents let their children stay out late.

"There's Brenda," Harry said, pointing to a picnic table. "Looks like Billy's there with her."

Evie peered through the crowd. Billy stood with his foot propped on a bench, his arm on his knee. Casual and at ease, he smiled at something Brenda said. Evie's pace accelerated.

Before Billy saw her, his head snapped around, and he stood at attention a moment before taking off toward the cement block restrooms down the beach. A girl had come out and was hollering his name and waving. Evie stared at the child until recognition dawned. She experienced a moment of panic. Billy was running toward Jane Hogan. And something was definitely wrong.

She and Harry raced to the picnic table. "What's going on, Brenda?" she asked.

"I don't know. Can't be anything too serious." She hooked a thumb at a nearby table where adults were gathered around a large cooler, laughing. "The parents are over there and all the kids have been playing nicely."

"I'm going to go after Billy," Evie said.

"No. He said to stay put," Brenda warned her. "Trust me. You'll only make him angry. When he says stay, you'd best do it."

Against her instincts, Evie remained at the picnic table. Jane looked fine. No injuries, so sign of trauma. She watched as Billy pressed the heel of his palm to his forehead for a split second before advancing the few feet to the lady's restroom. The last Evie heard—even from this distance—before he disappeared inside was, "Gemma Scarlett Muldoone! What do you think you're doing?"

Brenda seemed to shrink beside her as she mumbled, "Oh, dear."

BILLY COULDN'T BELIEVE his eyes. There, in the middle of the women's bathroom, his daughter crouched low like a pint-size Sumo wrestler, her little fist wrapped around a huge cedar limb she could barely hang on to, much less jab in the air as she was attempting to do. He didn't see any other girls in the restroom, but sounds coming from two closed stalls proved Gemma wasn't alone.

"Gemma, drop that stick."

She turned and glared at him.

"I said drop it now."

Whimpers filled the tiled room. Desperate, frightened sounds.

Still clutching her weapon, Gemma hollered, "Shut up. It's just what you deserve!"

One quivering voice filtered over the closed stall door. "Officer Muldoone, get her out of here."

Billy wrenched the limb from Gemma's hand and

laid it on a sink. Then he grabbed her by the arm and spun her around to face him. "Did you hit anyone with that thing?"

"No. They're just babies, crying for their mommies."

Billy pointed a finger at her. "Don't move." He went to the stalls and knocked on the doors. "Who's in there?"

"It's me, Alina Vasquez," a timid voice answered.

"And…me, Whitney Broadmoor."

Billy recognized the name of the girl who had left Gemma off the guest list of her sleepover party. "You did this?" he asked Gemma. "You backed these girls into these stalls?"

She pursed her lips.

"You can come out," he said. "She's not going to hurt you."

He heard the latches slide across and watched the doors creak open. Slowly, the two victims came into the open. Their faces were streaked with tears, but otherwise they didn't appear to have suffered any injuries.

"Are you both okay?" Billy asked, moving closer to check them over.

They nodded.

Whitney pointed at Gemma. "But I hate her. She's horrible."

Billy couldn't come up with a reason to argue that at the moment. He leveled a steely look on Gemma and said, "Stay here while I take these girls outside. Then I'm coming back for you."

She fisted her hands at her sides. "I wasn't going to hurt them. I could've, but I wasn't going to."

"We'll talk about that later. Stay put."

He escorted the girls outside where they immediately ran to the party of adults who were obviously celebrating Friday night and oblivious to the scene in the bathroom. Billy shook his head. There would be hell to pay once they realized what had happened.

He returned to the bathroom, grasped Gemma's hand and dragged her out behind him. They were halfway back to Brenda's table when George Broadmoor ran to intercept them. "Muldoone, you'd better keep that kid of yours caged from now on."

Billy stopped, tightening his hold on Gemma's hand with a fierce combination of anger and protectiveness. "Is your daughter okay?"

"She wasn't impaled by that brat of yours, if that's what you mean."

Something hot, alien and frightening flared up inside Billy. It was all he could do to keep from venting his smoldering fury on George. "I'll handle this," he said. "Gemma won't go near Whitney again."

"You see that she doesn't." With a final threatening glare, George returned to his party.

Billy continued to the picnic table where Brenda stood like the Muldoone family sentinel, poised to react, eyes watchful. And she wasn't alone. A few feet from the table Evie Gaynor waited, her hands clasped in front of her, her eyes brim-full of the one emotion

Billy hadn't expected to see from anyone in Point Park. Sympathy. For him. And, perhaps even for Gemma.

Brenda placed her hands on Gemma's shoulders. "What's happened, William? What did she do?"

He released his daughter to her grandmother. "I'll explain everything to you later, Ma. Can you take her home?"

"I don't have my Winnie." She looked at Harry.

"I'll drive you," he said. "Once I get them home, I'll come back for you, Evie."

"No need," Billy said. "I'll drive her." And then in a voice hoarse with emotion, he added, "But, Harry, if you wouldn't mind staying awhile at my house. Just until you know the situation's calmed a bit…"

"I don't mind at all." Harry waited until Evie nodded her approval. "See you at home, then, Ev."

They walked off, Gemma's hand held securely inside Brenda's, and Harry, who'd just come to Florida for a visit with his daughter and who hadn't planned on serving as family mediator in a crisis, beside them. Billy let out a breath as his shoulders slumped. "I'm glad you're here," he said to Evie. "I'm still on duty another few minutes at this end of town, but can you stay?"

She slid onto the picnic bench. "For as long as you need."

He sat across from her, knitted his hands together on the rough wood tabletop and inhaled deeply. "I need your help, Evie," he said hesitantly. He looked into her eyes and saw only understanding, not the slightest hint of condemnation. "Tell me it's not too late."

She covered his hands with hers. "Of course it's not too late."

His lips curved slightly, but there was no joy in his smile. "I don't know what to do anymore."

Evie knew how difficult this admission was for him. Keeping her hand steady on his, she said, "Would you be more comfortable talking with June Renniger, the school counselor, or Dr. Grey, the psychologist?"

His eyes narrowed. His fingers flexed beneath hers.

"Since you and I have a...complicated relationship," she continued, "I thought maybe..."

He pulled his hands free. "Are you refusing to help me now?"

"No. I'm giving you an out if you want to take it."

"Why would I want to do that? You know everything. You said you'd help."

Evie wrapped her hand around his forearm. "I will. I was just making sure that my advice is what you want."

"It is."

"Okay. Then why don't you tell me what happened in that restroom."

He nodded, pressed a button on the radio strapped to his shoulder. "Jack?"

When his boss responded he said, "I'm at Point Park. If everything's okay, I'm going to be here awhile."

Jack's voice crackled through the night air. "I'll

call you if I need you. Check in before you leave for the night."

"Will do." He stared into Evie's eyes, even attempted a smile. "Ah, the bathroom caper. Here's how it went down, at least what I know now."

"You saw what happened after I dragged Gemma out of there," Billy said. "Hopefully she's sound asleep by now and your father has escaped the clutches of both Muldoone women. And you haven't given us all up as lost causes."

Evie smiled. "I haven't given up on anyone."

"So, what do I do? Lock Gemma in her room for the next twenty years?"

Evie pretended to give his suggestion serious thought. "Not that long." She leaned forward. "Here are a few basic facts you need to know about children with Oppositional Defiant Disorder. They spend a great deal of their time trying to show that their parents don't have any power over them. You, as the parent, have to prove that you do." She shifted on the hard wood.

"And, not surprising to you, I'm sure, ODD kids are almost always intelligent and creative. Gemma is going to come up with all sorts of inventive ways to show you she's the boss. You have to be just as creative to establish that she's not. Gemma believes that if she simply ignores your rules, you'll grow tired of enforcing them. You have to prove to her you won't."

Billy rubbed his hand down his face. "Wow. Seems like we're drawing battle lines."

"It's not an unrealistic analogy. We do need a clear strategy to deal with this. The first thing you have to do is to establish structure in your house. Set yourself up as the one in charge. Brenda has to know that what you say is the rule of the house. She can still care for Gemma and provide for her, but she has to support your decisions."

He acknowledged his acceptance with a nod. "I need to discuss this with Ma before I talk to Gemma."

"Right. And you must speak to Gemma as soon as you can. Even if you're working tomorrow, you should get her up before you leave and lay some ground rules."

"I can tell you how it's going to go. She'll stare at the ceiling, roll her eyes. If I ask her questions, she'll say, 'I don't know' or 'just because.'"

Not surprised, Evie said, "Of course she will. She's her own boss. In her mind, she doesn't have to tell you anything. So here's what you're going to do. Establish two rules at the onset. One, you're going to insist that she look into your eyes when she's talking to you. And two, you won't take 'I don't know' for an answer."

"I could be there all day."

"You might be in a standoff for a while, but if you have to go to work, tell her she has to sit in one spot until she's ready to answer your question. For simplicity's sake, make it only one question to start.

Maybe ask her why she did what she did tonight. She can get up and use the bathroom. She can eat her meals in her chair, but she must remain right there until she's ready to answer the question. Let her know that she can call you on your cell when she decides to cooperate, and her confinement will end then."

"What if she truly doesn't know why she did it?"

"She still has to come up with an answer, and it will be more truthful than you might think. She's smart. She knows why she did it, and when she admits it, you've accomplished one small victory."

He rested his elbows on the table. "Okay. I can do this, but what about punishment? I can't let her think that sitting in a chair is punishment for what happened, can I?"

Pleased that Billy was not only willing to do what had to be done, but was thinking ahead of her, Evie said, "Oh, no. She's going to be punished. What's her favorite possession?"

Billy thought a moment. "The TV in her room, I guess. She plays video games and watches movies a lot."

"It's gone, as of tomorrow."

He sat back. "What?"

"Just for Saturday. Tell her you're taking the television out of her room for a day and warn her that each time she behaves badly, there will be a consequence to pay. The next time she engages in what she knows is unacceptable behavior, the TV goes for a longer period, along with something else, maybe a favorite snack. When she behaves appropriately, she gets her stuff back."

"She'll say her things were gifts, they're hers."

"Maybe they were gifts, but let's be realistic, Billy. Nothing in the house is really hers. You know that, and you have to make sure she knows it, as well. You own everything. You simply let her *use* it."

His eyebrows came together in a frown. "Boy, you're tough."

"Maybe. But the structure we're establishing is also going to be flexible. Think of structure as a big elastic band that fits all the way around Gemma. When she misbehaves, the band contracts. When she responds well, the band relaxes. Bad behavior means fewer privileges. Good behavior means the return of them."

He rubbed his forehead. "Maybe this is good in theory," he said. "But Gemma isn't like most kids. She's had a tough time. Her mother left her. The kids at school reject her."

"We'll get to that rejection thing later. Right now we're dealing with tonight's situation and your reaction to it."

"But she'll say it's not fair."

"And you'll say it is, because you're warning her of the consequences ahead of time. She knows exactly what will happen if she makes a decision to misbehave, like the one she made tonight. No surprises. And don't forget that in addition to returning her privileges, you have to praise her when she does well. That's very important."

He exhaled. "It sounds logical."

"It is logical. And it works. Not overnight, but gradually. We'll add some other proven techniques and, as we do, you'll start to feel more confident. You're fortunate Gemma's only nine. In the teen years, there can be more serious problems. I believe Gemma will respond."

"Okay. I'll give it a try."

"And, Billy, two more things, and that's enough for tonight. Never, *ever* yell. When you raise your voice, you relinquish control as the parent and an already tense situation becomes a shouting match between two equal competitors. You can't let that happen. Repeat yourself in a calm voice for as long as it takes Gemma to understand you're not backing down. You're not changing your mind."

"And the second thing?"

She gave him a smile of encouragement. "This is a process. Gemma's going to test you in many ways. Whatever she says, don't take it personally. You're a good father. Gemma loves you. I see that every time you're together."

Billy blinked hard, cleared his throat. "It's eleven o'clock. My shift's over. I can take you home now."

"Okay."

He took her hand as she rose from the bench. "I'm parked behind city hall. It's only a couple of blocks."

"I think the walk will do us both good."

He radioed Jack. "I'm going home now, if you don't need me."

"Go ahead. Everything's okay."

Evie squeezed Billy's hand. "If it doesn't violate any policy of the town's enforcement division, can you give Jack a private message?"

Billy raised his eyebrows. "What's that?"

"Claire wants him to bring home a pint of Rocky Road."

Billy chuckled, repeated the message into the radio and said, "Did you copy that, Jack?"

"One Rocky Road. Got it. Have a good one, buddy. And good night, Evie."

CHAPTER ELEVEN

WHILE CONCENTRATING on navigating his truck through the thinning tourist traffic, Billy summarized everything Evie had told him. He didn't admit it to her, but he wasn't confident that her suggestions would work. He'd pretty much run out of options, though, and after Gemma's stunt tonight, he knew he had to try almost anything.

When he pulled into Evie's drive, he asked, "So, what do you think? Have I passed my first lesson?"

She smiled. "You've taken good notes. Whether you pass or not depends on Gemma."

He chuckled. "Then I'm in trouble."

He stopped in front of the cottage, beside her father's Buick. "I see Harry made it back okay."

"That's good. It means the situation at your house is stable."

"Do you need to go in right away?"

"No. Not right away."

That was the answer he'd wanted, so he cut the lights, kept the air conditioning purring. With his hands firmly grasping the steering wheel, he stared out the windshield. He'd wanted some time alone with Evie, but he was suddenly hesitant to kiss her.

She seemed to sense his discomfort right away. Maybe she was *too* good at this psychological stuff. "You want to talk about it some more?"

The discussion at the park had changed their relationship, and Billy didn't see any point in denying it. "I don't know," he said. "I feel like something's different between us. Like maybe I've revealed more about my life than I'm comfortable with you knowing."

"Maybe it's just hard to admit you're actually starting to trust me."

He dropped one hand to his thigh. "I suppose, but I still find you sexy as hell."

She smiled. "That's a relief. It's nice to know I still have feminine allure while acting all official."

She was handling this better than he was. Billy put his hand on her shoulder and pulled her close. "You're luring me, that's for sure." He leaned in and kissed her. Maybe things wouldn't be so different, after all. "Is Pops going to turn on the porch light?" he asked.

They both glanced toward the cottage. Harry's shadow crossed the front window. "He could be heading to the switch right now," she said.

"Okay. I'll behave. But I expect a solid return of my privileges very soon."

"How about Sunday night? Do you want to have another lesson?"

He'd have preferred an invitation that didn't include the word "lesson," but he wasn't going to turn down any chance to be with her. "Sounds good," he said. "But this time in a more suitable location, maybe the Tail and Claw. And I'll have my mother invite Harry to fill my seat at the Sunday dinner table."

"Fine. I'll see you Sunday." Evie got out of the truck and started toward her front door.

Billy buzzed down the passenger window. "Hey, Teach."

She turned around.

"Thanks for tonight. If this works I'll find a more appropriate way to show my appreciation."

"And if it doesn't?"

"Aw, hell. I'll still want to thank you. I'll just come up with another reason."

SINCE THE NEAREST true supermarket to Heron Point was thirty miles away in Micopee, Evie and Harry set off early Saturday morning to buy supplies. They'd just crossed the bridge to the mainland and were driving past the Indian burial grounds when Harry cleared his throat—a sure sign he was about to broach a sensitive topic.

"So, Ev," he said, staring out his window as if the flat landscape was fascinating, "I know how everything turned out with Gemma last night, but how was Billy when he dropped you off?"

He was worried about Billy? "He was disappointed

in Gemma. And he was angry and confused about what to do."

"I guess you helped him out some."

"I tried. I gave him some pointers that have worked in the past with children who have similar problems to Gemma's."

"And did he listen to reason?"

"Yes, he did. He seemed grateful for my help." She took her attention from the road long enough to try to read his expression. No clues there. "How was Gemma once she got home?"

"She seemed fine to me. But then, she didn't have a big stick in her hand."

Evie smiled.

"I guess scaring people wears a person out, because she went right up to bed." Harry scratched the back of his neck. "That's not good what she did, though, Ev."

"No, it isn't."

He shifted in his seat.

"Dad, is there something else you want to say?"

He looked at the roof. "I'm wondering how serious you are about Billy. Do you like him?"

Bingo. Harry had never particularly liked anyone Evie dated. In most cases, he'd been right to be cautious. "Yes, I like him. We've gotten to know each other, and I enjoy his company. Why?"

"He's interested in you." Harry rolled his shoulders, unnecessarily checked his seat belt buckle. "I mean, in a serious sort of way."

"How do you know that?"

"I told you, Brenda has a loose tongue. And I don't think she knows how to tell a lie. Except about her hair color."

Evie had had several conversations just like this one in her thirty-four years with Harry. He couldn't help playing protector. "And you just came out and asked her what Billy thought of me?"

He nodded. "Apparently he feels strongly. And he's looking for someone to share his life with. He's approaching the high side of his thirties and wants to settle down."

Evie wondered if this summary of Billy's goals was more Brenda's desire than Billy's. He'd just told her on Wednesday that his life prior to gaining a daughter and a live-in mother had been close to ideal. She didn't think he wanted to hook up permanently with a woman at this stage. But she played along with Harry's paternal concern. "What would you say if I were interested in Billy in the same way?"

"Are you?"

"Actually, Dad, since you've gotten so friendly with Brenda, you'd be the next-to-last person I'd tell."

"Oh. Well, if you have set your sights on him, I guess I'd have to say he seems like a good man."

Evie's jaw dropped. "You actually approve of him?"

"At least he drives a Chevy truck. That's a point in his favor."

Evie couldn't stop a sputter of laughter. "That's

how you judge a potential son-in-law? By whether or not he drives a General Motors vehicle?"

He shrugged. "I'm still a company man, Evelyn. I know how we build 'em. A man who chooses a GM truck shows good sense."

Evie braked at the traffic light at the end of the two-lane road. The supermarket was just down the highway about a half mile. She turned on her blinker and waited for the green. "I'm glad I have your blessing, Dad…if I should ever need it."

He pointed to the light, which had just turned. "Don't get me wrong. I'm not giving my blessing. I just brought this up so you'd think about what you'd be getting into with that daughter of his. She's nothing like you when you were that age. I'm not saying I don't like her. In a way, I do. But she's a fireball, and I don't see her burning out for a long time."

She pulled into the parking lot and found a spot. When she turned off the engine, she looked over at Harry. "Would you really want all the sparkle to go out of Gemma? Wouldn't you want a few spit and crackles left to make life interesting?"

He laughed. "Yeah, I guess I would. I'm beginning to appreciate the same fire in her grandmother."

He was out of the car and grabbing a cart before Evie could comment.

Once in the store, she walked alongside the cart while Harry pushed. They'd only gone a few feet when he said, "You'd better get your own buggy, Ev."

She stopped, stared at him. "What? Why?"

He kept going. "I'm using this one."

"We can't share? You need a cart all to yourself?"

"As a matter of fact, I do."

Since he was obviously not waiting, she hurried back to the front and grabbed an additional basket. She caught up to him in the produce department. "What are you shopping for?"

"What's in season now?"

"I don't know. It's summer. Everything I guess."

He wandered down an aisle. "Ah. Here's what I need. Peaches." He squeezed a few and dropped them into a plastic bag. "You got a bag of flour at home, Ev?"

"No. I don't bake."

"A bag of sugar?"

"No. I use the artificial stuff."

"Bah! That's no good. How about lard?"

"Lard? I don't even know what lard is."

He tied off the bag of peaches and headed away. "Guess there's no point in asking about real butter."

She threw a few vegetables into her cart and trailed after him. "Dad, stop."

He did, reluctantly.

"What are you fixing?"

"Dessert. Peach cobbler."

She stared. "That's nice. I like peach cobbler."

"Not making it for you." When she didn't comment, he finally explained. "Brenda's asked me over for Sunday dinner. She said Billy's going out with you."

"Don't you want to go over there for supper?"

"Sure, it's fine. I told Brenda I'd bring the dessert. She's making some kind of grilled snapper. Healthy, I suppose. I didn't want to take the chance that she'd serve rice cakes for dessert."

Evie laughed and continued down the aisle. After a few steps, she looked over her shoulder and said, "How do you feel about Brenda? And don't just tell me she's talkative or bossy. I want to know how you *really* feel about her."

Harry passed her and stopped in front of the Hostess cupcakes. "Now who's being nosy?"

"Me."

"Okay, then. Brenda's interesting. You never know what she'll do next." He dropped two boxes of cupcakes in his cart and moved on to Little Debbie. "She's got wanderlust, though. Drives that Minnie Winnie all over, been to twenty states in it she told me."

"And traveling in a motor home seems strange to you?"

"No, not exactly. I appreciate anything with a 350 Chevy engine. Besides, where she goes or how she gets there doesn't matter to me. I'm going back to Detroit. I only hired the kid down the street to—"

Evie held up her hand. "I know. To cut the grass one time."

Harry smiled. "I mentioned that already, did I?"

"Yes."

"I've got to get cat food." He headed down the aisle but paused before turning the corner. "Ev, what would you think if I took Muffler with me tomorrow? Do you think Gemma might get a kick out of him? Or do you think she'll poke him with a stick?"

Evie caught up to him. "I think Muffler is just what Gemma needs right now. Along with some homemade peach cobbler."

BILLY MANEUVERED the golf cart down Beach Road, keeping close to the curb to let tourist vehicles go by. He passed the Tail and Claw Restaurant where he'd made reservations for Sunday night and smiled to himself. Great food. Even better company. If it weren't for the problems at home, life would be just about perfect.

Keeping a watchful eye out for pickpockets or the occasional tourist weaving along the sidewalk because of too many Bloody Marys, Billy felt for the outline of his cell phone in his shirt pocket. Other than calls from Lou and Gail, the phone had been silent. He'd left Gemma at eight-thirty this morning sitting on a kitchen chair with a bowl of Fruit Loops in front of her and a scowl on her face. She'd been told not to move from that spot until she was ready to answer his question.

He turned the golf cart around at the end of the road and glanced at his watch: Ten fifteen. Damn, that girl could be stubborn. An hour and forty-five minutes must seem like half a lifetime to a nine-year-old. Brenda had promised to make her sit, and Billy believed she was following through on that pledge. His mother had been pretty shaken up over what happened at the public restrooms last night. So why hadn't Gemma called?

He was pondering the wisdom, and compassion, of just letting her off the hook when the phone rang. Billy grabbed it out of his pocket. "Hello."

"Daddy, it's me."

Relief washed over him. "Hi, Gemma. You have a reason for calling me?"

"I guess so. I'm going to answer your stupid question. Nana thinks I should."

"Great. I'm anxious to hear what you have to say. Why did you threaten Alina and Whitney with that limb?"

"Because I hate them. Can I get up now?"

He gripped the phone tighter. "You'll have to do better than that, Gem. I think I already figured that out."

She exhaled a huge dramatic sigh. "Okay. I did it because Whitney was mean not to ask me to her party, and Alina is her friend, so she's mean, too. I showed them both that I could be mean back."

All right. Acceptable answer. "Hold on a minute, Gem." Billy pulled to the curb. He raised his foot to the cart's dashboard and took a deep breath. "Okay, Gemma. I get that. But do you think there was another way you could have expressed yourself?"

"I don't know."

"Gemma...you can't say that."

"But I answered the first question. I can get up now."

"Yes, but if you don't answer this one, you'll have to sit tomorrow. What else could you have done besides scaring those girls with the stick?"

"I could have stolen something from their backpacks on Monday."

Billy slapped his hand against his forehead. He deserved that. He'd asked the wrong question. He had a lot to learn. "I'm afraid that solution isn't any better than the stick. But you did answer the question, and I'm proud of you for that. Let me ask another one."

"Daddy!"

"Why do you think Whitney didn't ask you to her party?"

"I don't—"

"Gem..."

"Okay!" The uncomfortable silence stretched to nearly a minute. Finally, Gemma said, "She didn't ask me because I'm not popular."

His heart squeezed in his chest. "Do you want to be popular?"

She sighed again. "You're not going to like my answer."

"Try me."

"I don't know." She followed up with a string of anxious babble. "That's the truth, Daddy. I *don't* know.

If it means being like them, maybe I don't. But if it means getting invited, then maybe I do."

He closed his eyes against the weekend confusion all around him. Hell, someone could rob the golf cart right now, take his lunch cooler out of the back and he wouldn't chase them. This moment was about Gemma. "That's a fine answer," he said. "It's honest and truthful. You go play now. I'll see you later."

"Can I have my TV back?"

The word *yes* was on the tip of his tongue. But he had to make the word *no* come out of his mouth. "Not today, Gem. You're being punished for what you did last night."

Some of the hard edge came back to her voice. "That's not fair."

"Yes, it is."

"Then maybe I still hate you a little."

"That's okay. You can hate me a little. But you can't have your TV until tomorrow."

He disconnected, sat back and pulled a handkerchief out of his pocket. After wiping the sweat that had run into his eyes, he drove away from the curb. The past few minutes had been tenser for him than some of the standoffs he'd had on the job in the past few years. "Round one, Billy," he said to himself. "I wonder what grade Evie would give you."

RIGHT ON TIME at seven o'clock Sunday night, Evie heard Billy's truck pull up in front of the cottage. She took a quick last look in the mirror, smoothed a few strands of hair behind her ears and went to the door. She opened it before Billy had a chance to knock. *Way to show restraint, Evelyn.*

Oh. He looked good. Not just good. Spectacular. She just stared. He wore his hair slightly mussed, a few sexy strands meeting the straight lines of his eyebrows. He had on gray chino trousers and a striped gray-and-white knit shirt that accentuated every muscular attribute she'd been thinking about all day. She swallowed. "Hi."

He blinked once before letting his gaze wander from her hair waved loosely over her shoulders down the aqua sundress with tiny daisies she'd bought yesterday in Claire's shop. He smiled at the dainty yellow sandals framing her pink toenails. He leaned against her door frame and said, "You look beautiful. I'm glad I made the decision I did."

Confused, she stared back at him. "Decision? What decision did you make?"

"The one to keep this date instead of staying home for your father's peach cobbler." He curved a finger under her chin and lifted her face for a quick kiss. "When Harry first brought it in the house it smelled so good I have to admit it was a toss-up. But now that I've tasted you, I know I did the right thing."

Evie felt like she was a slowly melting confection of syrupy warmth. She shook her head. She couldn't remember experiencing this level of desire in…well, maybe ever. She licked her lips, savoring the minty freshness of his mouth again. "What time's our reservation?"

"Seven-thirty." He cocked one eyebrow toward the sofa as if he'd been reading her mind. "It's only a ten-minute drive."

She pressed her hands against his chest. "We'd better go. We can always have a drink at the bar if our table's not ready."

He shrugged one shoulder. "Or we could do that."

She walked across the room and grabbed her purse. As they went out the door she said, "On the way you can tell me how it went with Gemma yesterday."

He opened the truck door, waiting for her to settle in. "Okay. But I think I need a drink first."

GETTING A TABLE wasn't the most difficult part of dining out with Billy. Getting *to* the table was. Evie had never dated a man who knew practically everyone in the room. They were stopped on the stairs to the second-floor dining area a half dozen times, and flagged down several more as they crossed to their table with a view of the Gulf.

After they were seated, Evie waited for Billy to choose a bottle of wine before saying, "I guess I know who's going to win the popularity contest tonight."

He laughed. "Believe me, those weren't all favorable votes. You couldn't hear all the comments, but several of those good buddies you think I have were ribbing me about the warrior I'm raising as my daughter. Word gets around fast."

"Oh, sorry. But from what you told me on the way into town, I'd say you've accomplished a lot with Gemma in just two days."

He shrugged. "We're still speaking anyway."

"You're doing more than that. Now you know that Gemma wants to be liked and accepted. That's a significant confession, Billy. I can offer suggestions on how to make that happen."

Billy acknowledged the wine the waiter brought to their table and waited for the man to pour. They gave their orders and the waiter left.

"Don't be discouraged if Gemma backslides," Evie said. "It's expected."

"Wonderful. Something to look forward to." Billy lifted his glass. "Let's toast to good news for a change. I don't get dressed up often enough to waste my night discussing what might go wrong. And you're just too sexy for me to concentrate on any kind of backsliding." He winked. "I'm only thinking of moving ahead."

She took a sip. "Thanks. I was thinking the same about you, but tomorrow's a school day, the first since Friday night. You should prepare your daughter."

He sighed, knowing Evie was right. Gemma could face some tough criticism in the morning. "Okay. What's the next step?"

"Tell her when you're driving her to school that she may hear comments about what happened in the bathroom, but she should try to ignore them. Kids tire easily of teasing if they don't get a reaction. Then let her know you're aware her behavior in class has been unacceptable."

"I think she knows that."

"Yes, but you have to reinforce it. Tell her you're going to call Mrs. Haggerty every afternoon this week and get a report on how she's doing."

He narrowed his eyes and set his glass down. "I'm not really going to do that, am I? Every day?"

"I think you should. I'll tell Betsy to expect your calls. If Gemma's behavior has been unfavorable that day, you're going to take away one of her possessions or privileges. Make sure she understands that. If you get a good report, that elastic band we talked about stays loose, allowing her some freedom." Billy's expression conveyed his doubt. "Is something wrong?" she asked.

"I'm not happy about calling the teacher every day. I feel like I'm spying on my own daughter."

"You're not, though. Gemma is going to know you're making the phone calls and your purpose is to get the truth, good or bad. And she'll know there will be consequences, good or bad, depending on what Mrs. Haggerty tells you."

Still not convinced, Billy mumbled a curt response.

Evie smiled, trying to lighten his mood. "It's not like you haven't talked to Betsy before."

"I think she has a red phone direct-wired to my cell."

"Next we'll concentrate on Gemma's behavior at

home. There are certain techniques that work well in the home environment—warnings, time-outs…"

The waiter brought their dinners, huge platters of king crab claws, roasted potatoes and fresh asparagus. "These look delicious." Evie snapped her napkin open onto her lap and picked up a set of silver pliers.

Billy stared at his food. For a man who'd just ordered with enthusiasm, he didn't seem one bit hungry. Evie blamed herself. Billy looked like he wished he were anywhere but here, with anyone but her.

She reached over and took his hand. "Maybe going out wasn't such a good idea."

He pushed his plate a few inches away, put his elbows on the table. "Look, Evie, I appreciate what you're doing, but I have to tell you. I don't have your confidence that this will work out."

"Billy, these procedures do work. Truly."

"Maybe, but I went to police academy. I don't have your knowledge…"

She leaned forward. "And I don't have yours. As you pointed out the other day, I've never had kids. We have to work together on this. My expertise and your parenting skills. Together, we can—"

"That's just it. I've been a father to Gemma for four years, but I don't feel like I really know her. I've never been married. I have two brothers. What do I know about how women think?" He smiled in a self-depre-cating way. "According to half the people in town, I know less than nothing. I've let Ma handle so many of the details of raising Gemma while I went off to work or watched football games on Sunday…"

"There's nothing wrong with that," Evie said. "You're a guy."

"There seems to be plenty wrong with it now. Suddenly I'm supposed to know everything about my kid and experiment with the ways to do what's best for her. Hell, I don't know what's best. I asked you for help, but I'm not sure I agree with all this advice you're giving me about taking away her things and having her sit in a chair like she's a police interrogation suspect. I'm not sure I even remember everything you tell me and, if I do, how do I know I'm implementing these techniques the right way?"

Evie had known that Billy's insecurities might get in the way, so she really wasn't surprised by this reaction. "First of all," she said, "they're not *my* techniques. They've been tried and tested by professionals who know a whole lot more than I do."

"Yeah, I understand all that, but I could screw up royally, and end up with a kid who says she hates me and really means it."

Evie took a deep breath. "Billy," she said in calm voice, "you can't let your fear of failing as a father keep you from doing the right thing. Gemma's at a crucial time in her development. You can ignore her behavior and keep getting calls from teachers and parents, or you can deal with it."

He frowned before taking a sip of wine. "What

do we hope will happen? I don't want to take away her spirit."

Evie suddenly realized what failing as a father meant to Billy. What could be more of a failure than turning a bright, clever girl into a weak, ineffectual person who no longer resembled his daughter? She chose her next words very carefully. "No one wants to raise a powerless child, Billy. Having power is what kids are all about. They spend most of their time wondering how to get it and how to use it. You simply…" She smiled, realizing the irony of that word. "Your job is to steer her in the right direction, to teach her that power, used well, is good. Everyone needs power."

She nodded toward his plate. "I hope you haven't lost your appetite."

He frowned. "I'm not sure. Go ahead with what you were saying."

"In the end, your goal with Gemma is to encourage her to think for herself and to understand which behaviors get her in trouble and which ones don't. It's a matter of getting her to think ahead, anticipate the consequences of her actions and try to avoid the bad ones. But now, while it's so important, you have to show her the consequences are real." She gave his arm a squeeze. "It's an important job, and I know it's not an easy one. It's maybe the toughest job you'll ever have, but the rewards are worth the effort."

He remained silent for a moment and then pulled his plate back to the edge of the table. "Okay, I'll do the phone calls this week and I'll take the steps needed when I get the reports, but can we stop talking about this tonight?" His lips curved up in the first indication of a smile since they'd sat down. "I've always loved king crab claws, and I'd like to dig into these before the waiter feeds them to the cats outside."

DRIVING DOWN Gulfview Road an hour later after dropping Evie off, Billy contemplated how this evening could have turned out so badly. He'd parked in her drive and waited for her to say something other than another bland comment about how well-prepared the food was at the Tail and Claw. When she didn't, he finally said, "I suppose Harry could come home at any minute."

"Yes, I suppose he could."

"I should go then."

She'd looked over at him, clearly surprised and confused. "If you want to. Or you could come in for coffee."

And we could eventually return to a discussion of my daughter, which would ultimately lead to indigestion and a sleepless night. He'd explained lamely that coffee made him jittery and he'd have to pass.

Billy turned off Gulfview onto his street. He didn't want to go home. Hell, he wanted to retrace his tire tracks right back to Evie's, where he could drink as much coffee as she could percolate and hang a Do Not Disturb sign on her front door to keep Harry from barging in.

When he'd left his house earlier tonight, Billy couldn't wait to pick Evie up. He'd been pretty sure he was falling in love with her. Really in love this time. Not supposedly in love, or temporarily in love, or lustfully in love, although lust was part of it. And a big reason he was tense as a high wire right now.

So what was he supposed to think after tonight's fiasco? Evie had accused him of being afraid of failing as a father. The woman he was nuts about could read his mind, interpret his weaknesses—not exactly a morale booster. He hadn't asked to be a father, he hadn't prepared for it. How in the world was he supposed to recognize when or if he was a failure at it?

He hit the steering wheel with the heel of his hand. Not measuring up as a father was only part of his insecurity. He was also failing again with a woman, only this time it was even worse. Despite his constant struggle to decide if an allegiance to Evie meant he was betraying his daughter, he was definitely falling in love.

Seeing Harry's car still in his driveway, Billy pulled onto the swale. But he stayed in his truck for a few minutes to prepare himself for the inevitable questions he knew he'd face when he walked in. How was he to explain why he was home so early? How was a cop supposed to admit that Evie was right? He really was afraid. Afraid of messing up so badly that he'd eventually lose one of the two females who'd come into his life without warning and found a sure path into his heart.

CHAPTER TWELVE

BY THE TIME school ended on Wednesday, Evie knew how at least part of Billy's week had been going. She'd told Betsy Haggerty that Billy would be calling each afternoon to check on his daughter's progress. Betsy had taken it upon herself to keep Evie informed.

Monday's school day ended without incident, and Billy received a good report when he called. On Tuesday the teacher reported a minor confrontation, an incorrect math question and a stick of chalk crumbled on the floor. On Wednesday, Gemma refused to sit at her usual desk, claiming the girls nearby were teasing her. Evie figured that complaint was probably justified, proposed that Betsy move her to another location and not inform Billy at this point. Betsy had elected to tell him anyway.

Harry had a story of his own to tell at dinner on Tuesday evening. He and Brenda had gone to the Wal-Mart in Micopee to buy gardening supplies so Harry could help rejuvenate the beds around the Muldoone house. They'd picked Gemma up at school and taken her along. While they were selecting tools and ferti-lizer, Gemma had wandered off.

Torn between panic and anger when Gemma's dis-appearance was discovered, Brenda went immediately to the store manager and had a missing child alert an-nounced throughout the store. Since the description of the child included "extremely short auburn hair," Gemma was located by an employee immediately and brought to the service counter.

After scolding Gemma for doing what she'd been told countless times was a severe breach in any parent/child relationship, Brenda noticed bulges in the girl's pockets. She pulled out bags of candy. Enough, she'd claimed, to keep Heron Point's dentist in clover for the next year. Thinking Gemma had stolen the merchandise, Brenda was furious. Gemma, however, produced a receipt. This fact only slightly mollified Brenda, since having candy without permission was almost as serious as stealing.

"Needless to say, Ev," Harry had told Evie that night, "the ride home to Heron Point was an exercise in who could scowl the most and say the least."

Evie drove to the Island Market after school on Wednesday and picked up a few things she needed to make dinner that night. While driving back, her thoughts turned once again to Billy. He hadn't called her since Sunday night. She assumed he was angry at her about disciplining Gemma. She understood his reaction, but that didn't lessen her frustration. She could no longer fool herself. She was attracted to Billy. And he had to know that the chemistry between them was real and strong. She'd done everything but admit it to him.

So what was she to do? If a relationship with Billy could continue, Gemma's behavior as a student had to be addressed. And, if Evie allowed her imagination to reach its full limits, Gemma could mean more to her in the future.

Her mind wandering, Evie nearly passed Gulfview Road. She pressed hard on her brake before abruptly swinging into the turn. "Since when did you start thinking of Billy in terms of a husband?" Did she really believe they could have a future together? And did he even remotely feel the same?

Evie's hands began to shake on the steering wheel. Marriage. Had such a possibility been part of Evie's plan when she left Detroit for a new life? But now that hope seemed doomed to join the near-misses of her past. Billy hadn't called her. He was obviously done trying with her. She had to accept that and move on.

Flashing blue lights in Evie's rearview mirror deflected her attention back to her driving. She panicked for a moment until she reminded herself that this wasn't Detroit. Police cruiser lights didn't automatically mean trouble. Besides, there was only one patrol car in Heron Point, and usually only one person inside it.

She slowed to a crawl and pulled over. She hadn't

been speeding. She'd successfully made the sudden turn onto Gulfview without threatening anyone's safety. Feeling ridiculously nervous, more so than if she'd truly been driving like a demon, Evie shut down her engine.

From her side-view mirror, she watched Billy get out of his vehicle and begin a slow, decidedly coplike saunter to her car. She rolled down her window. He stopped, stared around the interior of her Malibu and pulled a ticket pad from his pocket. "Afternoon, ma'am," he said in an official drawl.

Two could play this game, she decided. "Hello, Officer. Was I doing something wrong?"

"You were driving okay, but your taillight is out on the passenger side."

"I find that hard to believe. You see, my father is staying with me right now. He used to work for GM, and he's thoroughly checked this automobile front to back."

Billy tapped his pen on top of a blank ticket. "Maybe that's not the problem then. I'm sure your tag's expired."

She flipped open her glove compartment and produced the registration. "No, sorry. Up to date."

"Oh." He scratched something over the top of the pad, but Evie couldn't tell if he was really writing. "I remember now. This car's in violation of island beautification policy."

She raised her eyebrows, stared back at him.

He stroked his hand down the side of the door and

showed her a film of dust on his fingertips. "It needs a wax job."

"I see." She bit her lip to keep from laughing. "By all means, then, give me a wax-needed ticket."

He appraised her with an official scowl, rolled his tongue around the inside of his cheek. Evie smiled down at her lap.

"You know what?" he finally said.

She looked up. "What?"

"You're probably a model citizen with the exception of this one violation. I think I'm kind of attracted to you…in cop-to-perp sort of way. I'm going to let you off with a warning this time."

She gave him her sweetest smile. "I really appreciate this, Officer."

"You run along then. And mind our traffic laws."

"I will. I promise."

He took a step away from the car, but immediately returned. "One more thing…"

"What's that?"

He propped his elbow on the roof of her car. "Maybe you could do a little something for me."

"Payback time, eh?"

"Something like that. Don't make any plans for Saturday. I'm picking you up at nine o'clock. And pack some sunblock. You're going to get wet."

"I am? How?"

"We're going camping."

"Camping?" Evie had never camped in her life.

She'd never wanted to. Until now. But even if she were the KOA queen, with her father here, the king of traditional·values, she couldn't steal away with Billy to share a sleeping bag.

"You have a problem with that, ma'am?"

"Well, as I said, my dad's here visiting. I don't know if I can get away overnight."

He made a big show of fanning his face as if his internal temperature had suddenly soared to a dangerous level. "I'm surprised by how your mind's working, ma'am. I didn't say anything about this being a sleep-away camp." He smiled. "I'll have you back by dark."

"Oh."

He leaned into her open window. "Disappointed?"

If he were any good at interpreting clues, he'd know the answer by the blush on her face. Her internal temperature had skyrocketed. She babbled a denial and continued chattering. "What else should I bring? How long a drive is it? Should I pack food?"

He patted her shoulder. "Look, lady, I know you don't do impulsive very well. So here's a suggestion. About that getting wet part I mentioned, you can bring a swimsuit if it makes you feel better. I'll try to remember to do the same."

He waved as he walked back to his car. "See you Saturday. And get that car waxed." He turned his cruiser around and headed in the other direction.

Evie started the Malibu and slowly proceeded along Gulfview. Suddenly she was glad she'd already made the turn toward her cottage. She wasn't sure now that she would even remember the way.

SATURDAY MORNING Billy walked out the front door of his house carrying a cooler. He set it in the cargo area of his truck next to the canoe. Gemma came up behind him. "Where are you going, Daddy?"

"The Myacki River." Knowing what her answer would be, he said, "You want to come?"

She made a face. "I don't like that place. There's nothing to do."

"I know you feel that way. You can stay home. I'll be back later tonight."

"Are you taking Miss Gaynor?"

"Yes. Is that okay with you?"

She shrugged. "It's okay. You need to think about someone besides me for a while."

He smiled. "Don't kid yourself that I won't be thinking about you, too. I'll be wondering what you're doing all day." He leaned against the truck cab. "Let's see, what have you given up lately?" Counting on his fingers, he said, "The TV, your CD player, your bicycle… Did I forget anything?"

Her mouth pulled into a perfect pout. "No. I don't *have* anything else."

He chuckled, turned around and checked the ropes on the canoe. "Yeah, right."

She tugged on the hem of his T-shirt, getting his attention again. "Yeah?"

"As long as you're going to be gone anyway, can I use my bike? You won't see me so you can pretend I didn't."

"No, you can't ride your bike. But if Nana says you're good today, you can get some stuff back tomorrow."

She picked up a rock and threw it into a bush across the driveway. "I'm starting to hate living here."

"I know, but the rent's cheap."

"It's not funny!" She stared at her feet. "You're never fair anymore."

He got down on one knee, thinking she would raise her downcast gaze to his face. She didn't. "I can be very fair, and you know how."

"Right. If I'm perfect or something."

He grasped her arms, waiting for her eyes to connect with his. "Look at me, Gem." She did. "Nobody expects perfect. But I do expect better. And you know how to do that. We went over all this yesterday afternoon before I went to work."

"I'm sick of hearing the same stuff. Do this. Don't do that. Be good...."

"I'm sick of saying it, but I'm not going to stop." He ruffled her scruffy hair. "I think it's growing back."

"Who cares?"

He stood. "I'm looking forward to getting a good report from Nana. And I'll know if she's lying to get you out of trouble."

Gemma frowned. "She doesn't lie for me anymore. She's still cheesed over the candy. But at least she'll be in a good mood today."

"Why's that?"

She thrust out one hip and replied in a nasally voice. "Her boyfriend Harry's coming over."

"Oh."

"We're going on a picnic."

"That should be fun, right?"

For the first time her pout almost transformed into a smile. "Yeah, I suppose. I'd rather go with them than to the Myacki River. We're taking Muffler. He has a leash, just like a dog, so he doesn't have to stay in a cage."

"That's cool for Muffler." Billy pulled his keys from his shirt pocket, leaned over and kissed the top of her head. "I'll see you later then. Be good."

"Sheesh! You have to spoil everything with those two words."

She stomped off toward the house. Billy waited until she'd gone inside before backing out of the drive and checking to be sure his cell phone was on the dashboard.

EVIE GLANCED out the window before cramming a bottle of sunblock into the stuffed nylon bag she'd packed with everything she might need for wherever she might be going. "Bathing suit, change of clothes, cell phone, a little cash…" She sighed with relief. It was a pleasure not to have to think of bringing a hair dryer or *real* shoes, or any of the contents of her briefcase. She was finally starting to feel like a Heron Point native.

Billy's truck appeared around the side of Claire's house right on time as usual. "He's here," she called to the kitchen where Harry was making sandwiches.

"Have fun. You know what time you'll be back?"

Standing in front of the mirror, Evie gathered her hair into a scrunchy, pulled the ponytail through the back of a ball cap and wiggled the bill over her forehead. "He said before dark. If it's going to be later, I'll call you." She went to the kitchen door. "Have fun yourself."

"Will do."

Billy was standing by the tailgate when she came out. "Ah-hah," she said. "A clue. You have the canoe."

He smiled. "Guess that eliminates mountain climbing."

"Yes. But it does make me wonder why you said I'm going to get wet." She worried her lower lip. "I'm not exactly a white-water-rafting gal."

"No? I suppose I'll have to cancel that trip to Colorado next weekend." He opened the passenger door. "Get in. I promise you'll return in one piece."

The morning air was still cool and fresh, so they opened the windows. When they reached Highway 19, Billy turned north.

"Still not telling me?" Evie said.

He kept his gaze straight ahead. "Isn't it enough that it's pretty country up here?"

She relaxed in her seat, turned her face to the window. "Yes, it is." They drove another forty-five minutes, past woods and picturesque small towns. Billy eventually turned off the main highway onto a narrow path bordered by palms and dense thickets of brush.

"Only a couple of miles to go," he said.

Evie peered through oak and cedar trees to glimpse a swath of open space where the vegetation abruptly stopped. "What's over there?" she asked. "A ravine or something?"

"The Myacki River. It wanders through a gully about six feet below the bank."

They passed a smattering of dwellings, some little more than well-established whitewashed cabins. At a mailbox decorated with palm trees, Billy said, "We're here."

The name Muldoone was painted on the side of the box.

Billy turned onto a rutted drive that wound toward the river. Sunlight glinted off the high-peaked roof of a structure barely visible through the trees. They soon cleared the foliage and stopped at an A-framed cabin.

Evie released a breath. "This is where we're camping?"

"This is it." He layered his arms over the steering wheel and looked at the clapboard house with its wide wood deck. "It's humble, to say the least. The view's better from the back."

"It's charming. Is it yours?"

"I bought it seven years ago from a guy who

moved up here from Heron Point to get away from the crowds. He was old then, over eighty, and when he broke his leg he had to move in with his sister. Said he didn't see a reason to keep the place so he let me have it for a fair price."

They got out and walked to the steps that led to the deck. "I don't doubt it needs a woman's touch," he said, "but since Ma and Gemma don't care much for the place, it's stayed pretty rustic." He took a key from his pocket and opened the door. "Don't expect much."

Evie stepped inside a wood-scented interior. The first level was one large room with a kitchen in one corner, a door in the other, which Billy said was the bathroom, and a sitting area in front of a large stone fireplace. The furniture, mostly solid pine, was old but clean and comfortable looking. Narrow stairs with a cast-iron banister wound from the first floor to a loft extending halfway over the main living space. "What's up there?" Evie asked.

"The bedroom. Has a king bed and a big closet." He walked to a window air-conditioning unit and flipped a switch. "It's going to be hot today, so we might as well be ready."

She set her bag on a chair. "Billy, this isn't camping. It's vacationing."

He pointed to a small television on a metal stand. "I only get three channels with the rabbit ears, and that's only if the weather is perfect. The phone blew out in a storm a couple of years ago, and I never reconnected it. If I ever get the chance to come up here more than every couple of months, I'll probably modernize the place, make it more kid-friendly to please Gemma."

"It's wonderful," Evie said.

"I like it." He smiled at her. "Feeling strong?"

"Sure."

"Let's get the canoe from the truck and lower it into the river. We've got some paddling to do."

They dragged the canoe to the bank and carried it down a flight of steps to the water. "I'll get the cooler and we'll set off."

In minutes they were traveling through unspoiled paradise. Nothing like the first canoe trip. This river trip was splendid because of its primitiveness.

Once out of sight of the cabin, Evie imagined they could have been winding through a Brazilian rain forest or a remote section of the Amazon. Heavy branches dipped so low over the water, she had to duck to avoid them. Critters scurried through the brush. Birds called from treetops. And in some places the river narrowed so she could practically reach out and touch both banks at the same time. Billy explained that this tributary of the Myacki River was closed to the public since inexperienced boaters might become grounded in the shallow water.

And then, after a mile of nothing but cool green shade and gentle breezes, they passed a crude wooden sign that read Myacki River State Park, and they reentered civilization, complete with a concession stand, a bathhouse and dozens of people. Billy pulled the canoe into a shaded cove and tied up. "The spring's busy today. But it's Saturday. Lots of kids. Even Gemma likes this part of our trips here." He tossed her bag onto shore. "Why don't you change? I'll find a spot for our cooler, and we'll go for a swim."

On the way to the bathhouse, Evie passed excited, screaming kids jumping from a rustic stone wall into the water. More cautious, the adults walked down a set of rock steps and floated toward the center of the pool. She changed quickly and walked around to where Billy had claimed a couple of lounge chairs. He stood when she approached and she nearly tripped over her own bare feet. In a swimsuit, his long, lean legs dusted with a light matting of dark hair, his chest and arms rippled with muscles, he was a fine-looking man.

She bit her bottom lip and dropped her towel on one of the chairs. "Is the water cold?" she asked, hoping it was.

His gaze swept over her with open appreciation. She couldn't understand why. Her skin was Detroit pale. And she certainly lacked the statuesque physique of a model. But seeing herself through Billy's eyes at this moment, none of that seemed to matter. She felt pretty, sexy and most of all, wanted.

"It's always cold," he said, grinning with mischief. "I'd advise just jumping in and getting it over with."

She pulled the band from her ponytail, shook her hair free and gave him a challenge. "I'm right beside you, big boy."

They found a spot along the rock wall not already occupied by other bathers. Evie stood with her toes wiggling over the edge. "This water's amazing," she said. "I can see the bottom."

"That's spring water in Florida. Clear and, need I say it again, cold." He grabbed her hand. "Ready?"

She nodded and they jumped.

The brisk, invigorating water stole her breath away. When her face broke the surface, she took a deep, quivering gasp, rubbed her arms and squealed.

Billy came up beside her and squirted water from his mouth. "You okay?"

"It's cold…"

"Don't say I didn't warn you."

They swam laps, stopping occasionally to toss a ball with kids treading water or secured in water rings. After half an hour they climbed out, toweled off, applied sunscreen and lay back on the lounge chairs. The hot sun was soothing. After a languid rest, Billy touched her arm. "You're not going to sleep, are you?"

"No. But I'm dreaming just the same."

He sat up, looked down at her. "About what?" His expression warmed with something primal, yet gentle. "The same thing I'm dreaming about, I hope."

Evie's blood heated and she knew it had nothing to

do with the sun. She smiled. "I think there's a good chance of that."

He took her hand. "Let's go back. I brought lunch. And afterward, we've still got some serious camping to do."

Two HOURS LATER Evie and Billy sat on the back deck of the cabin. Sandwich wrappers and two empty beer bottles were on the table between them. A warm breeze tickled the hair on Billy's arm, making his already tightly strung nerves come alive.

Since he'd picked Evie up this morning, neither one of them had mentioned Gemma, Brenda or Harry. It was as if they'd reached an unspoken agreement before the truck ever left Heron Point. This was going to be their day, without interference or conflict. They'd talked plenty about other topics—personal histories, fears, goals…even past relationships.

Billy looked over at Evie. Her body seemed relaxed, her hands hung over the sides of the chair, her eyes were closed, her lips full and moist. She was infinitely kissable. And though she might appear ready to fall asleep, he sensed that her awareness of him, of them, of the utter aloneness of this place, was every bit as palpable as his.

"We'll have to go in another few hours," he said. "Do you want to take a nap?"

Her head turned slowly. Her eyes opened. "No."

"Then, what…?"

"The clouds have rolled in," she said. "I was thinking about taking a look at the upstairs." She stood, reached for his hand. "I was kind of hoping you'd show me."

CLIMBING THE STAIRS with Billy behind her, Evie didn't look back. She wanted him now, in this perfect place on this perfect day.

In the loft, the air was cool. The sun, now shrouded behind clouds that would bring a late-afternoon storm, sent spears of soft gray light over the bed. Billy pulled back the covers and turned to her. Slowly, with deliberate tenderness, he lifted her shirt over her head. His hands roamed down her arms over her sides and cupped her breasts from beneath.

She placed her hands on either side of his face and pulled him to her for a shattering kiss she hoped would tell him all that needed to be said about her desire, about the rightness of what they were going to do.

He peeled her shorts and panties down her legs, and she stepped free of them. His eyes, warm and sensual, caressed her everywhere his hands did. Her skin tingled from his touch. Her heart raced.

She tugged his T-shirt from his shorts, pulled it over his head and then stood on tiptoe, offering not just her lips, but her whole body. He shrugged out of the rest of his clothes, picked her up and lay her on the mattress on cool, soft sheets. His hands brought her alive, stretched her longing to its limits, making every inch of her yearn for him.

He opened a nightstand drawer, took out a square package.

After a breathy chuckle, she nibbled on his earlobe. "A good camper is always prepared," she murmured.

He sheathed himself, nuzzled her neck. Laughing softly, he said, "A *really* good camper is prepared more than once."

"Are you a really good camper?"

He stroked her breasts, bringing the nipples to a taut, pleasurable ache. "I guess you'll have to be the judge of that."

The first raindrops, full and heavy, hit the back of the cabin as he entered her. The sky opened as she did, wrapping herself around him, pulling him tighter, deeper, meeting his thrusts with the rhythm of her hips. She called his name as the first crack of thunder rattled the window above their heads.

DARKNESS had just settled over the island when Billy brought Evie home. He parked between hers and Harry's car, pulled her close for a long, satisfying kiss. "Phone you tomorrow?"

She stroked his face. "Sure."

He waited until she was inside before turning the truck around and driving away. He blew out a breath and laughed out loud. How long had it been since he'd felt this good? This free of problems? A long time. Probably never.

He pulled into his driveway and got out. When he

opened the door and walked inside, his mother was waiting in the foyer. His heart hit his stomach. His blood turned cold. "What's wrong?"

"We've got trouble, William. This plan of Evie's isn't working."

CHAPTER THIRTEEN

SPOTTING HER FATHER under the pole light in the gazebo, Evie decided to take a shower before finding out how his day with Brenda and Gemma had gone. Ten minutes later, she headed through Pet's garden. Harry turned when he heard her approach.

"Nice night, isn't it?" Evie said, breathing in the fresh, rain-washed air.

"I suppose. It's quiet anyway, and that's what I need after the day I've had."

The first prickling of alarm made Evie pause on the steps. "Did something happen?"

Harry scooted over, giving her room to sit beside him. "I'll say."

"Gemma?"

He nodded. "Ev, you wouldn't have believed it. Everything was going fine. We got to the park early enough to claim a picnic table. Gemma played with Muffler, took him around on his leash. I fired up a grill."

Sensing this Norman Rockwell scene was about to take a drastic turn, she said, "And then?"

"All hell broke loose. Brenda and I didn't think

anything of it at first. Those two girls were there, the ones in the restroom last Friday night who Gemma threatened with the stick."

"Oh, no. She didn't do it again, did she?"

"No, this was different. In fact, they came over and asked Gemma if she'd like to play hide-and-seek with them. She looked at Brenda for permission, just as she should. Brenda gave it, told her not to wander off— you know, the normal stuff you tell a kid."

"And what happened?"

"Brenda and I both watched. One girl closed her eyes. Gemma and the other one dashed off to hide. Gemma went behind this tree, and a moment later she ran back screaming at the top of her lungs."

"Screaming? Was she hurt?"

"I'd say she was more angry than hurt, although she'd landed in a mound of fire ants on the other side of that tree, and she got a bunch of stings."

"Poor Gemma," Evie said. "Dad, do you think the other girls knew the ant hill was there?"

"I don't know, but Gemma sure thought that. And later she told Brenda that one of the girls had suggested she hide behind that tree."

Evie wasn't surprised. She was furious with Whitney and Alina. "What did Gemma do?"

"She tore after those girls, her fists flying. Her screams were loud enough to draw attention from everyone in the park."

Evie could picture Gemma's wrath. She squeezed

her eyes shut as she asked the next question. "Did she hurt anyone?"

"No, thank goodness. Brenda and I caught up to her before she could. But her language! Evie, I've spent forty years in an auto factory, and Gemma could hold her own with any of the guys I've worked with." He shook his head. "Made me blush, I'll tell you that. And made Brenda pack up and haul that child to the car in about three seconds flat."

"What happened when you got her home?"

"It was a bad scene. Gemma was blubbering like her life was over. At first Brenda called the girls little monsters, said she'd call their mothers."

Great. More trouble on Monday. "Did she?"

"No. I talked her out of it. There's no way to prove that the girls knew the ant hill was there."

Evie nodded. In cases like this, when tempers flare, it was often best to let things cool down before taking action. "Sometimes when the parents get involved, the problem just escalates," she said to Harry.

"I thought that, too. So Brenda sat Gemma in a kitchen chair and tried to put salve on her bites. The kid wouldn't have any of it. She kicked out at Brenda and released another blue streak."

Evie blew out the breath she'd been holding. "Oh, no."

"Then Brenda threatened her with telling her father, which would mean he'd take away more of her stuff. That really set the girl off." Harry shook his head sadly. "I'd say it was a good hour before Gemma calmed enough to even take a drink of water. I stayed until she finally just wore herself out and fell asleep in the living room."

Evie leaned back, pressed her hand to her forehead where a headache was creeping into her temples. "I'm surprised Brenda didn't call Billy," she said after a moment.

"She didn't want to ruin his day. But you can believe she's told him by now."

Billy would be extremely disappointed and discouraged. Evie couldn't help wondering what further consequences they'd all have to pay.

BILLY WAS UP at seven o'clock on Sunday morning to go to work. Brenda met him in the kitchen. "Did you sleep?" she asked him.

"Some."

She poured them each a cup of coffee. "What are you going to do?"

"I'll come home at lunchtime and talk to Gemma then."

"No, I mean, how are you going to punish her? Are you sticking with these ideas of Evie's? Are you going to take more away from her?"

He stared over the rim of his mug. "I don't know. I can't blame Evie's plan for this. I've only tried it a little over a week. But Gemma was the victim of a mean prank, and it looks like this time she was justified in getting angry. Still, she reacted too violently, even kicking at you. And she used language we can't let her get away with. She's got to learn to control her temper."

"But I'm not convinced Evie's plan is working," Brenda said. "You've had several calls from Gemma's teacher and this latest outburst yesterday."

"I know, but don't forget, Ma, Gemma's behavior has been bad since long before Evie got here. Nothing we'd been doing was having much effect."

Brenda shook her head. "I know things are different now. Parents are told to avoid corporal punishment, spanking, that sort of thing. But in my day, all I had to do was reach for that willow branch and you boys toed the line."

"Selective memory, Ma. We never toed anything. We ran as far away from you as we could and didn't come home until we were sure you'd put the switch back in the shed."

She gave him an impish smile, one he'd seen often enough in Gemma's features. "And you don't think I planned it that way? I never wanted to hit you with it." She took a sip of coffee. "I would have, though. I'd have done it if you hadn't run. And you knew it, too."

"Okay, maybe your plan worked, but I haven't been so lucky with Gemma. My discipline techniques have been hit and miss. I've threatened her with things I'd never really do. You've punished her by taking away her spending money. None of those things made an impression."

"So now your idea is to make her miserable."

"In a way. If she has to give something up that means a lot to her, and she knows she can give up a lot more, she'll change."

Brenda rattled her spoon in her coffee though she'd stirred in her sugar minutes before. "I think all you're doing is putting pressure on her. She's being picked on by the kids at school, her teacher is watching her like a hawk. And her father is spying on her and denying her the things that make her happy. It's too much, William. She's bound to crack."

He frowned. His mother was laying the guilt on thick, and he wasn't sure she didn't have a point. "She also might improve," he said. "I say we stick with the plan for now."

Brenda sighed. "You're her father."

He tugged on his hat, grabbed his gear and went out to the truck. When he got inside it occurred to him there had been one favorable result from all this psychology stuff. In the past week or so, Brenda had finally let him wear the pants in his relationship with his daughter. Not that he'd ever fought too hard for the privilege in the past. Evie's techniques were at least beginning to work on one Muldoone female. Unfortunately, along with his newfound power, Billy realized he now assumed awesome responsibilities. And he could be making the wrong decision.

GEMMA CALLED HIM at eleven that morning. "Nana says you're coming home for lunch."

"That's right."

"And you heard about yesterday."

"I heard Nana's version. I haven't heard yours yet."

"It's not that different from Nana's, I suppose. Except I swear, Daddy, Whitney knew that ant hill was there. She tricked me into stepping in it."

"That could be."

"I wanted to beat her up. I cussed at her."

"I heard you did. I'm hoping now that you've had a chance to think things through, you can come up with another way you might have handled the situation. Maybe I can help you with that."

"Are you going to take away more of my things?"

"It's a good possibility. I think you know that the way you acted yesterday was wrong. Violence is never the answer."

The phone went silent for a few moments. Finally, Gemma said, "If I come up with another way to handle Whitney, will you not take any more of my stuff?"

Don't give in, Billy. But, oh, it would be so easy. "We can talk about it."

"When?"

"When I get home."

"When will that be?"

He tightened the rein on his patience. "I'm just pulling into city hall now. I'll see you in a few minutes."

As soon as he was in the truck headed home, his cell phone rang again. He recognized Evie's number and, despite his problems, he experienced a jolt of desire. What he'd give to still be in the cabin in a rainstorm instead of in the center of the storm brewing in his own house. He took a deep breath. "Hey."

"Good morning. How are you?"

"I've been better. I suppose you heard."

"Dad told me. I'm sorry, Billy. Nobody said kids are fair."

"Right. And nobody said being a parent would be easy."

"That, too." She paused, then went on. "Billy, I might be able to help with the problems between Gemma and the other girls. I wish you'd let me talk to her at school tomorrow."

"I don't know. I think she's had enough adults influencing her behavior for a while."

"I'm not going to discipline her. I think what those girls did yesterday is despicable. I'm just going to suggest ways for Gemma to get along better, to cope with other people's attitudes. I'll be gentle, I promise."

Evie's voice was like a spring breeze, fresh and warm, and the first truly comforting balm to his wounded ego. He'd trusted her this far, with more than he'd ever imagined. He'd do it again. "I suppose it would be all right."

"Thanks. I'll let you know how it goes."

He disconnected as he pulled into his drive. Now the fun began. But at least some of the tension had begun to ebb from his taut muscles.

BRENDA SERVED SOUP and ham sandwiches. She ate quickly, filling the void of silence with idle chatter, before leaving the kitchen. Billy didn't know whether to be grateful or angry.

Gemma, who never wasted time or words, cut right to the point—*her* point. "Can I have my TV back today?"

He gave himself a few extra seconds by slowly sipping from a tall glass of iced tea. "Gem, I can't believe you're asking me that. I said if I heard a good report from Nana, I'd think about giving you some of your privileges. Swinging at classmates and swearing like a longshoreman is not a good report."

"I had a reason."

"You had a reason to be suspicious, even angry. You did not have the right to react as violently as you did."

"You said if I came up with another way I could've handled it, you wouldn't take away more stuff."

Her voice quivered as if she were on the verge of tears. Jeez, she made it sound like he burned her things in a pile in the backyard. "Gemma, you realize your belongings are still in the house, don't you? I didn't get rid of them."

"Yeah, a lot of good that does me."

Point taken. *Move on, Billy.* "Okay, then. Did you come up with something?"

"Yes. This is a good one."

Her expression was eager, her posture erect. Billy allowed himself to hope. "So tell me."

"I'm quitting school."

That faint flicker of hope was extinguished like a match tossed in the ocean. "What?"

"I'm not going back. I'm staying home with Nana all day. That way I don't have to see Whitney or Alina, or any of them."

"You can't quit school."

"Yes, I can. You said if I figured out how to stay away from Whitney…"

He held up a finger. "Wait a minute. I said a way to *respond* to Whitney. Not avoid her. You can't avoid her. You have to go to school."

Gemma's body tensed. He knew what was coming next. He'd used the same line himself a time or two growing up.

She leaned forward, challenged him with glittering eyes. "You can't make me."

"Yes, I can. So can the government. You will go to school tomorrow."

"I will not. I'll run away."

Now's where the old Billy would have threatened to tie her to a bedpost, which, now that he thought about it, would eliminate this problem. But not anymore. Now he needed to be real. "Well, you could run away, I guess. But that wouldn't be a smart thing to do. I'd just have to put out an all-points bulletin, and some cop, somewhere, would find you and drag you back. Besides, I don't think you'd make it past the cemetery before you got hungry."

She stomped her foot under the table. "I'm not

going back to school, and I want my stuff back. Or I'm running away!"

"Why don't I give you some suggestions about ways to…"

"What? Be nice to that bitch Whitney? No way!"

"Gemma…"

She stood and glared at him. Despite his superior size and supposed dominance over the nine-year-old, he actually flinched.

Her face grew red. Her lips pursed until the breath she was holding burst out with the words, "I hate you, Daddy! You don't care anything about me. I'm not going to school, and I don't care if you have a stupid daughter!"

She spun around and headed for the door. Now he was angry. "Stop right there, young lady. You will not speak to me like that." She kept going. He started to tremble. "You will do as I say in this house." *Oh, help me, God, I sound like my father.*

He heard her footsteps on the living room floor, heard them pound up the stairs. He clenched his fists at his sides. He wanted to go after her but didn't trust himself. So he sat, cradled his face in his hands. When a door slammed on the second floor, he jumped. He counted to ten. Counted again. The worst criminal he'd ever brought into jail hadn't rattled him like his own daughter just had. His head pounded. He was close to losing control.

He didn't know how much time passed as he sat

there, dreading his next move. He had no idea what it should be. Minutes, half an hour maybe. He was startled back to awareness when Brenda came into the kitchen. "William?" she said softly.

He looked up through veiled eyes. His mother's face was blurry.

"You'd better come upstairs," she said.

He stood woodenly and followed her.

She stopped at Gemma's door, pushed it open so he could see inside. Had a tornado gone through town while he'd been sitting in a stupor? Papers, pencils, notebooks, every school supply he'd purchased since Gemma had come to live with him lay scattered all over her floor.

Shredded pages from books and tablets littered her room. Bits of crayon had been ground into her T-shirt. And in the middle of it all, she sat, like a dictator among the ruins, her blunt-nosed scissors in her hands. Billy stared at the instrument of destruction. *How did those harmless-looking scissors do all this damage?* But he knew the truth. The scissors weren't to blame. But who was?

When no words would come, he simply stared. Finally, Gemma looked up at him, placid satisfaction reflected in her beautiful brown eyes. "Now I can't go to school."

Somehow he pulled himself back from self-recrimination. "Sorry, kid," he said calmly. "But you're still going to school. Tomorrow and the day after. And the day after that." A hint of the old Billy, the one who exaggerated about consequences that he prayed would never come to pass, crept in. "And after you graduate, I hope I'm not watching you go off to prison. Now clean up this mess."

Her eyes narrowed to slits. "I will, but I won't go to school. I'll run away and I'll never come back. I mean it. I hate this house and I hate you."

He didn't look away. He didn't even blink. And someday he would marvel at how he managed it. "Start cleaning," he said.

A chime sounded, as if from a faraway place. For a moment Billy didn't recognize it as the front doorbell. Gemma jumped up. "Somebody's here. I'll get it."

"No. You stay here." He grabbed for her arm, but she eluded him. A few seconds later he heard the front door open and Gemma's childlike voice, normal again, ask, "Who are you?"

He came down the stairs, stopped at the front entrance. It took him a moment to find a place for the vaguely familiar face in his befuddled brain. But when he did, his heart seized. "What are you doing here?"

Astrid Moonflower folded her hands at her waist. "Hello, Billy. Long time no see."

BILLY DIDN'T THINK he would have known her if he'd passed her on the street. A woman he'd once slept with, the mother of his Gemma. She could have been in the midst of a throng of tourists, and he would have stared right at her and kept going.

His arm went automatically around Gemma's shoulders. He tugged her close and forgot all about his anger toward her from moments before. Every one of his senses, every emotion, was suddenly targeted across the threshold. "You're damn right it's been a long time," he said. "Why are you here now?"

She tucked a strand of neatly arranged dark brown hair behind her ear and pulled the hem of a tailored jacket over a pair of perfectly creased slacks. There was no doubt she'd had a makeover—at least a surface one. This Astrid had lost her gaunt, waiflike features. Her skin no longer had an unhealthy yellow cast. She'd put on some weight and appeared fit, not to mention she was dressed like a model for business attire. But the eyes that had avoided looking at him four years ago were still vacant, dull. Nearly colorless.

She tried to smile, but managed only a twist of her coral lips. "Isn't it obvious?" she said. "I left something behind when I was last in Heron Point, and I've come back for it."

He squeezed Gemma's shoulder. She looked up at him. "Go to the kitchen, Gem."

"No. I want to stay. I think that's—"

"Go. Now. No arguments."

She huffed an indignant breath and stomped away. He glanced over his shoulder and mouthed the words, *And don't run away.*

"I won't!" she said out loud and pointed her finger behind a cupped hand. *She looks like Mommy,* she mouthed back.

"We'll talk about it later." She started to protest, but he cut her off. "And shut the door!"

"Okay!"

He waited until Gemma was out of hearing range before confronting Astrid. "Is this a joke?"

"Hardly. It looks like I got here just in time."

"Just in time? That *is* a joke. You're four years too late."

She came in without an invitation. "What have you done to my daughter, Billy? She's filthy. And that hair. It looks like a lawnmower…"

"Now just hold on a cotton-pickin' minute!" Brenda's voice preceded her down the stairs. "You don't have any idea what you're talking about."

Astrid frowned up at her. "Who are you?"

"I'm Brenda Muldoone, that child's grandmother." She reached the first floor and jabbed her index finger into her chest. "I'm the woman who's taken care of that girl ever since you left her on my son's doorstep. You've got no right to come in here and draw conclusions. You don't know anything about Gemma."

Astrid's cheekbones crested with scarlet. "No right? I'm her mother."

"Not in any way that counts," Billy said, keeping between the two women, but careful to stay clear of the fire coming out of his mother's nostrils. "You gave up any maternal rights four years ago."

"That was then," Astrid said. "I was in no position to raise a child. Now I'm in a better place."

Billy scoffed. "Don't use that New Age lingo on me, Astrid. Heron Point is not your 'better place' and it never will be." He glanced out the front door where a BMW sedan was parked at the curb. "You'd be wise to get into that fancy car of yours and drive off this island. There's nothing here for you."

"Don't be unreasonable, Billy." Her voice lowered in threat. "You can't keep me from my daughter."

Blood pounded in his head. "The hell I can't. Don't push me, Astrid. I'm a cop, and I can have you arrested for child abandonment."

"I didn't abandon her," Astrid snapped. "I left her with her father!"

"Who, as I recall, was practically a stranger to you."

"I knew you well enough to be certain you'd take care of her."

"And I have. And I have no intention of letting you take her back now."

Astrid stared over his shoulder. "You may not have a choice," she said in a harsh whisper. Her mouth lifted at the corners in another attempt at a smile. "Hello, baby."

Billy turned. Gemma stood a few feet from them, her eyes wide, her lips trembling. In that moment she looked like the child she'd been four years ago as she'd stood on his doorstep watching her mother walk away. "Gem, I thought I told you…"

She stared up at Astrid. "Mommy?"

"Yes, baby, it's me."

Gemma drew her bottom lip into her mouth. When she spoke, there were teeth marks on the tender flesh. "Where have you been, Mommy?" she asked in a quivering voice.

"It's a long story, Gemma." Astrid added to Billy, "Will you leave us alone?"

He crossed his arms over his chest. "Not on your life."

"I have a right to speak to her."

"Fine. But you'll do it in front of me. And not today." Suddenly all Billy wanted was to get Astrid out of his house. He needed to establish some sort of normalcy in the spiraling chaos. The events of the past twenty-four hours and now this was churning toward a sort of hysteria, and if he lost control, he might never get it back.

Astrid glared at him. "Then when?"

"Tomorrow afternoon. After things have settled down. Where are you staying?"

"The Heron Point Hotel."

"I'll contact you. We'll arrange something."

Astrid pursed her lips in a show of defiance, but she didn't argue. "All right. I'll hold you to that." She looked at Gemma. "Mommy will see you tomorrow, baby."

"Okay."

She walked out the door but stopped before heading

to her car. "I'm registered under Althea Hufnagle," she said. "It's my real name."

Billy shut the door with a hand that wouldn't stop trembling. How had his life gotten so complicated? He'd just heard the name of his daughter's mother for the first time.

He turned around, got down on one knee and looked into Gemma's eyes. "I'm sorry, Gem," he said. "I guess that was a shock."

"I wanted to go with her."

"You'll see her tomorrow after school. The three of us will sit down and talk then."

Gemma's eyes rounded. "School? I'm not going to school. I want to be with Mommy all day."

Billy closed his eyes and reminded himself to stay calm.

"Gemma, you don't even *know* your mother. Heck, I don't even know her. And until we both do, nothing is going to drastically change around here. Which means, you're going to school."

Her shoulders shuddered with a dramatic sigh before she suddenly smiled. "Oh, all right. At least I have something to tell that stupid Whitney Broadmoor. I have a mommy now, too. And she'll take me away from here, and I'll never have to see Whitney again."

Billy shook his head. "I wouldn't jump to conclusions just yet, Gemma."

"Why not? Kids are supposed to live with their mommies. Even when their daddy's not around, they still live with their mommy." She gave Billy a deliberate stare. "Mommies don't take stuff away. And they don't make their kids go to a school that has all mean kids in it." She nodded her head once decisively. "Mommy finally came to get me. She wants me to be happy."

"I want you to be happy, Gemma. You know that, don't you?"

"No, you don't, Daddy. You take away my things and make me sit in the chair."

Billy glanced up at his mother when he heard a sniffle. She dabbed at her eyes with a tissue. "Do something, William," she said.

CHAPTER FOURTEEN

EVIE DISCOVERED a break in her schedule by midmorning on Monday and asked Mary Alice to send for Gemma. Even though Billy hadn't called last night, Evie told herself not to assume something was wrong. He was probably busy, or perhaps he'd worked late, or spent time with Gemma. And since he'd clearly given her permission to speak to the girl, that's exactly what Evie intended to do.

Mary Alice opened the office door and poked her head inside. "I've got Gemma with me," she said.

Evie came around her desk. "Oh, good. Send her in."

Gemma entered, stood with her hands clasped behind her back. She looked cute in jeans and a glittery tank top under a floral camp shirt. "Hi, Gemma. How are you?"

She rocked back on her heels. "Really good."

The girl's smile came so easily, Evie couldn't help responding with one right back at her. "Want to sit down a minute?"

"Sure." She headed toward a chair and Evie walked back around her desk.

"Everything going okay today?" Evie asked when they were both seated.

"Great."

At this moment Gemma seemed like any normal, well-adjusted preadolescent. "That's wonderful," she said. "Have you had any trouble with Whitney or Alina today?"

Gemma shook her head. "Nope."

"I heard about what happened on Saturday," Evie said.

"Oh, that. It was all Whitney's fault. She tricked me into stepping in that ant hill."

"I think that might be what happened," Evie agreed. "And I wanted to talk to you about it."

"You don't have to," Gemma said.

"Why not?"

"Because Whitney won't ever cause me a problem again."

She sounded so confident, Evie wondered if she and Billy had come up with a solution to the problem. "I'm glad to hear that. Do you mind telling me what has changed?"

Gemma sat up straight, beaming. "I'm moving away from Heron Point."

Evie felt like all the air had been sucked from her lungs. The Muldoones were leaving? How was that possible? She stared at Gemma. "What do you mean?"

"I'm going away with my mother. She came to get me yesterday."

After several moments, Evie finally said, "Your mother is here?"

"Yep. And she wants me to live with her." She paused, gave Evie a great big grin and said, "So if it's okay with you, I'm going back to class now. It could be my last day."

None of this made any sense. Astrid was in Heron Point? Billy was letting her take Gemma? It couldn't be. If there was one thing Evie was sure of, it was Billy's love for his daughter.

"Miss Gaynor?"

Evie snapped to attention. "Yes?"

"Can I go?"

She nodded. When Gemma had left the office, Evie called for Mary Alice. "Take messages," she said. "I've got to go into town."

Her assistant looked confused. Evie never left school in the middle of the day. "Will you have your cell phone on?" she asked.

"Yes. But don't call it."

BILLY DRUMMED his fingers on the counter of the Heron Point Hotel lobby. The clerk looked up. "Hi, Mitch. Have you got a room number for an Althea Hufnagle?"

The young man pointed to the restaurant. "She's in there having breakfast. Just came down a few minutes ago."

Billy checked his watch. Ten-thirty. At least one

thing hadn't changed. Like the old Astrid, Althea didn't start her day until nearly noon. He went into the restaurant and spotted her immediately. There were only two other people dining, tourists.

She looked up, set down her fork and stared vacantly. She made no motion to wave him over. He walked to her table, pulled out a chair. "Mind if I sit?"

"Suit yourself. Where's Gemma?"

"I said I'd bring her after school."

"Oh. Then what are you here for?"

"To talk. Just you and me."

She picked up her fork again, shoveled a mound of eggs Benedict onto it. "So talk. But make it quick."

"You have a busy day?" he said, sarcasm dripping from each word. "You reading a few palms while you're here?"

"I gave that up. I don't need gimmicks anymore." She swallowed the egg and dabbed a napkin over her lips. "I'm only concerned with being a good mother."

"Yeah, I'll bet."

She targeted the empty fork at his face. "Don't start with me, Billy. I saw Gemma. You'll never convince me you've been Daddy of the year."

"That award would be for the past *four* years."

Ignoring the gibe she said, "I saw how our daughter looked yesterday. What did you do? Give her a bath in a paint can?"

He couldn't argue. Althea had seen Gemma at her tantrum-throwing, crayon-streaked worst. "It's a long story. There was a disciplinary incident yesterday. You arrived at a bad time."

She took another bite. "Spare me the details of how you discipline, please."

He sat back, gave her a thorough appraisal. She'd definitely acquired a hard edge. This wasn't the meek, insipid creature who'd dropped off an innocent child with a virtual stranger. "So what's your story, *Althea*? Why do you want Gemma back after all this time?"

"People change. I realize my mistake and now I want to correct it."

He repeated her word with damning emphasis. "Mistake, huh? Abandoning a kid is not like mis-adding a column of figures. What you did is more like a life-altering, no-going-back decision."

She gave him a frosty glare. "I'm getting tired of hearing you accuse me of abandonment. You're her father, for God's sake. You were the best person I could leave her with. I knew you were a decent, responsible man."

"The hell you did. You didn't know me at all. We hadn't spoken in six years." He gave her a half smile. "And for your information, ten years ago when we conceived a child, I wasn't a decent man. I was almost as much of a human wreck as you were. In fact, if you take a minute to remember how it was, that's what attracted us to each other. You picked me because I was the sappy, half-tanked cop. And you were one of a long line of women in my futile attempt to find one who'd get me on the right path."

He leaned over the table, commanding her attention. "Only you weren't the woman who did that for me. A five-year-old kid did. And I'm not about to give her up."

"That's a selfish attitude, Billy, and I should warn you not to let this get nasty. You won't win."

"Yeah? And what are you going to fight me with? Your stellar history?"

For the first time she smiled, a coy, catlike stretching of her lips. "Money. I have lots of it."

"Really?"

"Yeah, and if it'll make you happy, I'd even consider giving some of it to you. What do you think your time and effort taking care of Gemma the past four years is worth? Twenty thousand a year? Thirty?"

He dropped his hands to his lap and clenched his fists under the table. "Whew. Tempting. That's good money for a nanny. So where did you get all this cash?"

"Does it matter? I can take care of Gemma. That's all that should concern you."

"But it's not all that concerns me. I'm a cop, remember? You could have robbed a bank for all I know."

"I didn't." She pushed her plate away and folded her hands on the table. "Look, Billy, let's stop the war of words. We both want what's best for Gemma. At least we should. I can provide for her, give her anything she wants or needs. Private schools, a nice home, the best sorts of friends. I didn't do right by her at the beginning. I know that and I'm willing to admit it. But I want to make up for it now."

Billy slowly shook his head. "I'm not letting you take her, Althea. Heron Point, including my humble little house, is Gemma's home now. She's staying."

"And how does she feel about that?"

Billy knew the answer. If Althea proposed half of what she'd just laid out, Gemma would run to her like water down a mountain. Billy had just taken away half of everything Gemma thought she possessed. And Althea apparently was willing to give it all back with bonuses.

Suddenly his heart felt as though it was being squeezed in a vise. Althea appeared to be telling the truth. She seemed to have money. And she was going to use it to offer Gemma a life that would fulfill a girl's fantasies.

He couldn't help thinking about the way he'd been handling his daughter's behavioral problems. What had all this discipline been for, after all? Was Evie's version of tough love going to cost him his daughter maybe as soon as this afternoon? Even if he could keep Gemma here in Heron Point, would she resent him for the rest of her life? Could he prevent that from happening if he softened up on her now? At this point he was willing to try anything, even if that meant abandoning the techniques Evie had been so sure would work. What did it matter if something ultimately worked or not if he lost his child in the meantime?

Althea's voice brought him back. "Why can't you just believe that I want to make up for past mistakes?" she said.

"I just can't," he said simply. "Even if you'd had a heart transplant and pure gold beat in your chest, I still wouldn't believe you. I just can't figure out what your angle is."

"My angle is to provide for my daughter. And I can do that, Billy. She won't lack for anything."

"She doesn't lack for anything now." He frowned, knowing Gemma would argue that point.

"You can still be part of her life," Althea said. "She can visit in the summers. And you can come to Denver and see her."

Denver? This was the first time Billy had considered that Althea's plan included moving his daughter far away. A chill flowed through his veins. "That's where you think you're taking her? Colorado?"

"Of course. It's where I live."

"No, Althea. No way. You're not taking her across the country."

She smiled again. He was beginning to hate her smile. "I'll take this to court, Billy," she said. "You know judges usually decide in favor of the mother. And I can afford the best lawyer in the country."

Trent McElroy, Heron Point's only lawyer, would offer to help, probably wouldn't even charge Billy.

But what chance would a retired, sixty-eight-year-old recreational fisherman have against the legal mind Althea could afford?

All he had left was bravado. Billy stood from the table and blustered for all he was worth. "You're the one in for a fight, Althea. Gemma is my daughter and I'm not giving her up."

He started to walk away but she stopped him. "You'll bring her here this afternoon, right? You gave your word."

"*We'll* be here," he said. "And we'll both be listening to everything you say."

EVIE PULLED OVER in front of the city hall and got out of her car. She was just about to go inside when she saw Billy come out of the Heron Point Hotel across the street. She waited until he spotted her. His expression didn't change. In fact, his features seemed to be set in granite. His lips were drawn into a thin line. His eyes were narrowed in what appeared to be deep concentration. Such a somber demeanor was unusual for Billy, but after hearing Gemma's news, Evie wasn't surprised. He had a lot on his mind. She held her breath as he crossed over. He stopped in front of her, rubbed the back of his neck.

He nodded once.

"Can we talk?" she asked.

"It's not really a good time."

"Billy, I just spoke to Gemma. She had some startling news. I need to know if it's true."

He took her by the elbow, walked her around to the back of the municipal building. Motioning to a golf cart, he said, "Get in."

A silent and tension-filled sixty seconds later, he pulled under a palm tree next to an empty stretch of beach and turned off the cart. He put his arm across the back of the bench seat. "What did Gemma tell you?"

"She said her mother's in town. That she wants to take Gemma away from Heron Point."

He stared at the Gulf. A muscle flexed in his jaw. "That about sums it up."

"Can she do that?"

"I don't know. Maybe. She thinks she can."

Billy's voice was eerily calm, and Evie questioned his stoic attitude. He seemed tightly wound, as if his rage was about to combust. Without thinking of how her words might sound, she blurted the first thought that came to mind. "You're not considering it, are you?"

"Hell, no, I'm not," he said hotly. "What kind of a question is that?"

Evie inched away, putting space between them. "I'm sorry. I'm just trying to find out what's going on. I thought that with all the problems you're having with Gemma, you might be weighing all options."

He clenched his hand repeatedly. "Like what? Giving that witch my daughter? How could you think that?"

She hadn't thought that, not really. This conversation had started out badly, when all she'd wanted to do was to help. That was all she'd ever wanted to do for Billy and Gemma. Until Saturday. Now she wanted so much more for all of them, and that's what made this moment so difficult, her choice of words crucial. "Billy, you misunderstood. I know you love Gemma and you want her here."

"Of course I love her. I've raised her. And now I might be losing her."

"No one would give custody of Gemma to Astrid," she said. "She abandoned the child."

He smirked. "Her name's actually Althea, and she doesn't look at it that way. In her mind, she merely dropped Gemma off for a few fun-filled years with her daddy. Now, apparently, fun time's over."

"But she's not a fit mother, is she? From the way you described her the last time you saw her, I assumed she was down on her luck, maybe even addicted to something."

"She was all that. But she claims she's straightened out." He scowled. "And looking at her today, I can't question her transformation. She appears clean and sober, determined...and rich. Putting it simply, Althea has weapons, and she'll use them."

Evie placed her hand on Billy's shoulder. He immediately dropped his arm to his side, shrugging her off. Hurt but undaunted, she said, "You have weapons, too. You've done a good job with Gemma."

"What? Now you think that?" His eyes narrowed. "All of a sudden I'm this terrific father when just two weeks ago you couldn't wait to tell me what I've done wrong, what I need to do to make it better."

"I never said you were a bad father. I never once thought that. I admire you for what you've done to give Gemma a safe, secure life."

"Right. I've raised a well-adjusted, socially accepted angel. That's what you're telling me now?"

"Gemma's problems go back to before you got her. And you're trying to correct her behavior now. It's not too late, Billy. Gemma can grow to be…"

He held his hand in front of her face. "You know what, Evie? I know you're only trying to help, but it's time we canned the talk about Gemma's *condition,* about your expertise." He wrapped his hands tightly around the steering wheel and seemed to focus on his whitening knuckles. "What's it all been for anyway? I'm about to lose my daughter and the sad fact is, she wants to go."

Evie shook her head. "No, she doesn't. She's confused. She loves you—"

"She loves the guy who takes away her privileges? Who's ready to blame her for everything that goes wrong? Who takes the side of her teachers, her classmates —" he glanced at Evie quickly before looking straight ahead "—supposed psychological experts… instead of standing up for his own daughter?" He slowly turned to face her. The pain in his eyes made her choke back a sob.

"I don't think so, Evie," he said. "I don't think my

daughter loves me. She says she hates me, and I believe her. Sometimes we just have to listen to our kids and take what they say at face value, because what they say is what they mean. Maybe someday you'll have a kid of your own, and you'll see that I'm right."

Evie hurt, too—for Billy, for herself, for what they almost had and apparently were about to lose. Her eyes stung. She blinked back tears and stared at his rigid profile.

"And I know my daughter," he said, adding with sharp-edged emphasis, "better than anyone else who claims to know her better. And I'm damned sure she'll grab any chance to get away." He looked at the water, serene and calm, a marked contrast to the emotions roiling inside him. "And, just my luck, that chance showed up yesterday in a shiny new BMW, which probably has a trunk filled with everything a girl could want."

"Billy, let me help." Evie's voice sounded strained, like the untuned strings of a violin. "What can I do?"

Several anxious moments passed while she waited for his answer, the answer that might decide their future. "I think you've done enough, Evie. This is my fight now. Mine and a lawyer's. I've got to put some space between me and everyone who's tried to tell me how to raise my daughter. I've got to do anything I can to keep her...even if that means going against everyone's advice and being nice to her."

"You've always been nice to her, Billy," she said, her voice hitching. But she was determined to try one more time. "This whole discipline thing wasn't about nice. It was about fair. But you're not her friend. You're her father, and that means tough decisions sometimes…"

He squeezed his eyes shut. "How much longer?"

"What?"

"How much longer will I be her father? Do your textbooks tell you that? She already doesn't want me."

Evie clasped her hands in her lap to keep from touching him, comforting him. He didn't want her help, certainly not her advice. He turned the key and stepped hard on the accelerator. A minute later she was walking alone to her car.

CHAPTER FIFTEEN

BILLY WATCHED Evie drive away before getting Jack's permission to take off by two-thirty. Then, he went back on patrol. Unfortunately, the rest of his workday passed in a blur of misery, panic and regret. He'd spoken harshly to Evie and made judgments that weren't thought out. That was his problem, had always been his problem. He never thought before he spoke. He might have just sacrificed the only other relationship that had ever really mattered to him.

He'd blamed Evie because he didn't have the guts to blame himself. He knew he'd made mistakes with Gemma from the beginning, from those first breath-stealing moments of disbelief and uncertainty when he'd learned he was a full-time father responsible for shaping the life of a little human being he didn't even know.

He'd taken the easiest way out that day. He'd called his mother, who'd fired up her motor home and arrived two days later to a pair of anxious, floundering Muldoones who in their brief time together hadn't managed to discover any common ground. Brenda had taken over, put his house in order, established routine out of the chaos of her son's and grand-daughter's insecurity. And Billy had let her lead, even while he resented following. Now Brenda's heart would be torn apart if Althea took Gemma. And Gemma truly believed that all she had to do was to reach out and grab the brass ring. A ring Billy feared would tarnish the moment she touched it.

At two-thirty, he got in his pickup and headed toward the elementary school. As he drove, his thoughts vacillated between the difficult meeting ahead and the oddly comforting notion that in treating Evie so callously, he might have done her a favor.

He'd released her from anything she might have been feeling toward him and his family. Even if Billy did eventually pull himself out of the ruin Althea could make of his life, he didn't know what sort of man would emerge. But he probably wouldn't be the kind Evie deserved.

He pulled up in front of the school and waited. But it wasn't Gemma he saw first. It was Evie, standing by the door ushering her charges into the afternoon sunlight. She saw him, gave him a tentative smile, even after what had happened a few hours ago. Regret slammed him full-force once again. And so did the awful truth. Even though he loved Evie, if he lost Gemma, the best thing he could do for Evie, the only way he could wrestle with his feelings and not bring her down with him, was to let her go.

Gemma yanked open the passenger door, climbed in. "Hi, Daddy. Are we going to see Mommy now?"

"Yep. We're going."

"Goody. I can't wait."

ALTHEA WAS STANDING outside the hotel when they drove up. Gemma waved through the window when she caught sight of the impeccably dressed, cool-as-a-cucumber lady who refused to look wilted even in the heat and humidity. No doubt about it. Althea had an aura of confidence that made people take her seriously.

He got out and opened the passenger door. "Where do you want to go?" he asked.

She sat next to Gemma, gave her a squeeze and said, "This is your town, Billy, but I was thinking of ice cream. My treat."

Gemma, of course, seconded the idea.

He drove two blocks to the soda shop and followed them inside. Once the orders were placed, they sat at a bistro table and waited for the clerk to bring the sundaes. Althea broke the awkward silence by reaching into her purse. "I have something for you, baby," she said.

Gemma sat forward, a grin spreading across her face. "Really? What is it?"

Althea took out an envelope. "I wanted to bring you a present, but I didn't know what you'd like." She handed Gemma the envelope. "So I thought you'd enjoy shopping for something special. All us girls like to shop, don't we?"

Billy stared at the lightning bolts on the envelope and decided the gift certificate wasn't from Wal-Mart. And since that was virtually the only place Brenda and Gemma shopped, the piece of plastic might not be such a hit.

Gemma pulled out the card. She phonetically sounded out the words. "Elec-tron-ic World. Where's that?"

Billy looked at Althea. "We don't have an Electronic World in Heron Point."

She returned a condescending nod. "I'm not surprised. I'd forgotten how provincial this island is."

"What can I buy there?" Gemma asked.

"I'll take you to the store, baby," Althea said. "You'll find something wonderful to buy. A game system, DVDs, there's even enough money on the card to get an iPod."

Gemma looked up at Billy for clarification. He shrugged. "I don't think they have plastic bugs at Electronic World."

"I don't like those anymore, Daddy. I want a rubber snake."

Althea grimaced, but to her credit, she kept her opinion to herself.

By the time the ice cream bowls were empty and the bill was paid, Althea and Billy had reached a tenuous compromise. Althea would stay in Heron Point for a few days, visit with Gemma daily for a specified time period, and Billy would chaperone. He secretly prayed that Gemma would see through her mother's plastic veneer to the con under the surface. Billy wasn't certain of much, but his gut told him *Astrid Moonflower* was still very much alive and working an angle.

AFTER A TRIP to the market, Evie got home at five o'clock. In her kitchen she found Harry feeding Muffler. "I picked up some chicken breasts," she said blandly. She didn't think she could eat anything, but maybe later her appetite would return. "Would you mind if supper was late?" she asked. "There's something I want to do first."

"No, don't mind at all. I've got an errand to run myself."

She needed to escape this horrible mood she was in. Besides her constant worry that Billy would lose Gemma, she was desperately lonely, despite the fact that she and Billy had argued a mere few hours ago. According to Harry's original plan, his two-week visit would end on Wednesday. He hadn't mentioned leaving yet, but she didn't want him spending the last two days with his morose daughter who couldn't shake off her wounded pride...and broken heart. "Sure, go ahead," she said. "What I have to do won't take long, maybe an hour. I'll start dinner then."

"I expect I'll be back. I've just got to run over to the Muldoones' place." He filled Muffler's water bowl and set it down next to the cat's food. "I suppose you heard, Ev. Gemma's mother came for her."

"Yes, I heard. How is Brenda taking the news?"

"Not well. I don't know what I can do to help, but I'm going over there just the same."

I hope you have better luck than I did, she thought. She glanced at the phone on the wall just as she'd fixated on the one on her desk all afternoon, all the while listening for the familiar jingle of her cell phone. Wishing didn't make any of them ring. It was entirely possible that if Gemma left Heron Point, she and Billy might never speak to each other again. The way he felt about her now, Evie doubted he'd even pursue her if she drove down Island Avenue at sixty miles per hour.

Maybe Billy didn't want her help, and maybe she'd be risking what slight hope remained for a reconciliation with him, but she was determined to do something.

She reached down and patted Muffler's head. "I'll see you guys later then." The sun was still warm as she walked up the brick pathway to Claire and Jack's house. When no one answered her knock on the back door, she went around to the veranda to wait. Claire rarely stayed late at her office and she closed her shop at five on weekdays.

Evie sat in one of the porch chairs, wrapped her arms around her knees and gave herself a pep talk. "You've come this far, Evelyn. You've made this island your home. Now it's time for you to take a real stand and, for once in your life, leap before you look." She flinched. "What the heck? If you lose your job because of abuse of authority, maybe that gardener's job is still available at the Pink Ladies."

A few minutes passed before Jack pulled up in his SUV. Claire climbed down from the passenger side and Jane scrambled out the back. Claire immediately quickened her pace to the porch. "Hi, Evie. Is something wrong or is this a social visit? Either way I'm glad to see you."

"You were right the first time," Evie said, smiling at Jane and acknowledging Jack. "I suppose you both know what this is about."

A look passed between Claire and Jack before Claire spoke to her daughter. "Why don't you run inside and get the hamburger out of the fridge? And you can take a few potatoes out of the bin and wash them."

"Okay." Jane opened the door but turned before going inside. "I know you don't want me to hear what you're talking about."

"I really really want clean potatoes," Claire said.

The door closed behind Jane, and soon Evie heard the television in the background. "They're all too smart for their years," Evie said.

Claire sat beside her. "Let me guess. You're hoping that's true for Gemma, as well."

Evie nodded.

Jack remained standing and looked from Claire to Evie. "Do you mind if I sit in on this conversation?"

"No. I want you to," Evie said.

"You're worried about Billy, aren't you?" Claire said as Jack sat.

Evie sighed. "It will crush him if he loses Gemma."

"What do you want us to do?" Jack asked.

Evie braced herself. She wouldn't blame Jack if he turned her down. "I did some snooping around after school today," she confessed. "I saw Billy come out of the hotel earlier, and I figured that's where Gemma's mother was staying. I checked with the desk clerk if Billy had asked for anyone this morning."

Jack sat back in his chair. "You were right. That's where Astrid is staying."

"Yes, and the clerk gave me her name. I expected him to say Astrid Moonflower, since that's what Billy said she called herself before."

"We never knew her then," Jack said. "But I've heard Billy use that name."

"She registered as Althea Hufnagle with a Denver, Colorado, address," Evie said.

Claire sat forward. "Denver? That's practically across the country. No wonder Billy is so worried. We have to do something. If this becomes a court battle, chances are Astrid, or Althea, or whatever she calls herself, will win. Reformed mothers seem to be a favorite of our judicial system. Judges are too quick to reward them with innocent young lives."

"If, indeed, Althea is reformed," Evie pointed out.

"Right," Claire said. "What can we do to help?"

Evie looked at Jack. "I hope I'm not betraying a

confidence, but Claire told me you have an interesting background that involves some specially trained skills."

"I suppose," Jack admitted. "But my Secret Service days are long over, and I'm afraid my wife exaggerates."

"Not true," Claire said, taking his hand. "I'll never forget how you found Jane when she went missing last year."

Pride and gratitude shone in Claire's eyes, and Evie decided that someday she'd get her to tell that story.

"What are you thinking, Evie?" Claire said.

"I'm hoping Jack has a contact, someone who can find out intimate details about a person's life. Even a person who has had several aliases."

Claire stood and moved to where her husband was sitting. "Of course, Jack—that man, the one in—where was it, Virginia? He knows how to find out about anyone, doesn't he?" She tapped her finger against her bottom lip. "What was his name?"

Jack chuckled. "I could tell you, honey, but then you'd have to go into hiding."

She playfully slapped at his arm. "Call him, sweetheart."

Evie leaned toward him. "Please, Jack. I need to know everything about Gemma's mother. I can't ignore the serious doubts I have about her."

He looked from one to the other. "You're not playing fair, ladies. I've always been a sucker for a pretty face, and with the two of you staring me down, I'm toast."

"Then hurry," Claire said. "Call him now. Tell him it's top priority."

"Our national security is at risk, right?"

Evie gave him a guilty smile. "Our island security anyway. And it's your job to keep our citizens safe."

Jack pulled his cell phone from his pocket and headed toward the steps. Evie wondered if he was thinking that the speech he'd just heard was from an "islander" who'd only been in Heron Point a few weeks. What the heck. It had only taken a few days for her to feel as though she belonged here.

He strode out to the sidewalk to speak privately, but Evie watched his expression change from friendly greeting to serious business.

HARRY PULLED HIS Buick next to the Minnie Winnie and turned off the engine. Billy's truck wasn't in the drive, thankfully. He needed a few minutes alone with Brenda.

She came out before he'd even knocked on the door. He started to speak, but she wrapped her arms around his neck and clung to him as if she were sinking in the Gulf. He settled his hands on the small of her back and held her close.

"Oh, Harry, I'm so glad you're here." She sniffled into his neck, leaving a patch of his skin moist.

Brenda crying? He hadn't expected that. He'd come to think of her as the five-star general of Fort Muldoone, the lady who ruled with an iron fist, fierce determination and just a hint of redheaded temper. But she had a vulnerable side, a soft center that was all about family.

"What am I going to do, Harry?" she said. "If I lose Gemma, I've as good as lost Billy, too. He won't need me anymore. He'll want me gone, and I don't want to go. That little girl means more to me than…"

He stepped back, putting her at arm's length. Harry had never been adept at dealing with emotions. That was always Evie's department. She'd say the right thing at birthday parties and funerals. Harry was the one who stood silently by her side. He fumbled for words now, hoped he'd pick comforting ones and not cut the wound deeper.

"Now, Brenda, you're jumping to conclusions and that's not good," he said. "You don't know what's going to happen, but you need to have faith that Billy will make this all come out right."

"But you don't understand. Gemma is so mad at us. She wants to go with her mother. She thinks her life will be much better." Brenda grabbed his shirtfront, twisted the yoke in her trembling fist. When she expressed emotion, she didn't do it halfway. "But it won't be better. You should have seen that woman's eyes. They're empty I tell you, Harry. There's nothing inside her that's even remotely maternal." She dropped her hands and absently smoothed the wrinkles she'd made in his shirt. "We shouldn't have been so hard on Gem. Now she hates us."

Harry walked her away from the house. "You know that's not true, Brenda. Kids are put on earth to vex us. Gemma's just doing her part." He ran his hand through his thick hair. "You think I got this gray simply by growing older? No, ma'am. I was a single father and Evie turned every one of my hairs into this fine-looking garden of clover you see now."

He studied Brenda's fiery curls and said, "'Course that hasn't happened to you, now, has it?"

She gave him a playful jab to his ribs. "You know just the right thing to say."

Whew. Maybe being out of practice with women for twenty-seven years didn't render a man completely incompetent. He led her to his car. "I've got a present for you."

"A present? What is it?"

He unlocked his trunk, revealing two dozen colorful plants. "What do you think?"

She bent over and caressed a few silky petals. "They're beautiful. Are they for my garden?"

"Yes, they are, and I'm going to help you plant them right now, so you can water them and watch them grow." He stared into her eyes. "It's a sign of my confidence for the future. You see, Brenda, I don't anticipate you going anywhere soon."

She reached in and took the first pot from his trunk. "There's only one thing wrong with your plan."

"What's that?"

"You won't be here to watch with me. You're going home in two days, aren't you?"

He scooped an additional three plants into his arms. "That was the plan. But I called a young fella in my neighborhood today. Told him to mow my lawn an extra time or two."

Her eyes grew round. "Does that mean…?"

"Let's just say I'm staying a bit longer."

She set down her pot, reached up and pulled his face to hers for a loud, appreciative kiss that left Harry laughing out loud and fumbling to keep from dropping his plants. "Let's get these flowers over to the beds," he said, marveling that Brenda wasn't the only one who liked being needed.

On Wednesday afternoon Evie went out the back entrance of the elementary school and headed across the parking lot. Just as she reached her car, a black SUV pulled up beside her. She tossed her briefcase in the back seat and opened the passenger door of the SUV and looked inside. "Hi, Jack."

He held up a manila folder. "Get in." In what she imagined was typical Secret Service protocol, he handed her the file without speaking. It was marked "Althea Hufnagle."

Her hand trembled as she stared at the folder. "What did you find out? Is Althea on the level?"

His expression revealed nothing. "Look at it."

She opened the file and began speed-reading. The

report started with standard information. Althea's address, date of birth, matters of public record. Evie scanned down until she saw the name Carl Hufnagle, a man identified as Althea's father. "What do we know about Carl?" she asked.

"Only that he's the top sports agent in the Denver area. He handles contracts for the Broncos, the Rockies and the Avalanche. And he's a multimillionaire."

She checked Althea's address with her father's. "And Gemma's mother lives with him."

"She does now. But for years Althea was estranged from her family. She dropped out of the University of Colorado and began pursuing her various career choices, which involved questionable occupations across the country."

"Including her time as a palm reader in Heron Point."

"Exactly." Jack flipped a page in the folder and ran his finger down a column of names. "Astrid Moonflower, Devon Whitecloud, Tempest Honeywell—all aliases she used while masquerading as a sort of Gypsy fortune-teller. She read palms and tarot cards while avoiding the private detectives her father hired to find her. Eventually Carl gave up."

"What brought them back together?" Evie asked.

"Having run out of money and boyfriends, Althea returned to Denver to beg Daddy's forgiveness. She came home broke and addicted to prescription pain-killers. That was exactly one year ago."

"And Carl took her back."

"Yeah, till he realized she was only using him. Then he gave her an ultimatum." Jack turned another page, pointed to the name of a rehabilitation center outside of Denver. "Three months ago, Althea was released from this rehab facility, supposedly drug-free. Since then she's been living the good life in her father's house."

Evie perused the information, verifying the facts Jack had just related. "So, she's only wanted Gemma back for three months?"

Jack frowned. "If she truly wants her back at all."

"What do you mean?"

"One of my contacts talked to Althea's sister, who lives at one of the ski resorts. Our man identified himself as a headhunter investigating Althea as a candidate for a corporate position. Seems the sister was only too happy to tell the interviewer the real story behind the cozy father-daughter reconciliation."

"Sounds like the relationship between the sisters isn't a loving one," Evie said.

"Far from it. The sister has resented Althea all her life. She said Althea was a user, from the time she first learned she could shake down Daddy for candy money. She told the supposed headhunter she wouldn't recommend Althea as a short-order cook, much less an executive position."

Evie shook her head. "I still don't get it. If the father is a successful sports agent, he must be savvy. Why was he taken in by his daughter? Maybe he just wanted to believe she could change."

"That might be part of it. But according to the sister, Carl discovered Althea had something he wanted, something her sister had never given him."

"What was that?"

"A grandchild."

Evie said Gemma's name in a gasp.

"Right. Carl took Althea back and agreed to help her on two conditions. One—she complete her rehab. And two—she bring her child home." Jack stared out the windshield. "Billy told me Althea boasted she had enough money to fight him in court until she won. Apparently that's true. She seems to have fulfilled the first of her father's stipulations and, with his backing and financial support, it looks like she's going after the second. She has a reason to play mama again."

Evie closed the folder and squeezed it between her hands. "Unfortunately none of this indicates that Althea has any *desire* to be one."

"That's the sad part," Jack said. "And that's what scares me."

"So Althea is using Gemma as a bargaining chip into her father's life again?"

Jack nodded. "And his bank account."

Evie closed her eyes. A chill suddenly overwhelmed her and she shivered despite the afternoon heat. "We've got to save that little girl," she said vehemently. For the first time since Billy and Gemma had come into her life, she realized she was speaking for herself as well as for Billy.

In that moment of astounding clarity, Evie recognized she'd been rooting for Gemma since the first day she'd met her with her bagful of plastic bugs. She'd admired her spunk and her creativity as well as her tenacity to face her problems head-on. Maybe the child's choices hadn't been the right ones, but Gemma was a fighter, and Evie had no doubt that once her energies were channeled in the right direction, she could be a formidable champion of the underdog.

She was even more determined to try to keep Gemma where she belonged, with a father who would protect her and teach her right from wrong, and a grandmother who would love her with all of her wild Irish heart.

She was still formulating the execution of part two of her plan as Jack asked, "What are you going to do with this information? Are you going to share it with Billy?"

"I don't think Billy wants to hear from me just now," she said. "Maybe you should tell him what you found out, though. You're his best friend. But I'd appreciate it if you could give me a couple of days. I'm going to test Miss Althea Hufnagle. I have a few weapons of my own."

Jack nodded. "I was afraid you and Billy had had a falling out over this," he said. "That helps explain his bad mood lately, and it's just like him. He may be about to lose his daughter and, because of his own bull-headedness, if he's not careful, he'll lose you, the best thing that ever happened to him. I think it's time I told him what a jerk he can be."

"You might want to hold off on that jerk conversation for a while," Evie said. "I'll let you know how I do with Althea. If my plan backfires, I could be the one who deserves your speech." She smiled. "Besides, who said anything about him losing me?"

CHAPTER SIXTEEN

TWO DAYS LATER Evie received the reports she'd been waiting for. She carefully read the county school psychologist's detailed file on Gemma, called him to verify a few aspects that hadn't been included in her file and tucked the folder into her briefcase. Then she picked up her phone and dialed the number for the Heron Point Hotel.

While she waited for the desk clerk to connect her, she prayed that Althea hadn't heard that she and Billy had a relationship. It wasn't likely she had. Only a few friends knew they'd gotten close. And Althea wasn't privy to the Heron Point gossip trail.

A woman answered in a sleep-drugged voice. "Miss Hufnagle?" Evie asked. Ascertaining that she was indeed speaking to Althea, she identified herself as Gemma's principal and explained that she'd heard Gemma might be leaving the school system to live with her mother.

Althea confirmed, saying that, barring complications, she hoped to leave with Gemma by the end of the weekend.

Evie hid her shock at this revelation behind her cool, professional demeanor. "That being the case," she said, "I'd like to have a conversation with you as soon as possible."

"What about?" Althea asked, suddenly alert and on guard.

"The school psychologist and I would like to bring you up to speed." Before Althea could question her further, Evie quickly added, "This shouldn't take too long. Perhaps an hour. I was wondering if you could meet me at my home instead of the school at, say three o'clock? These matters are of a somewhat delicate nature and I want to insure complete privacy between us."

"But I was meeting with Gemma after school," Althea said.

Not until you hear what I have to say. "As I said, this won't take long. And it's extremely urgent."

Her interest obviously piqued, Althea agreed, asked for directions to Evie's cottage and promised to meet her there on time.

By two forty-five, the last student had left school. Evie grabbed her briefcase and headed for the rear exit. She prayed she was doing the right thing. She wouldn't violate Gemma's privacy any more than was necessary, and she justified her decision to inform Althea of Gemma's ODD by telling herself that Althea was truly Gemma's mother. If she did succeed in gaining custody, she should know all of the details of Gemma's history. Dr. Grey had agreed.

Evie shouldered her way out the back door, and ran into Billy coming the opposite direction. Her briefcase slammed into his thigh.

"Ouch!" He grabbed her by the arms. "Whoa. What's your hurry?"

She pressed her free hand under her rib cage as she sucked in a trembling breath. "Uh...I have a meeting. I'm late."

She certainly hadn't expected that the first time she saw Billy again, breathing would be so difficult, but she had to concentrate on forcing air into her lungs. She stared up at him, tried to think of something to say and came up with zilch. Deep down, she didn't want to talk at all. She wanted to touch. Events had taken their toll on him. His eyes were hollow and shadowed. His shoulders appeared slumped, seeming to sap him of his confidence. But his hands on her arms felt so sure and comforting, Evie wanted to drop her briefcase and just hang on to him.

He smiled, almost as if nothing had happened, the way he had at the cabin on the Myacki River. Almost as if he still cared about her. And Evie allowed herself to hope that maybe he did. And she became even more determined to help him keep his daughter.

"I want to talk to you," he said.

She closed her eyes. "I can't now, Billy. I really can't."

"But what happened the other day..."

"It's all right. I understand. You don't have to justify your feelings."

He released her, straightening. "I wasn't going to. But I wanted to tell you that when all this settles down, we should talk. I need you to know why I lightened up on Gemma."

She glanced at her watch. "I do know why, and it's okay, Billy, really."

"I've hired a lawyer," he said. "A guy here on the island. I don't know if he'll be able to stand up to Althea's legal power, but I've got to fight back."

"That's good," she said. "You have to do whatever you can to keep Gemma."

He frowned. Tension lines marred his full mouth. "I'm going to. Althea's not going to win, not as long as I have the means to fight her." He took a step back from Evie, gazed earnestly into her eyes. "But things between us… I never meant…"

She reached up, placed her hand on his cheek. "Billy, it's okay. I've got to go. But we'll talk very soon." *If I don't totally screw up this afternoon.*

"But do you still…?" The question, half-asked, hung in the air between them.

What did he mean? Do you still care? Do you still want to see me? Taking a chance, she said, "Of course." She stepped around him and hurried to her car. Her hand was trembling when she put the key in the ignition. Her dashboard clock read two fifty-three. "Don't fail, Evie," she said to herself as she backed out of her spot and drove from the parking lot. Now would not be a good time to get a speeding ticket.

She arrived home with a minute to spare and set a kettle on the stove before Althea pulled up in front.

"SO WHAT IS THIS Oppositional Defiant Disorder?" Althea said after she returned her teacup to its saucer.

Evie opened the folder and lay it on the coffee table between them. "I have the characteristics of the disorder here," she said. "Our psychologist, Dr. Grey, performed a comprehensive evaluation of Gemma. As you can see, he found all of these ODD indicators in her personality, some to a lesser extent, some more pronounced."

Althea picked up the top sheet and read it. As she progressed down the page, Evie noticed the first signs of uncertainty creep into the woman's otherwise composed features. "Gemma throws temper tantrums?" she said.

"Not so much at school," Evie answered honestly. "But you've certainly noticed her hair."

Althea's eyes widened. "She did that to herself?"

Evie just raised her eyebrows in response.

"And she blames others for her misbehavior?"

"Yes, although to be fair, sometimes it's justified."

Althea pointed to the paper. "It says here that ODD children argue excessively with adults."

"Yes. It's a matter of who has control. ODD kids hate relinquishing any, and they will argue despite clear knowledge of the outcome."

"And Gemma refuses to follow rules at school?"

"I'm afraid so."

Althea tossed the paper onto the folder. "This is ridiculous. The list takes practically an entire page. Gemma hasn't exhibited any of this behavior with me."

"That's understandable," Evie said. "Of the almost ten percent of school-age children who have ODD, nearly all of them only show signs of the problem at home or at school." Evie recalled the two incidents at the park. "Gemma has displayed tendencies in other places, however."

Althea sat back in her chair. "I'm shocked. I had no idea Gemma had this disease."

Evie quickly corrected her misconception. "It's not a disease, Althea. Hostile behavior in children can't, or shouldn't, be cured with a pill. The affected child must be conditioned to respond to adversity over time. ODD children can be helped, but it takes patience and a well-thought-out plan. That's why I'm acquainting you with the matter today. Dr. Grey would like to schedule a few meetings with you to prepare you for your role in Gemma's continuing therapy."

"What? I don't have time for meetings. I'm planning to go back to Colorado by Monday, with or without Gemma. If I have to come back for some sort of legal battle with her father, I will, but I'm not wasting time on meetings."

Evie exhaled a breath of relief. This was exactly the reaction she'd expected from a mother who had abandoned her child. Obviously in the past Althea had believed that her time, her priorities, were more important than her daughter's. "I'm afraid you'll have to meet with him sometime," she said, taking another paper from the folder and holding it up for Althea's inspection. "Dr. Grey has indicated here that he won't relinquish Gemma's records until he's spoken with her guardian as well as her future psychologist."

Evie hoped Althea wouldn't actually read the lengthy recommendation. The doctor had only strongly *suggested* these meetings take place. He actually had no legal right to insist on them.

Althea waved the paper away from her face. "What happens if Gemma's condition isn't treated?"

"It will get worse." Evie pulled out more documentation. "ODD often leads to something called Conduct Disorder, which is much more serious. Teenagers with this react violently, lash out in physical ways—even end up breaking the law." When Althea didn't reach for the file, Evie dropped it back onto the stack. "But you're fortunate with Gemma," she said.

Althea winced. "Yeah, how?"

"She's still young. If you participate in parent training programs in Colorado, enroll Gemma in behavioral therapy sessions, perhaps introduce her to social skills training…"

Evie stopped when she noticed Althea's eyes begin to glaze over. Evie was on shaky ground here. She hadn't suggested any of this to Billy because she believed Gemma could overcome this condition at home, without interference. But the psychologist had recommended these procedures if Gemma's behavior didn't improve, and Evie was determined to discourage Althea any way she could.

"How did Gemma get this?" Althea asked. "Did Billy do this to her?"

Evie tamped a spark of anger. She was playing the sympathetic adviser here, not the accuser. "No, I'm sure he didn't. In fact, in my dealings with Mr. Muldoone, I've found him to be a concerned and cooperative parent. He loves his daughter very much." She stopped, swallowed. *Don't lay it on too thick, Evelyn.* "Oppositional Defiant Disorder can result from both biological and environmental factors. Its roots can go back to early childhood, even pregnancy."

Althea sat forward. "Are you saying I caused this?"

"I don't know what caused it. I have no knowledge of your situation while you were carrying Gemma and afterward. But it's possible. It's also possible that an emotional trauma at some time in Gemma's life contributed to her problems now." *Like having a parent abandon her.*

Evie poured more tea into Althea's cup. "What caused Gemma to behave as she does isn't really important anymore. How to help her is what matters. I've told you what has to be done, what your part must be in Gemma's continued progress. I just want your assurance you will follow through with what we've started here." She picked up the folder. "I want to tell Dr. Grey that he'll have your cooperation." She picked up a pen and paper. "I'm going to write down the doctor's contact information. You can still reach him today to make an appointment—"

Althea stood abruptly. "I'll call you for his number."

Evie rose as well. "Do you have to leave? I wanted to talk to you about Gemma's academic record. I think she can perform at a much higher level. She's bright, but perhaps not as motivated as some of the other students."

Althea snatched her purse from the floor, made a show of checking her watch. "There's something I have to do. I'd love to stay but I'll have to get back to you."

Evie smiled. "Of course. You know where to reach me." She walked Althea to the door, closed it behind her and collapsed in the nearest chair. Raising her gaze to the ceiling, she said, "It's up to you now, Billy. I have a hunch that very soon your little girl is going to need you more than she ever has."

She picked up the teacups and took them to the kitchen. As much as she hated thinking of Gemma being disappointed again, she knew the child would be better off staying right here where she was loved and protected. Evie had made a tough decision today. She'd involved herself in matters that were beyond an educator's influence. But never once had she thought she was doing the wrong thing. She only hoped that when Billy found out, he would agree.

BILLY RUSHED HOME from work on Friday evening to get there before Althea showed up to take Gemma to dinner. So far the daily visits had been uneventful, as if both females were testing the limits of their new mother/daughter relationship. Gemma hadn't told him she hated him again, not since the first day Althea arrived. Neither had she received a bad report from her teachers all week or declared that she'd be leaving with her mother. Billy would have clung to these small victories as a sign that Gemma wanted to stay with him if she hadn't continued to be excited each time Althea was due.

Tonight could be a turning point. Althea had called Billy this morning and said it was time they talked seriously about Gemma's future. Billy had spent an hour with Trent McElroy preparing statements to counter Althea's attempts to take Gemma out of the state. If Althea insisted on it, Billy was prepared to go to court to stop her. Even if he didn't win custody in the end, Trent felt certain they would at least keep Gemma in Billy's care for the time being.

Feeling almost like a soldier preparing for the battlefield, Billy turned onto his street. He had a half hour or so to shower and gather his thoughts before Althea was due. But her BMW was already in the drive. He pulled around her car and parked near his mother's motor home. When he came through the back door, Brenda glanced over her shoulder at him. She pressed a finger to her lips and resumed listening at the kitchen door.

He walked up behind her. "What's going on? Why are you staying out here?"

"Shush, William," Brenda said, crouching low to give him room. "Just listen."

He peered out the cracked opening. Althea stood just inside the front entrance, her hands clasped tightly at her waist, her posture rigid, as if she were cornered and ready to bolt. Billy wondered why she hadn't entered the living room and taken a chair. Facing her, Gemma stood very still, listening intently. She scratched at her forearm.

"So you see, baby," Althea said. "I got that phone call earlier, and I've got to go back to Denver right away."

Billy gulped back a gasp. Brenda slapped at his knee.

Gemma shifted her weight from one foot to the other. "You mean, you have to go today?"

"Yes, I'm afraid so."

Gemma angled her head to the side, seeming to process this latest news. "Okay," she finally said. "I can pack my suitcase in a hurry."

Althea's cheeks flamed pink. "There's nothing I'd like better, Gemma, you know that, don't you? But you can't come with me this time."

"Why not? You came to get me, didn't you?"

"Yes, of course I did, but things have changed. I can't take you back as I'd planned. I'm sorry."

Billy's lungs burned with trapped air he hadn't even been aware he was holding. No wonder Althea had showed up early. She wanted to avoid Billy. What was she pulling now? Even as he allowed himself to hope that she was on the verge of another disappearing act, his anger wouldn't let him rejoice. It was one thing to walk out on Billy—twice—it was quite another to do the same thing to his child. He yanked on the door, but Brenda was holding it closed.

"What are you doing, Ma?" he asked in a hoarse whisper.

"She's digging her grave, William," she said. "I'd say we leave her alone and let her do it."

"But she's breaking Gem's heart."

"Maybe not as much as you think, son. And besides, you're here to patch it up again."

He opened the door despite her. "Yeah, and I'm on damage control starting now."

Althea's eyes rounded with surprise. Gemma, her face pinched with confusion, looked up at him. "Mommy has to go, Daddy."

He settled his hand on her shoulder and stared at Althea. "So I hear. What's the story, *Mommy?*"

"Something's come up in Denver that requires my immediate attention."

He clenched his free hand into a ball. "I'll bet. What is it? Somebody needs you to forecast a bright future like you did for Gem here?"

"Don't be mean, Billy. It's nothing like that. I have a job and I'm needed…"

Gemma stared up at her with glistening eyes. "Will I see you again, Mommy?"

Althea's motions were stiff and cautious as she reached out and touched Gemma's cheek. "Of course, baby. Just as soon as I get things under control. I'll call you, okay?"

Gemma's voice was as dry and coarse as winter grass as she whispered, "Sure, okay."

Althea tried to smile, but the attempt was a joke. "Well, you two take care, and I'll be in touch."

Billy tugged Gemma close, wrapped his arm around her. "Right."

Althea walked away, shutting the door. A moment later the BMW hummed to life, tires spit on the gravel drive and she was gone.

Billy knelt and turned Gemma to face him. He thought his heart would break. Her pain was so real, so intense. He put his hands on her cheeks and brushed silky patches of her short hair from her temples. Tears slid down her cheeks. "I'm so sorry, Gem."

She sniffed, blinked hard. "Did I do something *really* bad this time, Daddy?"

"What do you mean?"

"Well, Mommy took away the worst thing she could've. She took away herself. I must have been awful."

Billy, who had never been much of a hugger, pulled his daughter into his arms. He clutched her fiercely to his chest. "No, Gem. You didn't do anything wrong." He cupped the back of her head and nestled her close, and then realized his own tears were moistening her hair.

She straightened and backed away from him a step. "Poor Daddy," she said. "Are you crying?"

He thought about lying. Instead he sort of smiled, wiping his eyes with the pad of his thumb. "I guess I am."

"Why?" She shrugged her shoulders. "I guess I'm not going anywhere."

"It's hard to explain," he said between a sob and a chuckle. "I'm crying because I feel so sad for you. And because I'm really disappointed in your mother. But most of all I'm crying because I'm so damned happy you're staying here."

He pulled the handkerchief Brenda always made him carry out of his pocket and dabbed at Gemma's eyes. She leaned in close to him and spoke in his ear. "I'm damned happy, too, then. And, Daddy...?"

"What?"

"Here comes Nana. If she heard us use that word, we're both gonna lose our TVs."

He smiled for real this time. "I think she'll overlook it for now."

"Daddy?"

"What?"

"You won't go away, will you?"

"No, Gemma, I'm not going anywhere. I'm stuck to you like bugs on Bernard's shirt."

Brenda came up to them, put one hand on Billy's shoulder and one on Gemma's. Her eyes were wet and her lips trembled. "Who's up for helping me make chocolate-chip cookies with extra chips?"

Gemma scooted away from Billy and headed for the kitchen. "I am. And you'd better call Harry, Nana. He loves chocolate-chip cookies. And tell him to bring Muffler."

Brenda looked at Billy and a slow smile spread across her face, making her look ten years younger. "All's well that ends well, William."

Billy nodded. "I don't know if it's completely ended yet, Ma. But I think we just scored one for our team."

"I'm not a bit surprised by what that woman did. She didn't want to be a mother. I knew from the start she didn't have the heart for it."

Wondering what really caused Althea to change her mind, Billy put his arm around his mother. "Do you suppose we'll ever know why she left?"

They both looked toward the kitchen when Gemma came out. "Will you do me a favor, Daddy?"

"I imagine."

"Would you go over to Miss Gaynor's and tell her I'm staying at her stupid school? She's really nice and all, but I don't think this news will make her day."

Billy laughed out loud. "I think you're wrong, Gem. I think she'll be very happy to hear that. And I'll be glad to tell her. I've got a few things to say to her myself. I'm going to take a quick shower and head over to her place." He started up the stairs. "And save me some cookies. Don't let Harry eat them all."

CHAPTER SEVENTEEN

BILLY LEFT Gemma and Brenda in the kitchen with cookie dough up to their elbows, a burning desire consuming him. He couldn't wait to tell Evie the good news. Yes, they'd had words. He'd been angry and upset. He'd questioned her procedures. But now he just wanted to share everything with her—if she'd let him.

As he pulled out of his drive, his brain buzzed with matters that required his immediate attention. He needed to make sure Althea was really, truly gone. He had to contact Trent to tell him his services were apparently not needed, at least for now. He had to make a three-day reservation at one of the Disney World resorts for him and Gemma. That particular task made him smile as he drove away from his house.

First, though, he had to make things right with Evie. That scared him out of his wits. He hoped he hadn't blown his chance with her. When would he find a woman as patient, caring and as smart about kids? Never. And when else would a woman walk into his life who was as sexy as Evie and satisfied him as no other woman ever had? Never.

Billy headed straight for Tansy Hill. He hoped he'd find Evie home, and prayed he'd come up with the words to express what he was feeling.

When he pulled into the driveway next to Claire's house, he saw three people on the front porch. Claire, Jack and Evie. He parked behind Jack's SUV and got out. Evie stood as he approached. She looked from her friends to Billy and her worried gaze remained fixed on his face. She looked as he'd felt thirty minutes ago—uncertain, tense. But he was encouraged by the hope in her beautiful eyes. In a flowery dress that caught the breeze and showed off the shapely outline of her legs, and with her golden brown hair loose at her shoulders, she was as pretty as he'd ever seen her.

He climbed the steps and stopped by the porch railing. Jack pushed up from his chair. "Hey, buddy. Want a beer?"

Billy pretended to relax against a roof column. "Don't mind if I do. But first I've got news."

Jack seemed to be trying to suppress a smile. "This wouldn't have anything to do with Althea leaving town, would it?"

Billy dropped into the nearest chair. "How did you know?"

Giving up the effort to appear serious, Jack grinned. "I've had a hot line running between the hotel and my cell phone the past couple of days. Mitch just called a few minutes ago to tell me that one Althea Hufnagle just threw her half dozen suitcases into the trunk of her BMW and blew down Island Avenue like the last hurricane."

Relief washed over Billy. She was really gone. "So you know her real name?" he asked.

"Yeah. Seems that woman can't be honest about anything."

Evie approached him but didn't come close enough to touch. "How's Gemma? Does she know?"

"She knows," Billy said. "Althea stopped at the house a while ago and gave Gem a cockamamy goodbye. I'm amazed, but Gem took her mother's exit pretty well. A few questions, of course, a couple of tears, but now she's making cookies with Brenda like old times."

The worry lines didn't completely disappear from Evie's face. "You have to watch her closely, Billy. There could still be signs of stress."

"I know. I was thinking a visit with a certain central Florida mouse might cheer her up."

"That's a great idea," she said.

Jack opened the screen door to the house. "I'll get that beer. As long as our three other officers are patrolling the streets tonight, I'm proclaiming this a celebration."

"Wait a sec, Jack," Billy said. "What I can't figure out is what made Althea do this? Why did she give up on Gemma?"

Jack's hand tightened on the doorknob. "You know women," he said. "Can't figure them out no matter how hard you try. Just be glad she's gone and forget about it." He continued quickly into the house.

Evie backed away, and passed a quick glance at Claire, who seemed to be avoiding looking directly at Billy. Evie sat daintily in her chair and crossed her legs. She picked up her wineglass with a shaky hand, took a sip and nearly choked on it. Billy stared at her. Something was going on. He scratched his chin. "I'm the first to admit that I don't understand women," he said. "I never have and I probably never will, but I'm seeing two right now who are about as puzzling as any females I've ever come across."

Evie sputtered, released a breathy chuckle. "Who, us?"

"Yeah, but mostly you." He scooted his chair across the floor until their knees touched. She jumped as if the contact were hot as fire. "What's going on, Evie?"

A flush of color began at the roots of her hair. She set down her glass and sighed. "Oh, hell."

Jack returned and handed a bottle to Billy.

"Mind if I make this a take-out?" Billy said, cupping Evie's elbow and helping her from the chair. "Teach and I need to have a private conversation."

Jack smiled. "No. You two go on and have fun."

"Thanks. We intend to." He kept his hand firmly on her arm as she walked woodenly down the steps and around the side of the house. Once they were away from the others, Billy leaned over and whispered in her ear, "Are we having fun yet, sweetheart?"

THEY PASSED Harry who was headed to his car. "Don't wait dinner for me, Ev. I've been invited for chocolate-chip cookies." He gave Billy a light punch to his bicep. "Heard the good news, son. Congratulations. How'd that come about?"

Billy passed a quick glance in Evie's direction. "I think I'm about to find out."

Harry kept going. "You kids have fun."

They reached the gazebo and Evie stepped onto the deck ahead of Billy. "Nice people we know," she said. "They all want us to enjoy ourselves."

"Salt of the earth." He kept a keen gaze on her face, spiraling her anxiety to new heights.

She sat, smoothed her skirt around her legs and tried to look prim despite the wild pounding of her heart.

He remained standing, his features stern. She allowed herself to hope that he wasn't really angry. At least not yet.

"What do you know about Althea leaving town?" he asked.

"Nothing. I…"

"What did you do?"

Good grief. He wasn't even going to let her bluster with a good lie. Not that she had one. "I *am* Gemma's principal," she said as if that would explain every-thing.

"No one's doubting that. What did you do?"

She pressed on, keeping her voice composed. "As

her principal, I have a great deal of interest in her welfare."

"Right. What did you do?"

She blew out a frustrated breath. "Will you stop asking the same thing every few seconds?"

"Not until you answer me. What did you do?"

She released the tension building inside her with a squawk. "All right! I may have interfered slightly, but I swear, Billy, I didn't violate Gemma's privacy. I simply used what information I had about your daughter to try to scare the living daylights out of her mother." It felt good to confess. "And, thanks to Althea's selfishness, it worked."

He raised his foot to the bench beside her and leaned forward. His hair was damp and curled over the collar of his knit shirt. She breathed in his clean, pine scent, which reminded her of their afternoon in the cabin. All in all, Billy looked sexier than he ever had, maybe because his appeal was heightened by this oh-so-subtle streak of intimidation. "Are you saying you told her about Gemma's behavioral problems?" he asked.

"Yes, I told her, but not in a bad way. In a good way."

He repeated her, his voice rising with each word. "A good way? You've been telling me for weeks how Gemma's Oppositional Defiant Disorder could lead to serious complications, could worsen if not treated, could practically ruin her life—".

She held up a finger. "Billy, you're exaggerating. I never said—"

"And now you say her condition has a good side?"

She raised her eyebrows. "Well, for heaven's sake, look at the results."

The rigid line of his lips relaxed somewhat. "But what if Gemma had reacted differently? What if her mother's leaving had broken her heart?"

"I imagine it did to a degree. And I took a chance." When she saw his scowl return, she added, "Okay, a big chance. But I knew you'd be there for her. You and Brenda. You're all that child needs to feel loved and wanted. You're the best antidote for her mother's callousness and deceit." She curved her hand over Billy's bare knee, half expecting him to pull away from her. He didn't. "Althea was like a disease threatening to invade Gemma's life," she said. "You've always been the cure."

He swallowed, took a deep breath. "How much did you tell Althea?"

"Enough. Nothing that wasn't true, but not more than she needed to know. I discussed everything with the school psychologist beforehand. He agreed that anyone taking over Gemma's care should be advised of her progress and what still needs to be done. He would have told her if I hadn't."

"You should have talked to me. I was caught off guard by Althea's one-eighty."

"You're right," she admitted. "But we weren't exactly talking, and the subject of Gemma's ODD isn't one of your favorite topics. Besides, I was going to find you tonight and tell you everything, but then Jack informed me Althea had already left town. It all happened so fast—"

"Jack was in on this?"

"Yes, but only because I begged him to help. He had someone investigate Althea's background. I'll be glad to tell you what he found out, but believe me, Billy, if I'd heard one redeeming motive for what she was doing, I wouldn't have taken such a drastic step without consulting you first."

"But there was no redeeming motive?"

She shook her head.

A smiled started to crack his stony features. "So, once Althea found out she could be the target of bugs and spray paint, she hightailed it out of town."

"I didn't get that specific with her. Once she discovered Gemma was special in a way that required strong parental supervision, she pretty much lost her maternal instincts."

He thought a moment and then sat next to her on the bench. "You know, Evie, I'm the one with behavioral problems right now. I shouldn't be questioning what you did to get rid of Althea. I should be thanking you."

She clapped her hand over her heart, relieved to feel a normal beat again. "Oh, don't thank me. I—"

"I should be praising you."

A sputter of laughter escaped. "Well, if you really want to."

"I should be begging your forgiveness because I acted like a jerk."

"Don't be silly. There's nothing to forgive—"

"I should be telling you how grateful I am to you for helping me understand Gemma."

"Yes, I guess I did do that, so if you want…"

He placed his hands at her temples and held her face close to his. "Damn, I should be kissing you until we're both senseless with gratitude."

Her heart tripped into overdrive once more, but this time it felt right. "Well, now…that is the best idea you've had."

He expressed all his emotions in one heart-stopping kiss. His gratitude, appreciation, praise—she felt them all, along with something infinitely more profound, more lasting. And when he pulled away from her, she brushed her fingers against her mouth, still feeling the press of lips, the depth of his promise.

He smiled at her and her body became liquid heat. She nestled against him. "There's just one thing wrong with what you said a minute ago," he whispered.

"What's that?"

"You said Brenda and I were the only people Gemma needed to feel loved and wanted."

"But you are."

He chuckled, his breath fanning her neck, stirring her desire. "We're good," he admitted. "But you would make us even better."

"What do you mean?" She looked up at him, and

decided she would feel complete if she could see that wonderful smile the rest of her life.

His thumb caressed her temple. "Even if we had a kid of our own or, better yet, a few of them…"

"Kids? You and me? Billy, what are you—"

He placed his finger over her mouth. "And I hope we do, but will there always be a place in your heart for Gem?"

She started to answer, to tell him that she already loved Gemma, almost as much as she loved him, but once again he silenced her, this time with a kiss. "Never mind answering that. Who would've thought I could read minds? But I swear right now, Ev, I can read yours."

She smiled. "Will you let me ask a question for once?"

"Sure, go ahead. But hurry. I've got more to say."

"Are you asking me to marry you?"

He pulled back, clutched at his chest. "Now, where did you get an idea like that?"

"Billy."

"Okay, yes. I'm asking you to marry me. Now you've got all the time you need to say as much on that subject as you want to. Starting now."

She touched her lips to his and breathed, "Yes. Enough said."

The kiss became needy and even a bit dangerous, powerful for a girl who didn't take chances. But when Evie pulled back and smiled into the face she'd come to love, she realized that this time, she wasn't taking a chance at all.

"Hey, Billy!"

He turned but kept his arm around her. "Wonder what Jack wants." He hollered back to him.

"I just got a call from Gail, reporting in."

Billy frowned. "I hope this doesn't mean I have to go to work, because I certainly have other plans."

"You won't believe what she told me," Jack said.

"Yeah? What's that?"

Jack was laughing so hard, he could barely tell his story. "She gave a speeding ticket to a woman named Althea Hufnagle about an hour ago."

Billy laughed out loud. "No kidding."

"But Gail did us all a favor. She told Althea she could mail her fine in. She didn't have to come back to town to pay it."

Billy looked down at Evie and grinned. "It's a good thing. That would have been one fine I would have been happy to pay myself."

EPILOGUE

EVIE, BILLY, Jack and Claire sat on the back deck of the cabin on the Myacki River and watched the sun set. "This was a great way to spend the Columbus Day holiday," Claire said. "I just wish we didn't have to go back to work in the morning."

"And back to school," Evie said. She stroked Billy's arm. "It's almost a two-hour drive, honey. We'd better start soon."

He stood, stretched. Sounds of laughter came from inside the cabin. "Listen to those girls," he said. "After the canoe trip, swimming in the spring and now whatever it is they're doing inside, they'll sleep all the way back."

"They're making a scrapbook," Evie said.

"What's the scrapbook for?"

"They're doing pages about our girls' day on Saturday," Evie explained. "They each had cameras when Claire took us to that spa in Gainesville."

Jane's voice floated to the deck. "Look at this picture, Gemma. I told you Franco could make your hair beautiful. You'd never know you cut it all off that time."

"That was pretty stupid," Gemma said.

Jane spoke with the wisdom of her extra year of age. "Don't worry about it. You've matured a lot since then."

Billy squeezed Evie's hand. "It's amazing what can happen in a few weeks."

"Gemma's come a long way making friends," she said. "You put it best when you said, 'If you want to *have* a friend, you have to *be* a friend first.'"

"Maybe I'm getting the hang of this fathering business, after all." He kissed her cheek. "I hope I do as well in the husband department next month."

"I'm not worried."

Jack and Claire went inside to begin packing up. Billy took the opportunity to kiss Evie deeply. "I hope Ma and Harry are back from Pensacola when we get home. I wouldn't mind tucking Gemma in and coming over to your place for a few minutes...or so."

Evie smiled. "Imagine, Dad taking a trip in the Minnie Winnie. I could barely get him to the mall for new shoes when we were in Detroit."

"What's he owe that kid for cutting the grass now? A couple hundred bucks?"

She laughed. "At least."

He took her hand and helped her up from the chaise longue. "Only one more hurdle to cross, as far as I can see. I hope I made the right decision about Carl Hufnagle."

She put her hands on his arms. "I think you did. You'll be by Gemma's side for the entire trip to Colorado."

"Every conversation I've had with Carl, he's seemed like a good guy. It's not his fault his daughter turned out the way she did. And Gem deserves to meet her grandfather."

Evie patted his chest. "You can quit trying to talk yourself into this, Billy. The plans are set."

"Okay. I guess I'm still worried about Gemma seeing Althea again, but she doesn't appear to care either way. I think she has an extraordinarily grown-up understanding of her mother."

They walked together to the cabin's back door. Before going in, Evie stopped. "Aren't we going to be an odd sort of family," she said. "My guess is, Gemma will end up with two grandfathers, Carl and Harry, as well as her grandmother. She'll have a full-time Dad and stepmother, and a part-time mother. And once we have kids…well, it's almost too complex to think about."

"And don't forget a couple of uncles on my side," Billy said. "But when it comes to family, I say you can never have too much."

Evie sighed with contentment. Imagine this lonely, cautious girl from Detroit ending up in Heron Point, population two thousand, and almost every one of them like family. She looked up at Billy and smiled with all the tenderness in her heart. "I think it's time we started looking for a bigger house."

"What would you say if we got one with a view of the water?" He laughed. "And padded walls."

* * * * *

Happily ever after is just the beginning...

Turn the page for a sneak preview of
DANCING ON SUNDAY AFTERNOONS
by
Linda Cardillo

Harlequin Everlasting—Every great love
has a story to tell. ™
A brand-new line from Harlequin Books
launching this February!

Prologue

Giulia D'Orazio
1983

I had two husbands—Paolo and Salvatore.

Salvatore and I were married for thirty-two years. I still live in the house he bought for us; I still sleep in our bed. All around me are the signs of our life together. My bedroom window looks out over the garden he planted. In the middle of the city, he coaxed tomatoes, peppers, zucchini—even grapes for his wine—out of the ground. On weekends, he used to drive up to his cousin's farm in Waterbury and bring back manure. In the winter, he wrapped the peach tree and the fig tree with rags and black rubber hoses against the cold, his massive, coarse hands gentling those trees as if they were his fragile-skinned babies. My neighbor, Dominic Grazza, does that for me now. My boys have no time for the garden.

In the front of the house, Salvatore planted roses. The roses I take care of myself. They are giant, cream-colored, fragrant. In the afternoons, I like to sit out on the porch with my coffee, protected from the eyes of the neighborhood by that curtain of flowers.

Salvatore died in this house thirty-five years ago. In the last months, he lay on the sofa in the parlor so he could be in the middle of everything. Except for the two oldest boys, all the children were still at home and we ate together every evening. Salvatore could see the dining room table from the sofa, and he could hear everything that was said. "I'm not dead, yet," he told me. "I want to know what's going on."

When my first grandchild, Cara, was born, we brought her to him, and he held her on his chest, stroking her tiny head. Sometimes they fell asleep together.

Over on the radiator cover in the corner of the parlor is the portrait Salvatore and I had taken on our twenty-fifth anniversary. This brooch I'm wearing today, with the diamonds—I'm wearing it in the photograph also—Salvatore gave it to me that day. Upstairs on my dresser is a jewelry box filled with necklaces and bracelets and earrings. All from Salvatore.

I am surrounded by the things Salvatore gave me, or did for me. But, God forgive me, as I lie alone now in my bed, it is Paolo I remember.

Paolo left me nothing. Nothing, that is, that my family, especially my sisters, thought had any value. No house. No diamonds. Not even a photograph.

But after he was gone, and I could catch my breath from the pain, I knew that I still had something. In the middle of the night, I sat alone and held them in my hands, reading the words over and over until I heard his voice in my head. I had Paolo's letters.

Be sure to look for
DANCING ON SUNDAY AFTERNOONS
available January 30, 2007.
And look, too, for our other
Everlasting title available,
FALL FROM GRACE by Kristi Gold.

FALL FROM GRACE is a deeply emotional story
of what a long-term love really means.
As Jack and Anne Morgan discover,
marriage vows can be broken—
but they can be mended, too.
And the memories of their marriage
have an unexpected power to bring back
a love that never really left....

This February...

Catch NASCAR Superstar **Carl Edwards** *in*

SPEED DATING!

Kendall assesses risk for a living—
so she's the last person you'd
expect to see on the arm of a
race-car driver who thrives on the
unpredictable. But when a bizarre
turn of events—and NASCAR
hotshot Dylan Hargreave—inspire
her to trade in her ever-so-structured
existence for "life in the fast lane"
she starts to feel she might be
on to something!

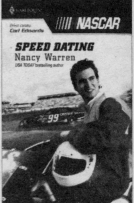

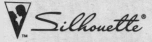

Silhouette®
Romantic
SUSPENSE

Excitement, danger and passion guaranteed!

Same great authors and riveting editorial you've come to know and love.

Look for our new name next month as Silhouette Intimate Moments® becomes Silhouette® Romantic Suspense.

Bestselling author
Marie Ferrarella
is back with a hot
new miniseries—
The Doctors Pulaski:
Medicine just got
more interesting....

Check out her
first title,
HER LAWMAN
ON CALL,
next month.

Look for it wherever
you buy books!

REQUEST YOUR FREE BOOKS!
2 FREE NOVELS PLUS 2 FREE GIFTS!

HARLEQUIN®

Super Romance®

Exciting, emotional, unexpected!

YES! Please send me 2 FREE Harlequin Superromance® novels and my 2 FREE gifts. After receiving them, if I don't wish to receive any more books, I can return the shipping statement marked "cancel." If I don't cancel, I will receive 6 brand-new novels every month and be billed just $4.69 per book in the U.S., or $5.24 per book in Canada, plus 25¢ shipping and handling per book and applicable taxes, if any*. That's a savings of close to 15% off the cover price! I understand that accepting the 2 free books and gifts places me under no obligation to buy anything. I can always return a shipment and cancel at any time. Even if I never buy another book from Harlequin, the two free books and gifts are mine to keep forever.

135 HDN EEX7   336 HDN EEYK

Name	(PLEASE PRINT)

Address	Apt.

City	State/Prov.	Zip/Postal Code

Signature (if under 18, a parent or guardian must sign)

Mail to the **Harlequin Reader Service®**:
IN U.S.A.: P.O. Box 1867, Buffalo, NY 14240-1867
IN CANADA: P.O. Box 609, Fort Erie, Ontario L2A 5X3

Not valid to current Harlequin Superromance subscribers.

Want to try two free books from another line?
Call 1-800-873-8635 or visit www.morefreebooks.com.

* Terms and prices subject to change without notice. NY residents add applicable sales tax. Canadian residents will be charged applicable provincial taxes and GST. This offer is limited to one order per household. All orders subject to approval. Credit or debit balances in a customer's account(s) may be offset by any other outstanding balance owed by or to the customer. Please allow 4 to 6 weeks for delivery.

Your Privacy: Harlequin is committed to protecting your privacy. Our Privacy Policy is available online at www.eHarlequin.com or upon request from the Reader Service. From time to time we make our lists of customers available to reputable firms who may have a product or service of interest to you. If you would prefer we not share your name and address, please check here. □

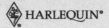

HARLEQUIN®

E V E R L A S T I N G   L O V E ™

Every great love has a story to tell ™

Fall from Grace

Kristi Gold

Save $1.⁰⁰ off

**the purchase of
any Harlequin
Everlasting Love novel**

**Coupon valid from January 1, 2007
until April 30, 2007.**

**Valid at retail outlets in Canada only.
Limit one coupon per customer.**

52607370

HECDNCPN0407

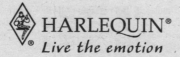

HARLEQUIN *Super Romance*

COMING NEXT MONTH

#1398 LOVE AND THE SINGLE MOM • C.J. Carmichael
Singles...with Kids
When Margo almost loses her bistro...and custody of her children...she realizes a real family is about more than owning a pretty house and being a perfect mother. And then there's Robert... But like the other single parents in her support group, she has to make sure he wants the whole package. Is it really possible to find true love the second time around when you're single...with kids?
The first in a wonderful new series!

#1399 THE PERFECT DAUGHTER • Anna DeStefano
Count on a Cop
Detective Matt Lebrettie can't be the man for Maggie Rivers. She just can't watch him face danger every day. But will keeping her heart safe rob her of her chance for happiness?

#1400 THE RANCHER NEEDS A WIFE • Terry McLaughlin
Bright Lights, Big Sky
After his divorce, Wayne Hammond resisted making anyone the second Mrs. Hammond. Topping the list of the women he wouldn't pick is Maggie Harrison Sinclair, who's taken refuge at her family's ranch until she can figure out which big city is for her. He's not about to make the mistake of picking a city woman again. Or is he?

#1401 BECAUSE OF OUR CHILD • Margot Early
A Little Secret
More than a decade ago, Jen Delazzeri and Max Rickman had a brief, intense love affair—and then disappeared from each other's lives. Now Jen's work as a TV reporter brings her into Max's world again, the world of smoke jumpers and Hotshots, of men and women who risk their lives to fight wildfires. Should she use this opportunity to tell him the secret she's kept for twelve years—a secret named Elena?

#1402 THE BOY NEXT DOOR • Amy Knupp
Going Back
In Lone Oak, Kansas, Rundles and Salingers don't mix. Not since the tragic accident involving Zach Rundle's brother and Lindsey Salinger's mother. But when the well-being of a young boy is at stake, Zach and Lindsey are unwillingly dragged together again. Fighting the same attraction they'd felt twelve years ago.

#1403 TREASURE • Helen Brenna
Jake Rawlings is a treasure hunter and Annie Miller is going to lead him to the mother lode. But what he finds with beautiful Annie is much more than he bargained for.

HSRCNM0107